THE PRICE OF M...

A totally grip... ...he mystery

BRIAN BATTISON

Detective Jim Ashworth Book 2

Originally published as *Fool's Ransom*

JOFFE BOOKS

Revised edition 2021
Joffe Books, London
www.joffebooks.com

First published in Great Britain in 1994
as *Fool's Ransom*

Cover art by Nina Kicul

ISBN: 978-1-78931-686-5

This book is dedicated to the memory of my late parents:
Frederick and May Battison

PROLOGUE •

The mock Tudor house stood well back from the road, nestled behind a vast expanse of immaculate lawns and flowerbeds. A wide gravel drive swept through the centre of the lawns, to a large parking area in front of the house whose facade was decorated with white stucco and dark oak timbers.

A fine Boston Creeper encompassed the building and now seemed set to encroach upon its roof. In summer these vines would envelop the structure in a green leafy splendour, in autumn a deep glossy red-brown, but now they merely appeared as fissures in the white mortar.

The drawing-room was grand, opulent, rich with the scent of cut flowers, but Barbara Edwards was impervious to it all as she nervously paced about the room. She was, thanks to money and hard work, a well-preserved woman of forty-five. The face beneath the short blonde bob was clear-skinned, and seemed to have escaped the usual ravages of age. Her figure was youthful, elegant in a Catherine Walker suit.

Her clear blue eyes showed signs of agitation as they flicked up the drive towards the entrance between tall privet hedges bounding the property. A dark blue Jaguar car came into view.

In the hall, Barbara slipped on a green quilted jacket and hastened outside to meet the visitor.

The Jaguar was parked beside her large Renault. The driver got out of the car quickly. He was a tall man, grey-haired, distinguished.

He came hurrying towards Barbara as she asked anxiously, 'Any news?'

The man shook his head grimly.

'Haven't they located his car yet, or anything?' she asked, concern and disappointment mingling in her voice.

'Calm down,' he soothed. 'The police won't even start looking for at least forty-eight hours.'

'I can't calm down, Dennis, I'm out of my mind with worry.'

'I know,' he replied patiently. 'Just come inside.'

Together they entered the house.

CHAPTER 1

Sarah Ashworth stood patiently on the landing, listening to her husband's size twelve shoes on the rafters in the loft, the drone of his voice as he muttered indistinct oaths.

The closer the sounds edged to the open hatch the more agitated Peanuts, their Jack Russell, became, and when her master finally began to descend the aluminium ladder, she gave full vent to her recently acquired ability to bark.

'Thank God we're detached,' Jim Ashworth grumbled above the din, as he folded the ladder back into the loft-space.

'Be quiet, Peanuts,' Sarah commanded, to no avail.

'Well, the tank jacket's all right,' Ashworth told her, slipping out of his overalls. 'The best thing we can do is leave the heating on low twenty-four hours a day.'

The weatherman on Breakfast News had just predicted a big freeze. Sarah, since their first year of marriage, had always taken appropriate precautions with the central heating system in such conditions. Nevertheless, Ashworth had always performed this ritual, during which Sarah would dutifully listen and nod agreement.

Following her husband down the stairs, she noted with some satisfaction that his hips and waistline now bore testament to the strict diet which had, in the ten days since

3

Christmas, trimmed seven pounds from his fourteen-and-a-half-stone frame. A further seven would need to be shed before he reached his ideal weight and these, Sarah knew, would prove more difficult due to Ashworth's growing disenchantment with low calorie meals.

In the kitchen she put before him one half of a huge grapefruit, which he consumed with neither relish nor comment. His expression was gloomy as he sipped his saccharine-sweetened coffee.

Eventually, he proclaimed, 'I'll go and work on the book.'

'Very well, dear,' Sarah replied brightly.

Ashworth had always regarded the study as his exclusive piece of world: his domain. But during the last few days, as he sat in the captain's chair behind his impressive mahogany desk, sorting through old press cuttings, he had come to regard it as his prison.

Here he was, Chief Inspector Jim Ashworth, head of Bridgetown CID, in the last few days of his leave, and after that — if no overtures for his return were forthcoming — he would be retired.

Not that he regretted tendering his resignation; in the circumstances there had been no alternative. How could he have continued after his Detective Sergeant, Owen Turner, had attempted to usurp his position; after almost the entire establishment had conspired in an effort to force him to charge an innocent man with murder?

He had proved them all wrong and had walked out with his dignity intact, which was important to him.

Far too outspoken to be truly popular, Ashworth knew there were those at Bridgetown Station who would not mourn his departure, who would feel that the force was better off without his outdated views — particularly his opposition to women serving in CID. It was debatable whether these people were interested in promoting sexual equality, or just wanting to make the workplace more decorative.

Still, he did not really want to retire, and now the question uppermost in his mind was: What the hell was he going to do with the rest of his life?

Chief Constable Savage wanted him back — no doubt about that. He had given Ashworth one month's leave initially, during which time the paperwork for his retirement was to have been sorted out.

When at the end of that month, Savage had called to inform him that the paperwork had still not been completed, Ashworth had grinned inwardly with relief. However, when Savage had paused — granting him the opportunity to reconsider, no doubt — Ashworth had maintained a stony silence, forcing Savage to suggest a further month of leave.

Now, with the time almost up, and having had no fresh contact with Savage, Ashworth was beginning to wonder whether he had blown his chances of staying in the job he loved so much.

With little enthusiasm he now picked up a discoloured half-sheet of newsprint and scanned it closely, searching for some small fact that could motivate him into putting pen to paper. After seven hard days all he had was the title and an overflowing wastepaper basket.

He was supposed to be compiling his memoirs. Indeed, there was a publisher — cheque book in hand — waiting to peruse the first draft. Ironic really, for Ashworth's son, John, a struggling but rising writer, would have given much to be in this position, and yet here he was, with not an inkling of an idea of how to start.

Ashworth would have been only too happy to hand the project over to him but would never have dreamed of broaching the subject, for John had inherited the fierce Ashworth pride, and would have interpreted such a gesture as an act of charity. At least, though, John had promised to read the manuscript when — if ever — it was completed, and offer advice.

Ashworth paused to stare out of the window. A squally south-westerly wind was sending the clouds scurrying across the sky; later, as forecast, it would veer round to the east and bring with it the snow which was creeping across Europe.

After moping around the study for a while, Ashworth picked up his pen and sat looking at the blank piece of paper; he leant forward, elbow on table, chin on wrist; then he sat back, then he replaced the pen and went down to the kitchen in search of coffee.

Sarah automatically filled the kettle as he entered, then returned to the sink where she had been peeling potatoes.

Ashworth moodily circled the room, pausing by the table to glare at his slimline brand meal, which consisted of a small piece of cod in sauce bundled inside its waterproof plastic bag.

As the kettle boiled, Sarah dropped a potato back into the bowl and began making coffee. 'Chief Constable Savage phoned about half an hour ago,' she said.

'Why didn't you fetch me?' Ashworth demanded, with a hint of accusation in his tone.

'Because . . .' Sarah paused to draw in an impatient breath, '. . . two days ago you told me not to disturb you when you're writing.'

The coffee jar was banged on to the worktop, and the sound of spoon hitting mug had an angry ring to it.

Ashworth had been married to this woman for enough years — twenty-nine, in fact — to know that when she began to bite back he was getting pretty close to the wire.

'I'm sorry, Sarah,' he mumbled. 'Trying to write this book is getting me down.'

Sarah's exasperation finally surfaced. 'That's not what it is, Jim, and you know it.' She poured water into the mug. 'You want to go back to work . . .'

Taking milk forcefully from the fridge she almost threw it into the coffee before stirring it vigorously. '. . . But you feel that unless they come crawling to you on hands and knees, somehow you'll lose face, and that offends your precious masculine pride.'

The coffee was slammed down in front of him. 'It's so bloody silly!'

Ashworth looked to where the mug was sitting in a puddle of coffee. 'No, it's not, Sarah,' he said, smiling sheepishly. 'Put like that — it's bloody childish.'

'Thank goodness.' Sarah laughed wearily.

Ashworth picked up the mug, his tastebuds already on standby against the harsh taste of sweeteners. He took a sip and was pleasantly surprised. 'There's sugar in this.'

'Yes, there is, two instead of your usual four. Now, will you ring Savage and arrange to go and see him?'

'No.' Ashworth shook his head resolutely. 'But I'll ring and ask if he'd like to come and see me.'

Sarah's 'Oh, my God,' muttered through clenched teeth, was hardly audible.

* * *

Chief Constable Ken Savage was in truculent mood as he stomped towards his vehicle in the station car park. A slight thumping headache accompanied his hangover; he was a heavy smoker, and the wintry weather was making the congestion on his chest worse, causing his breath to come in short shallow gasps.

Inside the car he attempted to clear the phlegm from his throat with a series of hacking coughs, before lighting a cigarette and starting the engine.

Skilfully, and with a good deal of aggression, he edged out into the mid-morning traffic.

Savage was, at heart, a city man, so as he drove along the high street its beauty was lost to him; the quaintness of it, the stone cottages and shops, the occasional thatched roof — all escaped his notice, as did the fact that despite its perimeter being surrounded by modern housing estates, Bridgetown proper had somehow retained its rural atmosphere.

His mood was not improved by having to stop at a pelican crossing while an elderly lady trundled across with her shopping trolley. So slow were her steps that she was barely half-way across when the amber light began flashing.

'Hurry up,' Savage muttered irritably as he pushed his cigarette filter into the overflowing ashtray, peppering the car floor with burning tobacco.

When, at last, the woman was safely deposited on the pavement, Savage accelerated the automatic car and sped away.

His mind focused on the man who had necessitated this journey: James Ashworth.

Savage knew that if he lived to be a hundred — and, with his lifestyle, that was unlikely — he would never fully see eye to eye with Ashworth. The arrogance of the man! That he should expect Savage to go to him was typical of his attitude.

However, the professional part of Savage's mind pushed to the forefront: he must not allow personal feelings to interfere with the job.

In his opinion Ashworth was a few years past his best, but recent events had proven that he was still head and shoulders above the average small-town policeman.

Savage now had at his disposal a young enthusiastic team, eager to take advantage of modern technology, but all new to the area. What they lacked was leadership, someone to give them a sense of direction. That was where Ashworth came in. Once the team was up and running, once things were ticking over, Ashworth could be moved to a job where his particular talents would be far from wasted.

Without conscious thought he indicated left and turned into Ashworth's drive. The detached four-bedroomed house befitted someone of the Chief Inspector's rank and status; the fact that Ashworth had purchased it while still on his way up was evidence of his thriftiness.

Savage's shoes crunched on the gravel. He rang the bell on the cottage-style front door. A dog barked within and the sound reached a high-pitched yap, then became muffled, seconds before the door was opened by Sarah.

Her face lit up with a smile. 'Ah, Chief Constable, do come in.'

'Thank you, Mrs Ashworth,' Savage said cordially.

'May I take your coat?'

Savage struggled out of the dark blue mackintosh which covered his uniform.

Sounds of the barking dog filtered through from the kitchen.

'The dog,' Sarah explained unnecessarily. 'She's very young, not out of that silly puppy stage yet.'

Hanging up Savage's coat, she favoured him with another radiant smile, saying, 'Jim's upstairs in the study. If you'd like to come with me . . .'

Savage followed Sarah up the stairway and as he watched her sprightly step and trim figure, he thought what a strikingly handsome woman she was.

Opening the study door and stepping aside to allow Savage to enter, she said, 'It's the Chief Constable, dear.'

'Jim,' Savage said with a curt nod.

Ashworth was sitting at his desk, and Savage shrewdly observed that the man's seven weeks of inactivity had not resulted in any relaxation of standards; Ashworth was attired as for a normal working day: dark grey trousers, white shirt and maroon tie with a thin grey stripe.

Ashworth rose from the plush leather chair. 'Ken,' he said, extending his hand.

Across the perfunctory handshake, Sarah asked, 'Can I get you coffee?'

'That would be nice, Mrs Ashworth,' Savage replied. 'White with two sugars, please.'

'The same for me,' Ashworth added hopefully.

When Sarah had gone, Ashworth said stiffly, 'Sit down, Ken.'

Savage settled himself in the chair. 'You're looking well,' he remarked pleasantly.

'I'm on a diet.'

'And keeping yourself busy by the look of things.' He indicated the cluttered desk and the pen with which Ashworth was toying.

'I'm writing a book. *The memoirs of a small-town policeman.*'

'Really?' Savage said with eyebrows raised. 'I'd like to read that.'

Ashworth glanced at the empty folder. 'The first draft's not finished yet,' he responded shortly. 'In any case, I'm sure you're not here to enquire after my health or how I'm filling my time.'

'Straight to the point, as ever.' Savage chuckled, then cleared his throat. 'You've almost finished your extended leave, and I wondered if you'd had any further thoughts about retiring.'

'Why should I?' Ashworth's eyes twinkled.

This display of reticence angered Savage. 'You asked me to come and see you,' he said heatedly. 'The significance of that wasn't wasted on me . . . the mountain must come to Mohammed.'

'I see your temper hasn't improved,' Ashworth said lightly.

'Nor is it likely to. Look, I sold the ideas for the changes in CID badly and you over-reacted. Now that's as far as I'm going along that road.'

Their incompatible characters clashed and threatened to ignite as they locked eyes. Savage was the first to look away as Sarah entered with the coffee. If she was at all surprised that the two men were already engaged in hostilities, it registered in neither her expression nor her manner. She quickly served the coffee, excused herself, and withdrew.

Silence reigned for a few moments after the door had closed. Ashworth broke the impasse by saying casually, 'What's happening at the station — case-wise?'

'Very little. The burglaries are still going on.'

'Yes, I gathered that from the local press. They're really roasting your carcass,' Ashworth remarked mischievously.

'What's new?' Savage complained morosely. 'About the only other thing is a possible missing person. Simon Edwards, the industrialist.'

Ashworth, after a sip of coffee, said, 'Oh, I know Simon slightly. What's happened to him?'

Savage looked around hopefully for an ashtray but was disappointed, so reaching forward for his coffee cup, he said, 'He went to London yesterday on business. When he's away he always phones his wife around 8 p.m. Anyway, he hadn't phoned by ten so she called the hotel but he hadn't checked in. She waited until this morning, rang the people he was supposed to be doing business with and it seems he hadn't turned up.'

Savage drained his cup and replaced it on the desk. 'He's very likely on a bender. He'll come back in a few days, no doubt.'

'He didn't seem like that sort to me.'

Savage studied the sixteenth-century framed map of Bridgetown which hung on the wall behind Ashworth before saying briskly, 'Can we stop sparring, Jim? I want you back at the station.' He searched Ashworth's face but could read nothing into his expression.

'What about Turner?' Ashworth snapped.

Savage smiled. 'I realise you could never work with him again, Jim. I'm not that insensitive,' he said benevolently. 'So does he, as a matter of fact. Offered his resignation — which I refused.'

Ashworth's eyes became hostile.

Savage jumped in quickly, 'He's a good man, Jim. He just made a mistake.'

'A series of them,' Ashworth replied gruffly.

'Got a list of people who haven't?' Savage countered.

'Point taken,' Ashworth conceded, and Savage relaxed slightly. 'So what's happened to him?'

'Transferred back to his old patch.'

'And who's replacing him?'

'I've got a new team, Jim. Four detectives.'

'So why do you need me?' Ashworth asked cautiously.

Savage leant forward. 'Because they're young . . . experienced, but new to Bridgetown. I need someone to pull them into shape.' He studied Ashworth's thoughtful, undecided face. 'But there's more to the job than that. I'm looking for someone to argue the force's case for funding with the Home Office.'

Ashworth gave him a sharp stare. 'Again . . . why me?'

'Jim, you're the most awkward bugger I know . . .' He deliberately omitted the world 'old'. '. . . But you're also honest and intelligent. You know what's been happening these last few years: the Home Office telling us to cut costs and put more coppers on the beat—'

'And when we do, Whitehall uses that as an excuse to cut our budget,' Ashworth concluded.

'Exactly, it's a vicious circle. That's why I want someone in there who'll fight our corner, not just fold up the first time some pumped-up, self-opinionated politician raises his voice.'

'This is a carrot.'

'Yes, it is, but it's a real one.'

Ashworth frowned. 'That wouldn't be a full-time job.'

'No, it wouldn't. You'd remain head of CID at the same time.'

Ashworth still appeared to be unsure as he asked, 'And when would that part of the job start?'

Savage shrugged. 'Three months . . . six at the outside.' He spread his hands. 'So, that's it, Jim, I can't be any fairer with you. I could get someone in from outside but if you want the job you can finish your leave and start back Monday.'

Ashworth slowly stood up and crossed to the window, his mind pulling him in opposing directions.

Along one path lay the thankless task of trying to maintain law and order, while fighting the system which funded the force, pledged its support, and then seemed to thwart the wheels of justice at every turn.

He peered down at his large garden, which promised a far more tranquil future; soon, in a matter of months, it would need constant attention; there was a growing dog to exercise; a chance to become involved in Sarah's projects.

The wheezing of Savage's breath seemed terribly loud behind him.

He made his decision.

Slowly shaking his head, he said, 'No, Ken.' Then he turned. 'I've had enough leave to last me a year. I'll start back tomorrow.'

* * *

Ashworth was sitting in the carver at the dining table. Outside the wind had finally swung round to easterly. It moaned, sighed, but as yet its arctic chill had failed to penetrate indoors.

He sipped his malt whisky appreciatively, then placed the glass on the table among his jumble of papers.

He liked the dining room; it was comfortable, relaxing. Whenever his children and grandchildren descended on the house, mealtimes were always happy, chaotic affairs, and the atmosphere seemed to linger, to become part of the room.

He had left Sarah in the kitchen, ironing a sufficient number of shirts to last for the rest of the week — and ironing was the one domestic duty which Sarah did not consider bliss.

As Ashworth studied the papers in front of him, an acrimonious oath sprang from her direction. With a knowing grin, he crossed to the doorway, and called, 'All right, Sarah?'

'Yes, I'm fine, Jim, thank you,' came the curt reply.

Ashworth chuckled as, returning to his seat, he continued to study the papers on which were accounts of the four new detectives. Names which tomorrow would have faces and characters, but for the moment Ashworth had only Savage's assessments to go by; assessments with which he would no doubt disagree.

Alistair Stimpson — Detective Sergeant, he read. Formerly with the Metropolitan Police. Joined as a cadet, fifteen years ago. Awarded a commendation for bravery, after tackling two men armed with sawn-off shotguns during a post office robbery.

Michael Whitworth — Detective Constable. Previously stationed in Manchester. Ten years' service; last two spent

13

with the Drugs Squad. Backbone of the team, according to Savage, and on paper Ashworth found it difficult to dispute.

Nevertheless, he had reservations. Both officers had spent their time in violent areas, and although Bridgetown was becoming increasingly so, compared with any inner city, it was still relatively peaceful and sleepy. These officers, in Ashworth's view, would have to make massive adjustments in their approaches to both public and suspects.

Next came Joshua Abraham — Detective Constable. Ashworth chuckled. This boy's parents must have had a wicked sense of humour, he thought — why couldn't they have called him Peter, David or John?

Savage had labelled him a maverick, and it did seem that the DC had lived up to his odd name, had probably been moulded by it. Abraham had joined the force straight from school where he had achieved an excellent academic record. Quiet and reserved, he had spent much of his career in a small Yorkshire village. Computers were his forte. A good base copper, but little to commend him in the field.

The last name on the list — Bedford — was the one which puzzled Ashworth. Savage, a man who usually went in for detail, had merely divulged that this Detective Constable was 'a plodder but useful'.

Ashworth was draining his glass — the drink had been his second, and therefore, under his present slimming regime, his last for the evening — when a thought struck him. 'You wouldn't dare, Ken Savage,' he said aloud. 'Would you?'

CHAPTER 2

If, next morning, Ashworth had been privy to the interior of a bedroom in a small semi-detached house on the outskirts of Bridgetown, he would have known that Savage had indeed dared to draft a female officer into CID.

Detective Constable Holly Bedford was desperately late, and in a panic. Slipping a bra over her small tender breasts, she fumbled angrily with the catch. Then, muttering crudely, she rifled through her dressing-table drawer in the hope of finding a pair of tights without ladders.

Holly was not a pretty girl and, this particular morning, she could not even lay claim to possessing a nice personality, her period being merely a stomach cramp away. At five feet ten she had a slim, almost boyish, body. Her brown hair, cut in page-boy style, detracted further from her femininity. Her green eyes exuded a haunting pain; her straight nose and thin-lipped mouth added to the plainness of the face.

Stepping into one leg of the tights, she exclaimed, 'Shit!' There was a hairline ladder the length of her shin. 'Shit,' she repeated, tearing them off and attempting to hurl them across the room, only to become even more angry when they fluttered, spread-eagled, to the floor just inches away.

She took another pair from the drawer and proceeded to examine them.

'You'll be late, Holly.' The accusing voice drifted up the stairs and continued in an exaggerated whisper, 'I never thought a son of mine would marry a girl who'd use language like that.'

Holly made a face with a good deal of venom behind it. 'Okay, mum,' she called back, tightly.

Mother-in-law and pre-menstrual tension! Singularly, either was insufferable, but combined they made Holly feel positively suicidal.

She finished dressing and took a quick look in the mirror, making sure her charcoal-grey suit and light blue blouse were free of wrinkles. Satisfied, she stepped into her flat sensible shoes, grabbed her shoulder bag, and left the bedroom.

Half-way down the stairs, she stopped, muttered, 'Tampons,' then careered back up to the bathroom, emerging moments later with a pack of eight which she endeavoured to stuff into her already overfull bag.

'Come on,' she implored her body. 'Just come on!'

She found her mother-in-law, Emily Bedford, in the long narrow kitchen. Emily was a small woman, with a podgy shapeless body. Her features were pinched, vindictive; her hair, a dull dirty-grey. She wore a shabby checked dressing-gown and a flesh-coloured elastic bandage on her right knee.

'I don't know how you manage to oversleep,' Emily chided, thrusting a mug of coffee at her. 'It's not as if you do anything. I keep the house nice and do the cooking.'

Because I bloody work full-time, Holly thought, but she simply said, 'Thanks for the coffee,' and stared through the window at her small rear garden as she sipped the hot drink.

Vainly attempting to remain pleasant, she asked, 'What are you going to do today, mum?'

'Some shopping, I suppose,' Emily replied, miserably. 'Not much else to do up here. I don't know anybody.'

'You'll settle in,' Holly said with feigned heartiness.

'No, I won't. I miss my Bill too much to settle,' Emily replied resolutely.

Holly wanted to scream. For forty years that woman had had a cat-and-dog existence with her husband, then when he'd had the luck to die she had taken to visiting his grave and doing what she should have done when he was alive — talking to him as if there was love in her heart. And ever since Holly had taken her in, she had done nothing but whine about the fact that he was gone.

For God's sake, Holly thought, take your guilt and frustration out on somebody else!

She poured her coffee down the sink, it was still too hot, and she suddenly needed to get out.

'I'll see you this evening, mum,' she said, hurriedly.

She was in the hall when Emily shouted, 'I don't suppose you know what time?'

'No, mum.'

'Well, don't mind about me. I'll be all right — here on my own.'

This, Holly thought, and an ogre of a Chief Inspector who apparently loathes women officers. Holly Bedford, this is your life!

In the quiet cul-de-sac snow had already begun to fall, hard tiny flakes that stung the face like hail.

Holly climbed into her ten-year-old white Mini, slipped the key into the ignition, and muttered warningly, 'Start, you cow.'

* * *

A solemn air of silence prevailed over Bridgetown CID. Even the usually effervescent Alistair Stimpson was subdued, his nervousness manifesting itself as he drummed his fingers on the desktop.

Well on the right side of forty, Stimpson was impeccably dressed in a dark blue suit. His blond hair was short, slicked back with gel. His height, at over six feet, his strong build and even features, made him a focal point for female eyes.

Michael Whitworth, in contrast, was shorter, five feet ten, with a slim, wiry body. His black hair was unconventionally long and fell over his forehead in an unruly mane. His features, with the large brown eyes which could flash humour or anger with equal speed and the mouth, with its hint of cruelty, were darkly Latin.

Michael Whitworth was a man who enjoyed boasting about his time with the Manchester Drugs Squad, exaggerating the dangers he had faced.

He sat at his desk, fumbling in the pocket of his crumpled suit for a cigarette. Once lit, it was left to dangle from his mouth as he fiddled with the knot of his tie.

Stimpson was married, but did not allow the fact to impede his quest in charming the knickers off beautiful women. Whitworth did not crave beauty but did like variety and in order to satisfy his requirements he had wisely remained unattached.

Holly had so far managed to fend off their more serious advances, and parry their suggestive banter, without having to become unpleasant. She was seated at a trestle desk, between the two men, and directly opposite Joshua Abraham.

The whole of Bridgetown nick, especially uniformed, were waiting with anticipation for Ashworth's return and — human nature being as it was — everything possible had been done to heighten the discomfort of the new detectives.

The station 'book' had Holly — because of what she lacked between her legs — as clear favourite to be the first to incur Ashworth's wrath.

But 'young Josh' was by no means regarded as rank outsider, for did not his VDU occupy the exact spot where the great man's chair had once stood, and over which his map, dotted with red and blue marker pins, still hung?

Holly liked Josh; he was quiet, well-mannered and definitely not a wimp as most people imagined. His reserve lent him a studious air but his six-foot frame, beneath casual leather jacket, brown roll-necked sweater and cord trousers, appeared to be well developed. His face was boyish yet strong, with a firm chin, full mouth, straight nose, and grey eyes that held a softness which often threw Holly's hormones into disarray, always causing the flush of guilt which came whenever she found a male attractive.

Surely this Ashworth could not be so bad? she reasoned. The anti-Ashworth movement described him as intolerant, insufferable, impossible; a man who ate females for breakfast. The others told a different story: yes, he was difficult, a perfectionist, unable to tolerate sloppy attitudes or practices, expected two hundred per cent loyalty from his people, which was always returned. But everyone, for or against, had to admit that the role of women in CID was a subject on which Ashworth held strong doubts.

Holly's pre-menstrual tension had reached screaming point, when the door opened. Although she had had no preconceived ideas, she was surprised by Ashworth's appearance.

As he strode purposefully into the room, followed by the Chief Constable, she stood up along with the others.

'Please sit down,' he ordered, his voice quiet yet firm, strong.

Holly saw that he was a large, well-built man, looking far younger than his rumoured fifty-three years. His weathered, heavily lined face, thick black hair flecked with grey, only added to his masculinity.

Had she imagined it or did his startlingly hostile brown eyes appraise her fleetingly?

Chief Constable Savage cleared his throat. 'This is Chief Inspector Ashworth. At his request I'm going to leave you alone with him.' He gave a quick nod to Ashworth then left.

Ashworth's eyes scanned the room, which had changed drastically since he had last seen it. 'Well, back in the fish tank,' he remarked, apparently to himself.

There was a door to the right of where Abraham was sitting at his VDU. Ashworth opened it and cast his eyes over his new office: desk and chair facing the door, new metal filing cabinet in the corner, new dark grey carpet; external walls — glass; all others — stud partitions.

'Right,' he said, turning back. 'This is going to be awkward for us all, so I think the best way is for me to see you one at a time in my office. I'll start with DS Stimpson, then DC Whitworth, followed by DC Abraham and DC Bedford.' He disappeared into his office.

Bloody typical, Holly thought, as she seethed. He could not have made it more obvious if he had refused to see her.

Stimpson's interview lasted about five minutes after which he emerged smiling, passing Whitworth who was on his way in.

Winking at Holly, Stimpson said, 'He's not that bad.' Then he slid behind his desk and launched into a lewd description of a sexual act, smuttily suggesting Holly should offer it to Ashworth in return for being allowed to stay on as tea-lady.

'Ha-bloody-ha,' Holly replied with rancour.

Ashworth had not been overly impressed by either Stimpson or Whitworth. Good sound men, he had no doubt, but he suspected both were influenced by popular television police series and, in the field, would attempt to emulate their fictitious heroes — a not uncommon occurrence in the police force.

He knew he sometimes had a tendency to judge a book by its cover, and for that very reason he had been surprised by DC Abraham. To interpret the man's natural quietude as weakness was a mistake, Ashworth now knew. When questioned about the use of modern technology in crime detection, Abraham had given strong, measured answers that reflected his own opinions, rather than ones which may have curried favour with his Chief Inspector.

After the relative peace of village policing, the young man would no doubt need to readjust, but Ashworth felt that he would quickly find his feet.

As Abraham left the office, Ashworth reflected on Detective Constable Bedford. Her expression had been sullen, and he wondered what she had been told about his views on women officers. He had deliberately left her until last because he had a statement to make about equality, and DC Bedford's reaction to that statement could well determine her future within Bridgetown CID.

Holly now sat facing Ashworth. Her first thought had been one of surprise that his battered waxed cotton jacket, which now hung on the coatrack, had been covering a well-tailored suit, staid as opposed to trendy, but smart and reasonably new. She was awkwardly aware of her hands.

'Well, DC Bedford, I'll come straight to the point. Have you heard anything about me which bothers you unduly; anything you feel could make our working relationship difficult?'

Holly met his gaze, determined not to avert her eyes. 'I'm sure you know the answer to that, sir. I've heard that you're not particularly fond of female officers — and that does bother me.'

'Yes, I imagine that it would,' Ashworth remarked kindly. 'And have you seen anything in my manner, so far, to suggest that it's true?'

The question threw Holly for a moment. Hesitantly, she said, 'Well, it didn't escape my notice that you left me till last.'

'I see. I'll admit that I don't like women in CID.'

Holly's heart sank; her tension soared.

Ashworth went on. 'There are two reasons, both of equal importance: firstly, society is becoming increasingly violent and I don't think women should be put in the firing line—'

'I think I can set your mind at rest on that point, sir,' Holly broke in. 'I hold a black belt in judo.'

It was Ashworth's turn to be taken aback. He considered this thin strip of a girl. 'Do you now?' He pursed his lips. 'I see. So what it really boils down to is — do I consider you to be the equal of, say, DC Whitworth?'

'Yes, sir, I think it does.'

Ashworth shook his head. 'I can't give an opinion yet. Before I can pass judgement on whether you're equal, inferior or superior, I'll need a lot more information than the mere fact that you're a woman and he's a man.'

Holly felt a warm wetness between her legs, and with it came a tremendous relief which pushed away her tenseness. She gave a tiny sigh of gratitude.

Seemingly oblivious to this, Ashworth continued. 'There will undoubtedly be times when you feel you're being passed over, not given your correct place in the pecking order . . .'

Holly was no longer listening for the euphoria which had accompanied the start of her menstruation had now been replaced with an urgent desire to collect her tampons and visit the lavatory.

She forced her mind back to the Chief Inspector.

'. . . because it happens to all of us, but I can assure you that it will have nothing to do with the fact that you're a woman,' he concluded, with the air of someone who had just made a great deliberation.

'Thank you, sir,' Holly said hurriedly.

'Has that put your mind at rest?'

'Yes it has, sir,' she confirmed, glad that the interview was over.

'Good, I hope we can work well together,' Ashworth said, pushing himself up from his seat. 'Well, thank you.'

'Thank you, sir.'

Holly bustled towards the door, closing it loudly behind her, and — certain in the knowledge that Messrs Stimpson and Whitworth would put their own interpretations on her dash to the lavatory, and build a whole collection of witticisms around it — she collected her handbag and left the room.

Ashworth, never one to make snap judgements, had to admit that he found DC Bedford a strange young woman. As the interview began he had felt — sensed — her hostility, then she seemed to become almost benignly happy, a state which had been quickly followed by what he could only describe as a nervousness which carried with it an urgent desire to leave the room.

Rifling through the papers on his desk, he came upon the one bearing Holly's name; the one that Savage had conveniently forgotten to give him the day before. Long ago he had conceded that there were many things about women he would never comprehend, but by the time he had finished reading that file, he knew the reason for the pain that resided in her green eyes.

* * *

Ten minutes later Ashworth's appearance in what was now termed 'the main office' turned the banter into a stony silence.

'Right,' he said, 'bring me up to date with what's happening.'

Alistair Stimpson spoke up. 'We're working on the burglaries, sir. DC Abraham is sorting through juvenile offenders, and DC Whitworth and I are leaning . . .' a flustered pause '. . . interviewing them. Without much joy at the moment.'

'Nor will there be,' Ashworth said shortly. 'Why are you still doing that?'

'Last orders we were given, sir,' Whitworth chipped in. 'Everything's been on hold — waiting for your return.'

'Has it now?'

Ashworth walked to where Joshua Abraham was sitting at the VDU, its cursor flashing impatiently. He stood looking at his wall-map for some moments before tapping the VDU's screen, saying, 'Useful things, these, for storing information, but personally I find an old-fashioned map far more informative.' Adding tartly, 'But of course with a map one has to use one's powers of reasoning.'

He returned his attention to the map. 'Forget the juveniles. These villains are fully grown, and my guess is, they live somewhere here.' He indicated the large council estate to the north of Bridgetown. 'Now, the red pins indicate the burglaries that took place up to when I went on leave. If DS Stimpson and DC Whitworth would like to fill in the map up to the present time . . .' he turned to look at the two officers, 'I'm sure you'll see the pattern. If not, I'll point it out to you when I come back. Then a little surveillance this evening should sort out the problem. DC Abraham, if you could find out known offenders living in the area, that could narrow the field.'

'Yes, sir.'

'Good. Now, the missing person. What's been done about him?'

'Nothing, sir,' Holly replied. 'The Chief Constable told us to leave it alone for forty-eight hours. See if he turns up.'

Ashworth glanced out through the glass wall of the building and observed the steady advance of angry snow clouds.

'I'll overturn that order. We start looking now,' he said. Then to Holly, 'I want you to come with me to interview the wife. Give her a ring to let her know we're on our way.'

'Yes, sir.'

Ashworth vanished into his office. Some five minutes later he reappeared, struggling into his battered jacket.

Holly, having telephoned Mrs Edwards, had donned her thick black padded anorak and was standing waiting for him.

He gave her a nod and marched to the door. As he was about to leave, he turned and pointed a finger at no one in particular. 'One other thing,' he said. 'There's something wrong with these offices: this one is too cramped and there's too much space in mine. I'll sort it later.'

When they were certain he had gone, Stimpson and Whitworth exchanged a derisive glance. Whitworth began drumming out a rough rock-and-roll beat with both hands on the top of his desk, singing, 'I know everything, man. I know everything . . .'

The computer bleeped its annoyance at the speed with which Abraham was typing his questions, attracting the attention of the two officers.

Whitworth immediately slowed his beat and crooned, 'Joshua, Joshua, sweeter than lemon squash you are . . .'

'Shall we stick pins in the map?' Stimpson asked amiably.

'That's what I joined the force for,' Whitworth replied.

CHAPTER 3

Barbara Edwards was in her elegant lounge. She was pacing, wringing her hands, too restless to sit.

She turned to her brother, Dennis Paine, who was reclining on the sofa. 'But they must have discovered something, Dennis. Why else would they want to see me?'

'Sit down Babs,' Paine said irritably. 'They haven't discovered anything. They would have said.'

Barbara continued pacing. 'Something must have happened. Where is he?'

The front doorbell rang, causing her to jump.

'It's all right, Babs, I'll get it.'

Paine opened the door to Ashworth and Holly.

Ashworth produced his warrant card. 'Chief Inspector Ashworth, Bridgetown CID. We've called to see Mrs Edwards.'

'Yes, yes, come in. I'm Dennis Paine, Mrs Edwards's brother and Simon's business associate.'

'And this is DC Bedford, sir.'

Paine gave Holly a brief glance before saying, 'I'm afraid my sister's a little keyed up.'

'That's perfectly understandable in the circumstances, sir.'

Paine ushered them into the lounge, where the distraught Barbara Edwards was waiting expectantly. 'Have you found him? Is it bad news?'

'Nothing to alarm yourself about, Mrs Edwards,' Ashworth reassured her. 'We're just here to ask a few questions.'

The woman was looking wildly from one to the other, certain that they were concealing something.

'Look, Babs, why don't you go and make some tea?' Paine ventured.

'I can't, Dennis, they want to ask me questions about Simon.'

Holly stepped in. 'Why don't we go into the kitchen, Mrs Edwards? I can help you make the tea and ask questions at the same time.'

'Yes, all right,' Barbara answered absently. 'It's this way.'

Dennis Paine indicated an armchair. 'Sit down, Chief Inspector.'

'Thank you, sir.' Ashworth settled into the chair and unbuttoned his jacket. Paine stretched out on the sofa.

'Just a few routine questions really, sir,' Ashworth said. 'Do you know of anywhere your brother-in-law is likely to have gone?'

'That's a bloody silly question,' Paine flared. 'If I thought I knew where he was, I wouldn't be sitting here.'

'Mr Paine,' Ashworth began patiently, 'I've got to ask these questions, and losing your temper isn't going to help.'

Paine's look was contrite as he said, 'I'm sorry, Chief Inspector. This is a great strain.'

Ashworth took a moment to consider the room. The carpets and lavish furnishings must have cost a small fortune; the porcelain figurines, expertly displayed in glass-fronted cabinets, were so obviously antiques. Ashworth now saw the necessity for the elaborate alarm system he had noticed on his way to the lounge.

He looked back to where Dennis Paine was now sitting rigidly on the sofa. He said, 'That's all right, Mr Paine. I just want to know if there is anyone your brother-in-law might have gone to see. Someone who he'd rather your sister didn't know about.'

'A woman, you mean?' Paine shook his head. 'No, I wouldn't think so.'

'But you're not sure?'

'Well . . . not really. I've never thought about it. We go on a lot of business trips, to London, and abroad.'

'Yes?' Ashworth prompted.

'Often our hosts lay on hospitality . . . visits to strip shows and anything else. I'm a single man, Chief Inspector.'

'It's not your behaviour that's under scrutiny, sir.'

'I'm not my brother-in-law's keeper, Chief Inspector, I really don't know.'

Ashworth felt it unlikely that the two men could spend time together without each at least having some idea of what the other was doing, so he had to conclude that Simon Edwards did on occasions avail himself of the hospitality offered.

He asked now, 'Your business is what, sir?'

'Fashion wear. Mostly leather belts and handbags for the export market.'

'Does Mr Edwards have any financial problems?'

'Is the business broke? I take it that's what you're asking?' Ashworth nodded.

Paine considered the question for longer than Ashworth would have expected. 'We're solvent,' he said slowly, 'but like so many other businesses, we've had a few bad years recently. We'll survive though.'

'Sorry to have to ask you this, but is the financial situation acute enough to have caused your brother-in-law any amount of anxiety?'

Holly came in then, with tea in delicate china cups, and sugar lumps in a matching bowl.

Paine, with a great show of gallantry, rose to help, quickly moving a coffee table, and relieving Holly of the tray. All the time, his eyes appraised her.

Ashworth watched him. It was difficult to determine the man's age. His iron-grey hair suggested years which the almost wrinkle-free face denied, but he could not have been younger than mid-fifties. Somehow Ashworth felt that no woman would be safe from his advances.

Paine continued to stare at Holly until she had left the room, no doubt assessing her 'entertainment' potential.

Ashworth found he disliked the man. His oily manners barely concealed an abrasive attitude, and Ashworth sensed that sudden displays of temper would probably be the norm for him. He coughed to bring Paine's attention back to the matter in hand.

'Forgive me, Chief Inspector,' he said, sugaring his tea before settling back on the sofa. 'Financial worries . . . yes, both Simon and I have them, but not to any great degree. If I needed to raise money, I might have to mortgage my house.'

'And Mr Edwards's situation would be the same?'

'It had better be,' Paine laughed, 'because if it's not he's taking more money out of the business than I am.' He sat stirring his tea for a time then asked, 'Where is this leading?'

'Just routine questions, sir. Tell me what happened on the day Mr Edwards went missing.'

Once again Paine's good manners slipped. 'I've already been through that with someone else,' he snapped.

'Well, go through it again for me,' Ashworth said firmly.

Paine's sigh, as he began, indicated that he was not accustomed to being spoken to with such authority. 'It was late afternoon on Monday. Simon came into my office and said he'd had a call from one of our exporters in London — Horrocks International. They wanted him to go up to town for a meeting the next morning. Well, I was a little miffed that he had arranged it all without informing me first. And to add insult to injury, he asked me to come here and pick up a change of clothes and his overnight bag.'

'And Mrs Edwards can confirm that you did this?'

Ashworth feared for the safety of the china cup as Paine banged it into the saucer. 'Why should my sister have to confirm anything? I'm not under suspicion for any reason, am I?'

'Of course not, sir,' Ashworth replied, evenly. 'I was merely asking if your sister was here when you called.'

'Oh. No, she wasn't, actually. She was at a Women's Institute tea, or something like that. God, the rubbish women fill their heads with.'

Women's Institute, thought Ashworth; so Barbara Edwards could possibly be known to Sarah.

Paine had ceased to recount, so Ashworth prompted him. 'And then?'

'What do you mean, and then?' Paine snapped as he leant forward to replace his cup next to Ashworth's, which remained untouched.

Ashworth was fast becoming irritated by this man's lack of manners, and making no attempt to conceal the fact, he asked curtly, 'I mean, what happened then, Mr Paine?'

'I rang Babs early evening to tell her what had happened, and then at ten p.m. she rang me. I was still in the office. She said she was worried to death because Simon hadn't been in touch and she'd called the hotel but he wasn't there, he hadn't checked in. You see, Chief Inspector, my sister is a little neurotic.'

'So none of this worried you at the time.'

'No.' Paine then looked furtive, as he said, 'As I told Babs, Simon could easily have checked into another hotel. Rather unwisely, I realise now, I gave her the name of the people Simon was doing business with. In the morning she phoned them, panicked when Simon wasn't there, and called you in.'

'And Mr Edwards's disappearance still didn't bother you?'

'Of course it bothered me,' Paine spat. 'I was going to wait until later in the day, then phone all of our business contacts and try to locate him.'

'Did you do that?'

'Yes, I did. None of them had seen or even been in touch with Simon. The fool must have taken off somewhere. Just wait until he gets back. There — are you satisfied?'

'No. Far from it,' Ashworth replied frostily. 'You seem to be asking me to believe that in this climate of recession, Mr Edwards, on his way to a business meeting, suddenly decides not to bother, and instead, goes gallivanting off, and then doesn't take the trouble to phone his wife, not even to keep up the pretence. But the hardest thing for me to believe, sir, is your obvious lack of concern for your brother-in-law. You don't seem in the least bit worried.'

'Are you calling me a liar, Chief Inspector?'

'Yes, sir,' Ashworth replied bluntly. 'Or something close to it. Try 'not telling me the whole truth' — see how that fits.'

Paine chewed on his bottom lip as he considered the situation then, although there was no likelihood of their conversation being overheard, he spoke in a hushed, hurried whisper. 'This is very delicate. I feel I'm walking a tightrope here.'

'Could you speak up, sir?' Ashworth asked, stoutly.

Rather than raise his voice, Paine leant closer to the Chief Inspector. 'Look,' he said. 'I don't know what it's like to go to bed with the same woman almost every night for twenty-five years . . .' His expression indicated that the thought held little appeal for him. '. . . but I would imagine it to be monotonous, to say the least.'

As Ashworth had gone to bed with the same woman for almost thirty years, the remark annoyed him. 'What has this to do with anything?' he quickly asked.

Paine let out a long breath, before saying, 'Simon has done this sort of thing before. He isn't exactly a paragon of virtue when he's away from home.'

'He picks up women?'

'Not in the kerb-crawling way you're insinuating. There are women — society women — who are only too happy to accompany us at business dinners, that type of thing. Respectable women . . . not at all out of place.'

'And good to their mothers, no doubt,' Ashworth muttered, with heavy sarcasm. 'You think that's where Mr Edwards is now, then? With some high-class prostitute?'

'Or a succession of them . . . yes.'

Ashworth was far from convinced. 'No wonder your business has financial troubles. Why hasn't he contacted his wife?'

Paine now had the air of a man who, finding himself in a compromising situation, was doing his level best to extricate himself from it.

He smiled fawningly, then said, 'Chief Inspector, my sister may tell you differently, but believe me, once Simon is away he never feels any compelling urge to contact Babs. I'm always having to remind him. There have been quite a few occasions when I've had to make the calls myself, on the pretext that Simon is in a late meeting.'

'Why didn't you go with him this time?'

'I told you, I didn't have the chance. It was put before me as a *fait accompli*. Anyway, we were expecting a buyer from Brewsters — the chain store — yesterday; we're trying to expand our home market. I had to be here to deal with him. Are you satisfied now, Chief Inspector?'

'I'm satisfied that you've wasted a lot of our time,' Ashworth replied sharply.

'I refute that,' Paine said angrily. 'My sister reported Simon missing . . . what could I do? I couldn't tell her the truth. If Babs ever finds out what Simon gets up to, she'll have a nervous breakdown.'

Although Ashworth disliked the man he felt forced to concede that Paine had simply been acting in his sister's best interests.

He cut short Paine's earnest protestations that he was doing all he could to find his wayward brother-in-law, saying, 'All right, Mr Paine, I think we can leave it there.'

'You'll call the whole thing off then and wait for Simon to turn up?'

Ashworth shook his head. 'We can't do that. Mr Edwards has been reported missing, and until he turns up, he remains a missing person.'

'This is bloody ridiculous. What are you intending to do?'

'We have a procedure that has to be followed.'

'And what does that involve?'

Ashworth sighed; this was an area he would rather not go into. 'We drag the waterways, sir. Lakes and rivers. Send frogmen in, if we can. Then—'

'What?' Paine exploded, before glancing at the closed door and lowering his voice. 'Do you realise the effect that would have on my sister? I promise you . . .' He stabbed a manicured forefinger at Ashworth. '. . . if anything happens to her because of this, I'll sue the police for mishandling the situation.'

'And if your theory — because that's all it is — proves to be incorrect,' Ashworth said, his temper beginning to fray, 'and Mr Edwards is in some sort of difficulty, you'll sue us then for not acting quickly enough. Am I right?'

Paine slumped back on the sofa and said with exasperation, 'It's all a waste of time. Later today or tomorrow, Simon is going to walk through—'

'Then there's no problem,' Ashworth snapped. 'This type of search takes a couple of days to organise, and there's a big freeze on the way.'

'I have your word then that nothing will happen today or tomorrow?'

'You have,' Ashworth confirmed. 'And after that the utmost discretion will be used. No television. No press.'

'Good,' said Paine, much appeased.

The door opened and Barbara Edwards followed Holly into the lounge.

She immediately reproached her brother. 'Did I hear you raise your voice, Dennis?' Turning to Ashworth, who had risen from his seat, she said, 'You must excuse my brother, Chief Inspector, but this is all so trying.'

'That's all right, Mrs Edwards. I wouldn't worry. I'm sure everything will be just fine.'

'Yes,' Barbara agreed, a touch doubtful. 'You haven't finished your tea.'

'No, I'm sorry. Now, if DC Bedford is finished, I feel we should be on our way.'

Holly nodded. 'Bye. Barbara,' she said, kindly. 'Don't forget to phone if you need me.'

Barbara managed a weak smile. 'Thank you, Holly.'

Paine let them out. They stood for a moment in the open porch. It was bitterly cold, and Ashworth wished he had taken off his coat inside the house so that he could now feel the benefit of it.

Snow was still threatening, occasional flurries being buffeted about by the strong east wind that cut through clothing and flesh to chill the bone beneath.

They hurried to the car, frosty gravel crunching with every step. As Ashworth held open the passenger door, he quipped, 'This isn't regarded as patronising, is it?'

'Of course not, sir,' Holly replied icily. I'm not a bloody feminist, she thought, I was just waiting to come on — men have no idea!

Ashworth looked rather embarrassed as he climbed into his seat. He shot Holly a repentant smile. 'Sorry, that wasn't very funny.'

'It's all right, sir,' she said in a non-committal way.

She was feeling quite good now; the two paracetamol tablets she had taken back at the station had eased her stomach pain, and restored her equilibrium.

Ashworth struggled into his seat belt and started the engine. All at once the radio spluttered. A countrified voice came through. 'Foxtrot Tango to Delta One. Come in, please.'

Ashworth started at the radio, bemused. The coded message was repeated four times before he reached for the handset. 'Bobby,' he barked. 'What's all this Tango Delta business?'

The voice became hesitant. 'I'm sorry, sir . . . I . . . well, er . . . actually, DS Stimpson and DC Whitworth said that's how I'd got to do it.'

At Ashworth's exasperated sigh Holly quickly turned to face the side window, lips clamped tightly together to stop herself laughing out loud.

They had been winding up Bobby Adams, the naïve new recruit.

'I don't think so, Bobby,' Ashworth said briskly. 'Just stick to what we usually say: Bridgetown Station to Chief Inspector Ashworth. All right?'

'Yes, sir. Sorry, sir.'

Ashworth waited, and after a few seconds' silence, asked quietly, 'What did you want, Bobby?'

'Oh yes. Sorry, sir.' Bobby Adams was flustered. 'Um, there's been another break-in, sir, and DS Stimpson says it definitely looks like juveniles this time, sir.'

'Well, tell Stimpson and Whitworth to get on and investigate . . . and stop wasting my time.'

A whispered, 'Yes, sir,' and the radio went dead.

'Roger and out,' Ashworth said, with a hint, of humour in his voice. 'Morecombe and Wise . . . that's all I need.'

Holly was laughing. 'It was funny though, sir.'

'I know,' Ashworth chuckled. 'A little cruel but funny, I grant you that. I'm not without a sense of humour, you know. Despite what you may have heard.'

He steered the car along the drive. 'I think we've got off to a bad start, so why don't I take you to lunch, and we can discuss what we've found out about Simon Edwards? Perhaps that way we can begin to develop a good working relationship.'

'Thank you, sir. I'd like that.'

Ashworth fell silent as he manoeuvred the car along narrow twisting lanes, leading back to the heart of Bridgetown.

Holly noticed two cassette tapes stored beneath the dashboard. As one was Pavarotti and the other Handel's *Water Music*, she assumed that her new Guvnor was a classical music fan. However, if she had lifted them up, she would have found a third: *The Best of The Four Tops*.

It was very difficult to fit Ashworth into any particular slot. These apparently conflicting tastes in music reflected his character perfectly: Ashworth liked what he liked; full stop.

Once in Bridgetown he shunned the two smart restaurants in the high street, ignored the upmarket café with the

Continental look, and opted for an apparently shabby eating house, with the glorious name of The Crispy Bacon Café, which was hidden away down a side street. The inside was scrupulously clean, filled with the pleasant aroma of fried food.

Because it was early — only just twelve noon — lunchtime proper had not yet begun, and only two of the ten yellow-Formica-topped tables were occupied.

Ashworth steered Holly towards a rear table. The owner greeted Ashworth loudly as they sat. 'Hello, Jim, haven't seen you for a few weeks.'

He came from behind the counter: a large man, in his fifties, with the build and broken nose of a boxer.

Ashworth seemed pleased to see him. 'Hello, Bill. How are you keeping?'

'All right, Jim, all right.' He beamed down at Holly; his smile was warm, friendly. 'Is this young lady one of your policewomen . . . or your latest mistress?' he asked with a chuckle.

Ashworth was laughing as he removed his jacket, draping it over the back of his chair. 'This is DC Bedford, Bill.'

'It's Holly Bedford,' she interjected.

'And this old rascal's Bill Willis,' Ashworth informed her, genially. 'He does the best fry-up in town. And you can see from his waistline he consumes too many himself.'

'Hello, Bill,' Holly said, laughing, for she found his warm smile infectious.

'Nice to meet you, Holly. Usual for you, Jim?' Ashworth nodded. Bill looked questioningly at Holly who was studying the single card menu.

'I'd rather have something light,' she said, her eyes scanning the list of dishes, all of which seemed to contain an unappetising fried egg.

'I could do you a salad bap.'

'Lovely, thanks.'

'Right. Tea to start with?'

'Yes, please, Bill.'

Neither spoke until Bill had served the large mugs of strong steaming tea.

After Holly had declined the sugar and Ashworth had heaped two spoonfuls into his drink, he said, 'Now. Mrs Edwards.'

Holly felt, quite rightly, that her effectiveness as a police officer would be judged on what she put forward during the next hour or so.

Making an effort to remain cool, she retrieved the police notebook from her shoulder bag and began slowly. 'I don't think the marriage is an unhappy one, but I got the impression that Mrs Edwards is far from fulfilled. Their sex life is non-existent, although they do still sleep together. There are no money problems as far as she knows, but that's not very reliable information—'

'Why?' Ashworth sipped his tea.

'She's been cushioned for the last five years or so, hasn't had to work, and her husband has taken care of the finances. Within reason she's always had anything she wanted, and since that's still the case she assumes there are no money problems.'

Bill served the food: Holly's — white salad-filled bap on a small plate with paper napkin; Ashworth's — eggs, bacon, sausages and baked beans.

Ashworth tucked in as Holly continued. 'Now . . . other women. I don't know about when he's away, but when he's at home, definitely not. It's work, sometimes goes to the pub for a drink, and fishing . . . he belongs to an angling club at the factory. I've got a recent photograph if we need it. Do you want details of when he went missing? When it was reported?'

Ashworth shook his head. 'No, I'm familiar with those. What you've given me so far is more or less what I expected.' He cut into one of the sausages. 'Mrs Edwards . . . would you say she was neurotic?'

'No, sir, she's a very nice person, a little bit on the shy, nervous side, but not neurotic.'

Ashworth mounted an assault on the pile of baked beans. 'So you wouldn't say there have been other occasions when Edwards has forgotten to ring, and this time, for some unknown reason, his wife just panicked?'

'Definitely not, sir.' Holly consulted her notebook again. 'If her husband couldn't make contact, because he was in a meeting or whatever, he would always get her brother, or someone else, to telephone and let her know everything was all right.'

'Yes, Paine told me as much, and it would seem there were other women.' Ashworth gave her the information derived from Dennis Paine.

Holly listened and, although she found the thought of food nauseating, began to nibble the bap.

'Paine seems to think his brother-in-law will turn up today or tomorrow,' Ashworth concluded.

'But you don't?'

'I hope he does.'

Having despatched the last of the bacon, Ashworth put his cutlery on the plate. 'But there are several things I don't like about this. If Simon Edwards knew he was going to be away for two or three days, why did he take only one change of clothing with him?'

'Perhaps he planned to spend a lot of time undressed, sir,' Holly quipped.

Ashworth laughed. 'Now I hadn't thought of that. But there's something else. Surely a man would know that if he drops out of sight for a few days his wife would be likely to report him missing. He'd need to have a damned good explanation ready when he got back.'

He drained what was left of his tea and sat back, full up and satisfied. 'You'll hear a lot in future about my gut feelings. Well, I've got one about this . . . there's something wrong with it.'

Holly dabbed at her mouth with the napkin then hastily dropped it on to her plate so that Ashworth would not see she had left more than half of the bap.

'Did you get Paine's address?' Ashworth asked.

'Of course I did, sir,' Holly answered testily. 'I take the names and addresses of all interviewees as routine.'

Ashworth felt he had been put in his place.

CHAPTER 4

Stimpson and Whitworth fully expected some form of mild rebuke for the radio trick, but on Ashworth's return the incident was not mentioned; he simply asked for their conclusions on the burglaries, listened to their theories, and seemed satisfied.

He then went on to enquire about the juvenile break-in which, it turned out, had only been attempted; the offenders — two boys aged fourteen or fifteen — had not been detained.

Then, to their surprise, Ashworth suggested that, as they would both be working that evening on the burglaries, they should take the afternoon off.

He entered his office, leaving the door open, deposited his coat on the rack, then sat at his desk. The newness of the furniture irritated him beyond measure. He drummed his fingers lightly on the desktop. What to do now?

The workload — one person who may or may not be missing, a series of break-ins that would soon be cleared up — was light, even by Bridgetown standards, and at a time when personnel had been increased by some forty per cent. This irony was not lost on him.

Having a group of people idle led to the light-hearted raillery he was now having to endure.

Through his open door he watched Stimpson and Whitworth as they pulled on their overcoats. Stimpson was making one of his half-joking propositions to Holly.

'Look, Holly,' he was saying earnestly. 'We can get these burglaries wrapped up by nine p.m. Why don't I pick you up then? We could go for a meal, a few drinks, then I can show you what you've been missing.'

Holly snorted. 'Thanks, Alistair, but I've got something far more exciting to do.'

Stimpson raised his eyebrows inquisitively.

'We're having chips tonight,' she confided, sweetly, 'and I like to sit and watch the fat cool.'

This brought a guffaw from Whitworth.

'Lovely girl,' Stimpson observed, 'but so lacking in taste.'

'Yes,' Whitworth agreed. 'I can understand her not fancying you, but she doesn't even fancy me!'

Their noisy exit followed, and then peace, the only sounds the tapping of a computer keyboard, a drawer being opened and closed, a slight traffic hum from the expressway.

When, a few weeks later, Ashworth looked back on that afternoon, he would ask himself if there was anything he could have done to alter the outcome of so many subsequent events, and he would conclude that there was nothing.

Several unrelated incidents, all linked to Bridgetown CID, had already taken place; the chain of events was already set in motion. Ashworth was soon to find himself powerless, able only to sit and watch as the consequences devastated the lives of so many.

He picked up the telephone and dialled a number.

'Hello, Miller here.' The voice matched the character of Sergeant Ron Miller, the wiry, energetic man in charge of the police frogmen team.

'It's Jim Ashworth, Ron.'

'Hello, Jim, welcome back. What can I do for you?'

'I've got a missing person, one Simon Edwards . . .'

'And you want my lads to go looking,' Miller assumed.

'Good guess,' Ashworth grinned. 'He's only been missing a couple of days.'

'That's not long, Jim, and I don't think my lads will be keen on going underwater. It's brass monkey weather out there, and they're rather fond of their wedding tackle.'

'Dragging?' Ashworth asked hopefully.

'I can make a start on the lakes and ponds tomorrow if they're not frozen.'

'The river?' Ashworth feared he knew the answer before the question was asked.

'The river? Who do you think I am, Jim? Paul Daniels? Do you know how much water that is?'

'Not a lot,' Ashworth joked.

Miller groaned. 'God, I didn't think your quips could get any worse, Jim, but they have. Sorry, my old mate, but you've got no chance with the river.' Miller's tone bore an air of finality. 'If you knew exactly where and approximately when the body went in we might be able to work something out, but even then we'd probably have to wait the six to ten days it would take for him to pop up on his own accord.'

'I haven't got six to ten days.'

'If he's in the river, he'll wait, Jim, believe me.'

'All right then, Ron, whatever you can do will be fine. Thanks.' He replaced the receiver with resignation.

To while away the time, Ashworth spent the rest of the afternoon mapping out a new plan for the office. The sooner he got back to his old desk in its old position the better. This new office was too isolated, made him feel apart from the hub of operations, and therefore unable to function at maximum efficiency.

Holly was relieved when, at five p.m., Ashworth said they should call it a day. Josh Abraham said he was staying on, there was some computer work he wanted to finish. But Holly grabbed her coat and was off.

She was glad that this first day with Ashworth was over, but what had she to look forward to? An evening with mother-in-law!

A slight dusting of snow lay on her Mini. She got into the car, shivering in the cold seat, and activated the windscreen wipers which cleared the glass with a single stroke. Then she tried to start the engine; it turned over but failed to fire. After a few seconds she had another go, but still it refused to bite.

'Damn the bloody thing!' she cursed.

This time she kept the key turned and the engine ground over again and again until a slowing signalled the draining battery.

She struck the centre of the steering wheel. 'You bastard!' she said with feeling.

A tap on the side window startled her. Holly turned to see Ashworth's rugged face framed there. She wound the window down, saying feebly, 'It won't start.'

'Lift the lid up,' Ashworth said briskly.

'The lid?'

'The bonnet.'

Holly pulled the lever.

'Have you got a screwdriver?'

'No, sir.' She felt utterly hopeless.

Ashworth selected a suitable screwdriver from the tool kit in his car and was quickly at work under the Mini's bonnet.

He was at the window again. 'Push the accelerator down to the floor to clear the carburettor, and give it another try.'

Holly did as he instructed and the engine spluttered into life. With a huge sigh of relief, she said, 'Thank you, sir.'

'You were still on summer running but it should be all right now.'

None of that meant anything to Holly, so she just repeated, 'Thank you, sir.'

He pushed down the bonnet, leaning on it heavily until it clicked shut. As he walked towards his car, he called lightly, 'And don't keep upsetting it by suggesting it doesn't know its father.'

Realising that he had overheard her outburst, Holly felt the blood rush to her cheeks. But the remark made her feel better for, contrary to what she had been told, her new boss did seem to possess a very good sense of humour.

* * *

Ashworth and Sarah were beginning to find that walking the dog was more gruelling than pleasurable.

Peanuts, not yet old enough to interpret the aromas left by other dogs as sexual, was rather like a young child who is sexually inquisitive without knowing why; her instincts told her that the messages promised pleasure so she was forever eager to investigate.

'Walk, girl,' Ashworth muttered, jerking the lead for the umpteenth time.

The dog obliged for a few yards then stopped again, black nose plunging into frosty grass.

A huge pale moon rested just above the horizon, its white light illuminating the lane and surrounding fields in an unnatural eerie glow.

'Walk, girl.' This time the dog heard the firmness in Ashworth's voice and condescended to trot along.

He turned to Sarah. 'Do you know a woman named Barbara Edwards?'

Sarah, her face almost lost behind a large woollen scarf, mumbled, 'Yes, I know Barbara. Why?'

Ashworth ignored the question. 'Would you say she was neurotic?'

'Neurotic? Most certainly not. Nervous, perhaps . . . reserved, I'd say. Oh, let's turn back, Jim, it's too cold for this.'

As they began walking the two hundred yards back to the house, Sarah said, 'Why do you ask?'

'Her husband's gone missing.'

'That's awful. Doesn't she have any idea where he might be?'

'No, he told her — or rather, he told her brother — that he was going on a business trip. That was two days ago.' A

42

thought struck Ashworth then, a thought which would keep returning to his mind.

'Do you think something's happened to him?'

'I don't know, Sarah. Tell me, does she ever talk about him?'

'Now you come to mention it, I don't think she does. I mean, at meetings I often say, 'Jim said this . . .' or 'Jim said that . . ."

'I can understand you wanting to show me off,' Ashworth laughed.

'Yes.' She put a doubtful intonation on the word. 'Anyway, I'm sure Barbara never mentions her husband. I know he's something to do with the leather factory but I don't even know his name.'

They turned into the drive and, anticipating the comfort inside the house, quickened their pace. At the front door Sarah fumbled for the lock, then the warmth of the hall met the cold night air.

* * *

Alistair Stimpson's assumption that the burglaries would be cleared up by nine was proving to have been a little optimistic. It was nine fifteen now and nothing had happened.

Stimpson, sitting in Michael Whitworth's battered Cortina, was cold and bored. Whitworth broke the monotony as he clambered into the car with a large brown paper bag. Delving into it he brought out a cheeseburger and passed it to Stimpson.

'Anything?' he asked, biting into his own hamburger.

'No,' Stimpson replied.

The car was parked in a quiet street on one of the large estates. Double-bay-fronted terraced houses stood behind large front gardens. Many bore red security alarm boxes, their newness gleaming in the moonlight.

Stimpson was the more intelligent of the two men. Ruthlessly ambitious, he saw this backwater that was

Bridgetown as an easy route to promotion. Even the emergence of Ashworth had not bothered him, in fact he had not given it a thought.

When he chose, Stimpson had the ability to charm the birds from the trees; an ability he exercised frequently with the female officers back at the station, and he had made two conquests already. Friends and enemies alike described him as vain, arrogant, and selfish.

Whitworth, despite the rather villainous appearance, was the more trustworthy of the duo. He held little interest in rank, wanting only to earn a decent salary. Excitement was what he craved. Although, as many of his new colleagues suspected, he was inclined to glamorise his exploits, he did not have to colour them overmuch.

The high he experienced when — with adrenalin pumping — his team forced entry into premises suspected of harbouring drug dealers, was greater than any other — better even than sex. The scar tissue above his left eye, the ugly scar high up on his right cheek, bore testimony that reception committees at such events could often be somewhat less than friendly.

The stresses of the job had begun to take their toll, however, and Whitworth's term of duty at Bridgetown had been ordered by his superiors in Manchester as a form of rest and recuperation.

Off duty he liked loud rock-and-roll music, very strong ale, and women — in the strictly physical sense!

Both officers felt, with some justification, that they were over-qualified in the streetwise department for a hick place like Bridgetown.

Here, the uniformed branch — most of whom, from sergeants downwards, were used to being spat on, sworn at and ridiculed by the local youths — regarded the two men with a certain degree of awe. The fact that they seemed to be in complete control of the 'yob element' had brought them the dubious honour of being christened Starsky and Hutch.

Neither man held Ashworth in high esteem, in fact they had awarded him the derisory nickname, Dixon of Dock

Green. They were judging the package by its wrapping, a mistake made by many, and a rude awakening lay ahead.

'What time do we give them to?' Whitworth asked.

Stimpson glanced at his watch. 'Ten . . . quarter past,' he mumbled.

'Hello, looks like we could be about to get our string pulled,' Whitworth said, in a voice edged with excitement. 'White van . . . just turning into the road . . . moving slow.'

'Got it,' was Stimpson's curt reply.

They watched as the large van slowly cruised along the road as if selecting a property. It stopped and four men emerged, looked left and right, then vanished behind a high hedge surrounding the garden of the house.

'They're going in,' Stimpson reported coolly.

Whitworth threw the remains of his hamburger into the bag, opened the car door, and knelt on the pavement behind it.

Flicking the radio on, he said into it, 'DC Whitworth to Bridgetown Station.' Nothing. 'Come on. DC Whitworth . . .'

'Sergeant Dutton here, DC Whitworth. What can I do for you?'

'What can you do for me? God!' Whitworth exclaimed. 'We've got a happening at . . .' He calculated the number of the house being broken into. '. . . 105 Denmark Road.'

'Right, back-up will be with you in three minutes. Don't do anything till then. Repeat . . . don't do—'

'Bollocks!' Whitworth hissed, and turned the radio off.

Peace was shattered by the clanging of an alarm bell, its box flashing red, lighting up the houses opposite.

'They're coming out.' This was Stimpson.

Whitworth was back behind the wheel, starting the car. Its modified engine purred into life.

The roar of the powerful motor, the piercing glow of headlights on full beam, panicked the already startled men. They bundled themselves inside the van.

Whitworth, with a sardonic grin, waited until the vehicle had pulled away from the kerb, then he let the clutch out.

'Come on, baby,' he said as the car jumped forward, tyres screaming, aiming straight for them.

Just at the moment when a head-on collision seemed imminent, he stamped on the brake pedal, swung the steering wheel hard to the left and, with the stench of burning rubber all around, he executed a perfectly timed skid out of the van's path.

The other driver, possessing neither Whitworth's driving skills nor his iron nerve, was partially blinded by the Cortina's headlights, terrified of the car hurtling towards him, and, in his panic, he steered the van on to the pavement.

The dull, sickening thud as metal smashed into brick, the sounds of breaking glass, and a cry of human anguish, all did battle with the noise from the alarm as the detectives sped towards the van.

CHAPTER 5

Holly Bedford's father had always described home as a haven beyond the reaches of life's woes. But for Holly, her bedroom was the only place where any tiny vestige of peace remained, even though life's woes still followed her there, and its domain was far from sacred as, unannounced, Emily would often violate its sanctuary.

Holly had arrived home to find almost sub-zero temperatures over the whole house, apart from the kitchen, where, in addition to heat being generated by the cooker, an electric fire was fully on. Emily was in there preparing chips and battered fish.

'Mum, the house is freezing. Why haven't you got the heating on?' she said, flicking the switch and turning the thermostat to high.

'We haven't got money to burn,' Emily sniffed, 'have we?'

This innuendo was a direct reference to a discussion they'd had a few days ago, during which Emily had complained about being left on her own all day in a strange place. Holly had impatiently explained that the only money they had coming in was Emily's pension, and her own salary. There was the mortgage to pay, food, and other living costs — it would be impractical for her not to work.

47

It had ended with Emily's brisk retort, 'You should have thought of that before you asked me to come and live with you. I only had my pension then and I managed.' Followed by, 'If you ask me, I think you like working with all the men.'

Culinary skill had never been Emily's forte and this meal had not provided a breakthrough: the chips were soggy, the fish overcooked to the point of being burnt.

Holly ate as much as her jaded appetite and indifferent tastebuds could tolerate, before pushing the plate to one side.

Emily's sideways glance at the discarded food did not require words to convey its message.

'There's one of them ballets on Channel Four tonight,' Emily said, in a conversational tone which Holly had learned to dread. 'Don't know what you see in them. They're boring. All them men prancing about in tights, showing all they've got.' She paused to eat a soggy chip. 'Anyway, it clashes with *Coronation Street*.'

Trying to sound cheerful, Holly said, 'I don't feel like watching television tonight, mum, I'll listen to some music in my room, then have a shower.'

It seemed that the more tolerant, considerate and patient she was, the more cantankerous, unreasonable and bloody-minded Emily became. The trait had been there for some years now, but it had definitely worsened since the move to Bridgetown. Holly knew there was an almighty row brewing and she did not want one this evening.

Emily stood up and began clearing the table. She was engaging in one of her more irritating habits: making muttered statements not directed at anyone and not requiring answers.

'I suppose the days when children sat with their parents have gone,' she mumbled, hobbling to the sink, her limp too exaggerated for the pain caused by her slightly arthritic knee. 'They're too selfish nowadays.'

Then tutting as she scraped Holly's almost untouched meal into the waste-bin, she went on, 'There's them in Africa that would murder for a meal like this . . . and there's them here who turn their noses up at it.'

Holly spent the evening lying on her bed, listening to Radio 5. It relaxed her a little and at ten p.m. she showered. She was back in her bedroom, naked, searching through the dressing table for her long flannelette night-shirt, when, unheralded by a knock, Emily opened the bedroom door. She viewed Holly's nudity with distaste. 'I'm off to bed. I've got fed up sitting down there on my own.'

Holly was glad when she found the night-shirt, and quickly pulled it over her head to cover herself up.

'You want to be careful with all this Aids about. They've just said on the news it's an epidemic.'

Holly had reached seven in her count to ten when she heard the door close.

How was it possible to have loved, body and soul, the off-spring of someone she now viewed with a feeling akin to hatred?

But it had been so. Holly had met Jason Bedford when she was nineteen; he was twenty-one. She was a WPC; he was a long-distance lorry driver.

Jason had definitely veered towards his father's side of the family: outwardly jovial and very good company; inwardly sensitive and caring.

Their courtship had been unremarkable, like many others, much planning and saving, and when they walked to the altar eighteen months later, they had a house, furniture and most of the things they needed.

The first two years of their marriage had been idyllic. Even their jobs had been compatible, as often Holly's spells of night duty would coincide with Jason's nights away from home.

His father, Bill, had taken to Holly from their first meeting, but Emily never had, although in the early days she had been far too astute to allow it to show.

Then a chain of events began which shattered Holly's life.

Jason lost some of his sparkle. At first, Holly put it down to overwork. They had decided — with the ambition of the young — to save enough money to move into a larger house and start a family, so Jason was working all the hours the law allowed, and although he stopped doing this, his condition deteriorated rather than improved.

He postponed it for as long as he could, but finally made an appointment with his GP. The doctor appeared disinterested, non-committal as he carried out the examination, refusing to be drawn on the series of tests he wanted Jason to undergo at the hospital.

In contrast the hospital staff were cheerful, reassuring, and they both reasoned that if there was anything wrong — really wrong — the occasion would have been far more solemn.

They used this thought to nourish themselves during the sleep-disturbed nights that followed, and finally came to believe it . . . until the GP insisted on seeing them both at the surgery.

Holly remembered little of what happened — only 'leukaemia' and 'successful treatment possible' had survived in her memory.

The possibility of a successful treatment sustained them until it became obvious that the disease would not be halted.

In desperation Holly turned to the power of prayer, but as the disease and the drugs began to disrupt the mental stability of the man she loved, she abandoned any hope of divine intervention and prepared herself for the inevitable.

Even now, more than three years after it had happened, the memories could still cause dry sobs to rack her body. Tears no longer accompanied the sobbing, for her heart told her it had wept enough — it was time to live again.

When Jason finally died, a few days before Christmas, Holly's overriding emotion had been relief. She told herself at the time it was because Jason was now beyond suffering — which was true — but it was also relief for herself.

That was the beginning of the guilt from which she still could not escape. To admit to oneself that the demise of a loved one heralds the opportunity to begin living again sets into place a number of obstacles which prevent one from doing so.

Her parents, wonderfully supportive, had argued that at twenty-four she was still a young woman, and no one would expect her to waste the life which lay before her. And with the candour that befits the modern woman, Holly admitted that she had physical needs which were only remotely attached to the spiritual aspect of love; but those needs remained unfulfilled — she felt that her body belonged to the man who lay deep in the earth, beneath a marble headstone.

Little by little, she managed to pick herself up, returning to work where she swiftly gained promotion to the rank of Detective Constable.

After a time, as fond memories of Jason mellowed, she began to resent the grave, seeing it as the manifestation of all her emotional problems. The feeling grew inside her that, if only she could get away from that plot of land, she would be able to put her past life into perspective. But before such an opportunity could present itself, fate dealt her another cruel blow; one which further entwined her with a husband who had been dead for a year.

Jason's father died from a heart attack. It struck suddenly, swiftly, granting him only enough time to savour the prospect of escaping from the terrible woman he had married.

Out of some misguided sense of duty, Holly felt obliged to offer Emily a home, and although her own parents counselled strongly against it, she remained insistent.

From the start it was apparent that the situation could not work. Emily Bedford was a woman who demanded her own way. All through her married life she had achieved that end by giving full vent to her dominant personality. When Holly would not succumb, Emily resorted to every possible type of emotional blackmail.

Then the opportunity of a career move to Bridgetown came about — with rapid promotion prospects for the right applicant — and Holly jumped at it, hoping that her mother-in-law, not wishing to uproot herself, would apply to the council to be rehoused.

But Emily, true martyr that she was, forsook her roots, relinquished her memories, and stuck — leech-like — to her daughter-in-law.

No one in CID yet knew that they would soon be spending several evenings away from home. Holly would be the only member of the team to rejoice at the news.

CHAPTER 6

Ashworth was breakfasting lightly on crispbread, low-fat margarine, sugar-free marmalade, and coffee with skimmed milk and sweeteners. The diet, despite his excesses when away from the fold, was still working.

It was eight thirty. He rather absently kissed Sarah's cheek, reminded her to leave the heating on low all day, and left for the station.

Front reception seemed quiet and normal. Young Bobby Adams was behind the desk, his uniform neat, his mane of blond hair parted on the right and — to use a phrase from Ashworth's youth — 'larded down'.

A slight colouring crept into his young face when he saw Ashworth walking towards him.

'I'm sorry about yesterday, Chief Inspector,' he stammered, as Ashworth leant on the desk.

'It's all right, Bobby,' Ashworth cajoled, then, motioning to the boy, he said kindly, 'I just want to have a word with you, son. When you first join the force a lot of people try to wind you up. It's happened to all of us.' He laughed, expecting Adams to laugh with him. The young constable, however, merely swallowed loudly.

'Anyway,' Ashworth persevered, 'if you don't let them see it's upsetting you, after a time they usually stop being silly.'

'Yes, sir.' Adams clicked his heels as he stood to attention, interpreting the Chief Inspector's speech as a dressing-down.

Ashworth sighed and turned to walk away.

'Sergeant Dutton would like to see you, Chief Inspector,' Adams informed him nervously.

Ashworth turned back to the desk. 'Well, where is he, Bobby?'

'Oh, sorry, sir.' Adams marched stiffly to a door at the rear of the reception area. He gave a cautious knock, then popped his head round to announce Ashworth's arrival.

Sergeant Martin Dutton emerged and came round from behind the desk to where Ashworth was waiting.

'I'm off duty actually, Jim, but I waited for you. I think you've got problems.'

'Yes?' Ashworth asked as Dutton guided him away from the desk.

'It's Starsky and Hutch . . .' Dutton stopped and cast Ashworth an apologetic look. 'Sorry, that's . . .'

'Yes, I think I know who Starsky and Hutch are.'

'Well, the good news is, last night they arrested four men for burglary.'

'And the bad news?'

'They ignored a command to wait for back-up. Two of the men are in hospital, and the two we've got in the cells claim Whitworth drove straight at them, forcing their van off the road and into a brick wall.'

Ashworth digested this. 'Is there anything else?'

'With that pair there's always going to be more.' Dutton studied Ashworth's stony expression before continuing. 'We've had a social worker in, complaining that DC Whitworth stamped on the foot of one of her charges, badly bruising it.'

'This was in the station?'

'No, Jim, in an amusement arcade. The Chief Constable isn't due in till eleven, so I thought I'd forewarn you.'

'Good man.'

Dutton shuffled his feet, seeming reluctant to walk away even though he was already an hour late going off duty.

'Is there anything else, Martin?'

'Yes there is . . . This may sound like tittle-tattle . . .'

'That doesn't matter.'

'It's young Bobby — DS Stimpson definitely told him you'd ordered the radio messages to be coded from now on. I don't like telling tales, Jim . . .'

Ashworth knew that Dutton felt a responsibility towards every raw recruit who enlisted in the police force, and any complaints about the behaviour of CID were prompted by his sympathetic nature, rather than by maliciousness.

'You're not, Martin, those two have got to be sorted out. Leave it with me. And thanks for waiting for me to come in. I appreciate it.'

Ashworth shunned the lift and quickly climbed the stairs, all the time thinking of how he should handle the situation, for — contrary to general belief — he did not like being at odds with anyone; it did nasty things to his blood pressure, disrupted his digestive system, but he accepted that it was part of the job.

Being a scrupulously fair man, he held himself partly to blame — as head of a team of officers he should have stamped his authority upon them from the outset.

Acrid smoke from Whitworth's cigarette stung his nostrils as he entered the office. Of the four pairs of eyes focused upon him, he noticed that only Whitworth's were without apprehension.

'DS Stimpson and DC Whitworth in my office. Now!' he said stiffly.

His tone caused Stimpson's face to lose a little of its colour. But Whitworth, mostly for the benefit of the others, gave a wicked grin as he stood up.

Ashworth was taking off his waxed jacket as the men entered his office. He ignored them until he was seated at his desk.

55

He had noted that Whitworth had bruising round his left eye and that Stimpson was walking with a slight limp.

'Right, what the hell happened last night?' he barked.

Ashworth's abrasive manner brought Whitworth's volatile nature rushing to the fore. He ignored Stimpson's wave of the hand, urging caution. 'I'll tell you what happened, sir. Last night we solved a series of burglaries that have been baffling this nick for months. And after sitting there for hours, with my balls freezing off, then having some son-of-a-bitch trying to crack my head open with an iron bar, I'm not going to be dragged in here for a bollocking, because that gets right up my nose!'

'I don't know how you've behaved in other nicks you've worked in,' Ashworth thundered, 'but in this one you do not speak to a superior officer in that manner.'

He locked eyes with Whitworth, whose expression contained scorn, defiance and hostility.

Ashworth realised he had subdued the man only by pulling rank, by stating, 'You will do as I say, because I hold higher office than you.' This did not rest easily on his masculinity. A pulse beat in his forehead, heavy veins stood out in his bull-like neck.

When he spoke his voice was calm, but firm. 'I think there's something we have to clear up, DC Whitworth. From your record, and, indeed, your attitude, it seems you think you're some sort of hard man who's seen it all. I get the impression you regard your term of duty here as little more than a holiday with the yokels.'

He stood up now and leant forward to lock eyes with the DC. 'Well, I'll tell you something, son, I've had my moments, and although I'm a little overweight and a few years past my best I'm still quite capable of having a go, so any time you find me getting up your nose, just let me know. Do you understand what I'm saying, son?'

Whitworth was noticeably shaken by Ashworth's onslaught. In the past his behaviour had often given rise to criticism and reprimand, but never before had a Chief Inspector offered to fight him; but then, never before had he met a Chief Inspector named Ashworth.

He said, stonily, 'Yes, sir,' but this time the 'sir' was uttered without an insulting ring to it.

Ashworth sat down. 'Then I'll ask you again. What happened last night?'

Stimpson cut in smoothly, determined to twist the facts and show himself in a favourable light. 'We apprehended four men for burglary, sir. The two detained in the cells have already made statements admitting to most of the outstanding break-ins on our books.'

'Fine, but it's the manner in which you apprehended them that concerns me. Why didn't you wait for back-up?'

'We saw them going into the house, sir, and we radioed in. While we were doing that they set the alarm off.'

'They've coped with alarmed houses before,' Ashworth remarked dismissively. 'You should have waited. Instead, you over-reacted.'

'With all due respect, sir, both DC Whitworth and I are fully aware that a good team of burglars can have a normal household alarm disconnected inside ten seconds . . .'

Ashworth began to relax now that he sensed there was going to be some plausible explanation with which to pacify Ken Savage. 'So why couldn't they do this one?'

'Because the guy who owns the house works for a security company. He'd cobbled up the alarm from bits and pieces. To condense it, sir, he'd fitted the type of alarm used in banks and business premises: it had a battery fitted in the box on the outside wall, so whatever is done to the main power supply or the control box inside the house, the alarm keeps going off until the code is punched in.'

'I see.'

Ashworth was about to ask the men to sit down, but then thought better of it. 'And why did the van crash? You should have followed it, kept in radio contact with the station.'

'That's what we intended to do, sir,' Stimpson lied. 'But they realised we were police and drove straight at us. If it hadn't been for DC Whit—'

'Why wasn't the alarm still going off when back-up arrived?' Ashworth cut in.

'Simple, sir. Two of the suspects were slightly injured in the crash, but the others became very violent when we tried to arrest them—'

'That's not answering my question,' Ashworth said harshly.

His curt manner was now beginning to ruffle Stimpson but he did not let it show. He said earnestly, 'While all this was happening, sir, the next-door neighbour, who knew the alarm code, went into the house and turned it off because he was watching the test match and the noise was disturbing him.'

Ashworth had to swallow a smile; he knew from experience that at times the behaviour of the general public could appear farcical.

'And another thing, sir,' Stimpson continued in his obsequious manner. 'We'd arrested the two men, put them in the car, and called an ambulance before back-up arrived. It had been promised for three minutes, but took closer to six. We had to go in or risk losing our suspects.'

'Yes, all right,' Ashworth conceded impatiently. 'Make out your reports . . . and really go into detail about the alarm system.'

He paused and allowed his eyes to skim over Whitworth. 'Now, there are a couple of other matters . . . We had a complaint that a lad came away with a bruised foot after talking to you, DC Whitworth. What explanation have you got for that?'

'I think you're referring to an incident that took place in the Vegas Amusement Arcade, sir,' Whitworth replied, his manner still hostile. 'I was investigating the attempted break-in when this lad accidentally spat on my jacket. He explained that no offence had been intended, it was just that

I was standing between him and the spot he wanted to spit at. Immediately after that, I accidentally stepped on his foot. There were a lot of accidents that day . . . sir.'

'So it would seem. Don't do a report on that. Now the last thing is, if you want to wind a fellow officer up, pick on somebody with the confidence to look after himself. You both know who I'm referring to. And just remember not to step on any toes . . . especially mine. Right, that's it.' He motioned for them to leave.

Back in the main office the detectives strolled casually back to their desks.

'He's a right do-it-yourself merchant,' Whitworth remarked casually.

Puzzled, Holly said, 'A do-it-yourself merchant?'

'What Mike is saying, in a very polite way, is that our lord and master is a wanker,' Stimpson answered jauntily, although his tone was hushed.

'That's not what it sounded like from out here,' Holly said scornfully, for she was already beginning to develop a loyalty towards Ashworth.

If any of them had harboured any illusions that their new Guvnor's reputation had been exaggerated for their benefit, then the last ten minutes had dispelled them.

Stimpson was, even now, rethinking his earlier assessment of Ashworth; although he still did not really regard him as a force to be reckoned with, he had to admit that the man was not the country bumpkin he had at first assumed.

Another thing was plainly obvious: Ashworth's opinion carried a lot of weight, and Stimpson now saw him as a useful ally in his fight for promotion.

Whitworth watched with distrust as Stimpson returned to Ashworth's door, flattening his tie and buttoning his jacket before knocking firmly.

'Come.'

'A word, sir, if I may,' said Stimpson, closing the door quietly.

'Yes?' Ashworth invited him to sit.

Stimpson settled into the chair facing his superior. 'I'm a little concerned about these attempted break-ins.'

'Why?' Ashworth asked bluntly.

Stimpson had heard that Ashworth preferred feelings as opposed to theories, so that was the route he pursued. 'I've got a feeling about them, sir.'

'Be precise,' Ashworth snapped. He had little time for the man, recognising him as a climber who would jettison his own mother, if he considered that to be a good career move.

'There was someone in all three properties at the times of the attempted break-ins. All of them women, late twenties, early thirties.'

Stimpson had expected some degree of interest, congrat-ulations, perhaps, on his insight, but all he got was a puzzled expression.

'I'm not following you,' Ashworth said stiffly.

'Aggravated burglary, sir,' Stimpson explained politely. 'In London we call it 'Rape and steal the shopping money'.'

'Rape? How old are these kids?'

'Fourteen, fifteen, sir.'

'And you think they're looking around for women to rape?'

'Nowadays, sir, lots of fifteen-year-olds have very full sex lives.'

Ashworth knew Stimpson was right, of course, but when faced with this truth, his initial reaction was always one of sor-row at the passing of the moral values attained in his own youth.

'So maybe they're just trying to spice it up a little,' Stimpson speculated, trying not to sound patronising.

Ashworth looked at him. 'What are you basing these assumptions on?'

'It's just too coincidental that lone women were in all three properties. If the burglars had chosen at random, I'd have expected at least one to have been empty.'

Ashworth grunted. 'Any description of the youngsters?'

'Very scant. Three different descriptions with only one common factor: the two lads were wearing balaclavas.'

Ashworth could remember most of Bridgetown's mid-teen population being escorted, by their mothers, to primary school, and he found it difficult to associate any of them with the crime of rape. But in the light of what Stimpson was saying, he realised it was a possibility he would have to take seriously.

'Right, you and Whitworth handle it, and report anything back to me.'

He was on the point of dismissing the detective when he changed his mind, asking, 'What do you make of Whitworth?'

Stimpson framed his answer carefully, realising that too strong a condemnation of his colleague's behaviour would bring his own into question; far better to concentrate on the problems it might cause in the future. 'He's good, sir, but . . . how can I put this so it won't seem like a stab in the back?' He hoped that the conflict between doing his duty and betraying a friend showed in his face. 'His methods are too extreme for a place like Bridgetown. My own approach is to try and contain the local element without antagonism.'

I prefer him to you, Ashworth thought; at least he comes up with straight answers.

'Very commendable,' Ashworth remarked, cynically. 'Well, I'm looking to you to keep him in check.'

There was a knock at the door.

'Come,' Ashworth called, hoping this would bring their discussion to an end.

A pale-faced Holly entered the office. 'Excuse me, sir, we've just had a call from Barbara Edwards. Someone's telephoned her, claiming to have abducted her husband.'

CHAPTER 7

Holly sat silent in the passenger seat of Ashworth's Sierra as he drove to the Edwardses' residence.

Snow was steadily falling, but the large flakes, as they hit fields and pavements made warm by a weak sun, quickly dispersed into sparkling droplets, and did not hamper the car's progress.

At the driveway to the house, however, it had begun to take hold, clinging to the tarmac and making slow progress across the path.

Barbara Edwards was waiting for them on the porch. Ashworth noted that she looked agitated — quite understandably — but there was no sign of the neurosis from which Dennis Paine insisted she suffered.

As the car drew to a halt in front of the house, Barbara, despite the fact that she was wearing carpet slippers, ran towards it.

Holly was first out. 'Come on, Barbara, let's go inside,' she coaxed, shepherding the woman towards the house.

'Thank goodness you're here, Holly,' she cried.

By the time Ashworth had locked the car and followed them into the lounge, Holly had seated Barbara in a large armchair by the fire and was crouching down in front of her.

She was saying, 'Right, Barbara, tell me what happened.'

Ashworth felt like an onlooker as he remained standing by the door.

Barbara, trembling violently, said, 'I know it sounds silly but I felt so happy this morning. Last night, Dennis — he's my brother, if you remember.'

'I remember, Barbara. Carry on.'

'Well, Dennis convinced me that Simon would come home today and everything would be all right. When the phone rang I picked it up, thinking it would be Simon . . .'

Her voice cracked and Holly had to wait a moment before she continued falteringly. 'There was nothing for a few seconds. Then a man's voice said, 'I've got your husband, Mrs Edwards. These are my instructions: Don't go to the police or I'll kill him. Be by the phone tonight."

Holly — aware that, even now, Ashworth would be assessing her ability — asked, 'Were those the caller's exact words?'

'I can't remember, Holly,' she sobbed. 'It was all such a shock.'

'But he definitely said — be by the phone tonight?'

Barbara nodded furiously, causing hot tears to escape her eyes.

'The voice, Barbara . . . what was the voice like?'

With a shudder, Barbara said, 'It was horrible . . . muffled . . .'

Then the door burst open.

Ashworth stepped aside just in time to clear the path of Dennis Paine who stood framed in the doorway, his face white with anger. 'What the hell's happening here?' he stormed.

The outburst brought Barbara's attention swiftly to her brother. She ran to him, threw her arms about his neck, and cried pitifully into his chest.

He patted her back, awkwardly. 'There now, Babs, I came as soon as you called.' Then to Ashworth, 'I'm still waiting.'

'If you've already spoken with your sister you know as much as we do,' Ashworth replied gruffly.

'That's not what I asked,' Paine said harshly.

'Don't, Dennis. Don't . . .' Barbara pleaded. Then she ran from the room and her muffled footfalls could be heard on the stairs.

'Look what you've done now,' Paine said accusingly. 'Don't you bloody people realise how serious this matter is?'

'We're well aware of the gravity of the situation,' Holly threw in, 'but your rudeness is only upsetting your sister.'

'My brother-in-law has been kidnapped, and you people are doing nothing about it. I think that entitles me to ask questions.'

'If we're finished here, sir, I'll wait in the car,' Holly stated flatly.

Ashworth nodded.

'God,' Paine muttered. 'How much of the council tax goes on funding the police?'

With temper rising, Ashworth retorted, 'Mr Paine, a lot of people might claim your behaviour was unreasonable. Yesterday, you didn't want me to do anything about Mr Edwards's disappearance. Today, you're lambasting me because I haven't. Like I say, there are those who would claim that was unreasonable. But being less charitable, I'd say you were behaving like a bloody fool!'

Paine glowered at the Chief Inspector. 'You'd better watch it. I know the Chief Constable.'

'So do I,' Ashworth responded hotly. 'Now, what I want from you is permission for my officers to be here tonight, for the kidnapper's call.'

'Yes, yes, of course,' Paine snapped. 'I won't be able to be here. Someone has to run the factory, or Babs would starve to death.'

Making no attempt to conceal the insult, Ashworth said, 'It may be just as well you won't be here.'

'You're getting on my nerves—'

'And you're getting on mine,' Ashworth confirmed briskly. 'If we're not too careful, we could fall out. We'll be here about five.'

Outside, the snow was settling; it crunched beneath Ashworth's shoes.

Holly, unable to gain access into the car, had been forced to stand in what was fast becoming a blizzard.

She looked thankfully at Ashworth as he held open the passenger door, saying, 'I'm sorry, sir, I just couldn't stay in there with that man.'

Ashworth, settling behind the steering wheel, glanced at the large house. 'He is a charmer, isn't he?'

'You can say that again,' Holly agreed. 'And have you noticed how Barbara seems to be all right till he appears on the scene?'

'I have. Yes, I think I'll ask a few questions about our Mr Paine. He seems too hostile to me. It might be a good idea to get someone to stay at the house with Mrs Edwards . . . another relative.'

'There is no other relative, sir . . . just the three of them. They've no children, and both sets of parents are dead.'

'Fancy having Dennis Paine as your only living relative,' Ashworth mused. 'Holly, can you be available for duty tonight?'

'Of course, sir.'

'It could be a long one.'

'No problem, sir.'

'Good. So, it'll be you, Josh, and myself. I don't want Starsky and Hutch anywhere near this. If Whitworth finds out there's been a kidnapping, he'll probably start taking hostages.'

Holly laughed, surprised that her boss knew about the nicknames, let alone used them.

She wondered if he knew hers: Pussy Galore. A natural title, given that she was an expert at martial arts.

Stimpson and Whitworth, however, after having had all of their sexual advances rejected, were forever throwing grave doubts upon its accuracy. Holly never bothered to respond, much to their chagrin.

The snow had already covered Paine's incoming tracks. As Ashworth eased the car along the sweeping drive an uneasy silence settled upon them; each was lost in their own thoughts, Holly anticipating Emily's reaction on hearing she must spend the evening alone, Ashworth thinking of all he had to do, with little time to do it in, and cursing the snow which dictated their slow return to the station.

* * *

The afternoon proved hectic.

Ashworth reported to Chief Constable Savage, who sat with lips pursed as the situation was explained to him.

'I'll leave it all to you, Jim,' he said, neatly shouldering the responsibility on to Ashworth and leaving his own evening free. Nothing displeased Savage more than a night of sobriety. 'Do you think this man could be a crank?'

'As no one outside his immediate family knows Edwards is missing, I very much doubt it. I want to keep this out of the news for the moment, Ken. No media coverage.'

Savage lit a cigarette. 'Right. If you handle the newspapers, I'll contact the television people.'

When Ashworth made no move to leave, Savage asked, 'Is there anything else, Jim?'

'Yes. I believe you know the brother-in-law, Dennis Paine.'

Savage caught the irritation in his Chief Inspector's tone. Ah, Paine's sharp tongue has already ruffled his feathers; a little diplomacy is needed here. 'Yes, I do. Paine by name . . . as they say. He's a very abrasive man, Jim. Self-made; works like a Trojan, but finds it difficult to delegate. He simply doesn't think anyone can do a job as well as he can.'

'Well, if he continues being abusive towards me or my officers, he can have the job of finding his brother-in-law,' Ashworth stated flatly.

Savage laughed. 'I'll have a quiet word with him. It's so much a part of the man's nature, he probably doesn't realise he's doing it.' Then, hoping to change the subject, 'By the way, Stimpson and Whitworth did a fine job on those burglaries. When I first heard about the crashed van, people in hospital, I thought, God, what's happening? But when I read their reports . . . They acted very well, Jim. Perhaps you'll pass on my congratulations.'

'Yes, Ken, of course,' Ashworth muttered with a strained cheerfulness.

* * *

Later, with road conditions hazardous, Ashworth steered his Sierra through the mounting traffic and parked at the Bull and Butcher public house in Bridgetown High Street.

It did not take much to make this man happy, and a walk along the high street was always guaranteed to lift his spirits.

He loved what he called 'Bridgetown proper': the small nucleus of shops and cottages; the maze of narrow roads and alleyways. Each building had retained its original character. Even the town's two banks still had the appearance of crofters' cottages. Take away the cars, street lighting and telephone wires and one could easily be transported back to the eighteenth-century.

Ashworth was lucky: he had Bridgetown, a happy, secure homelife, and a job he loved.

He always needed a problem to unravel, though. When his workload was light, he became bored, crotchety and ill-tempered. He was always at his best when embroiled in what others would regard as insurmountable problems; then his step became jaunty, his sense of humour keen, his brain alert.

He was on his way to the offices of the town's two newspapers: the old-established *Bridgetown Chronicle*, and the more recent free newspaper, the *Bridgetown Post*.

The editors — both of whom, in print, were pugnacious crusaders, ever willing to highlight the shortcomings of the police and politicians — proved to be charming, helpful and co-operative.

Ashworth approached the third call of the afternoon with mixed feelings. Even though he had never been unfaithful to Sarah, he still had an appreciative eye for a beautiful woman.

The opportunities to stray had been there, but he had always stopped to consider the consequences, had seen a fleeting sexual experience for what it was — trivial.

Still, there had been times when the chemical reaction had been so acute that the urge to resist had proved difficult.

Such was the case with Dr Gwen Anthony, GP and locum pathologist. The fact that the attraction was mutual made it doubly embarrassing.

Married to her partner, in a practice they had taken over five years ago, Gwen had often dealt with Ashworth during the course of her work. She was highly knowledgeable, totally professional, and a flirt, who — in Ashworth's opinion — was hard to resist.

Although he was resigned to the fact that some things can never be, the romantic in Ashworth still yearned for just one hour free from conscience and commitments.

With his thoughts running along these lines he approached the doctor's surgery. It was a beautiful building, originally a large cottage, and the quaintness of it held an appeal for him. The living room was now the waiting area, from where patients trooped up winding creaky stairs to what had once been the master bedroom, which had hardly changed at all over the last hundred years.

An early Victorian fireplace graced the chimney breast. An old porcelain washstand filled one corner. The white plastered walls were decorated with the doctor's framed qualifications. The dark stained floorboards were bare. A cheerful coal-effect gas fire seemed to be the only concession to the present day.

The centre of the room was home to a cluttered redwood desk, and a comfortable, highly scuffed, green leather chair.

Gwen Anthony was scrubbing her hands as Ashworth entered. Straightaway she smiled. 'Hello, Jim. What a lovely surprise,' she enthused, drying her hands hurriedly on a paper towel.

Ashworth felt the usual surge of desire as he watched her. She was in her late forties, tall — perhaps five feet eight. Her loosely tailored dark grey suit did little to conceal the swell of her voluptuous breasts, the curve of her hips and buttocks. Her thick dark hair was tied back, but the severity of the style was softened by a hint of amusement in her clear blue eyes and the permanent half-smile on her lips.

She crossed to Ashworth and kissed him lightly on his cheek, moist lips just brushing his skin. She smelt clean, fresh, her natural odour unmasked by perfume; it was how Ashworth liked a woman to smell.

'Sit down,' she said, indicating the chair in front of her desk.

As he settled into it, Ashworth watched her returning a patient's notes to their file.

Gwen sat down with a sigh. 'People,' she said lightly. 'I've just had a woman in here — thirty-five years old — who's missed three periods, hoping with all her might that she's in the change of life. She's pregnant, of course.' Gwen huffed. 'Can you believe unwanted pregnancies in this day and age?'

'Actually, Gwen, I've never given it a great deal of thought,' Ashworth replied, smiling.

Gwen laughed. 'No, I suppose not.' She sat up straight and gave him her full attention. 'Right, you look perfectly healthy to me, and I presume this isn't a social call, so what can I do for you?'

'Gwen, I know I can rely on you to be discreet—'

'My God, Jim,' she said, with mock horror, 'what are you going to suggest?'

Ashworth chuckled. 'Relax,' he said, then sobering, 'I've got a kidnapping.'

Gwen's smile faded abruptly. 'I see. How can I help?'

'Well, with your knowledge of psychiatry, I wondered if you could provide me with some sort of profile on the type of person who's likely to carry out a crime of this nature. And, of course, advise me on how to deal with him.'

She thought for a while, then said, 'A lot of this is going to be generalisation, Jim — rather like those serial killer profiles.'

'I realise that, but anything you can tell me will help.'

'Okay. Firstly, you were right to assume that it's a man — the strength needed indicates as much. He's highly intelligent. In fact, his intelligence could probably border on genius.'

'Marvellous,' Ashworth interjected morosely.

'But for some reason he's never fulfilled his potential. How can I put this? He may have a physical deformity, or a speech impediment. But whatever it is has grown out of all proportion in his mind.'

'And he sees it as holding him back?'

'Not quite, Jim. Because of it he has to try harder, prove how clever he is. Remember you're dealing with a personality disorder. If you or I couldn't say our 'r's, for instance, we would simply tackle the problem and put it right. Our man can't do that and is convinced that no one can see beyond the disability — that's the real problem.'

Gwen noticed Ashworth's blank expression. 'I'm not explaining this very well, I know.' She tried another tack. 'You're seeing this as a crime committed for gain, but it's not—'

'You're saying the ransom money isn't important?'

'No, I'm not,' she stated emphatically. 'It's vital, but not in the way you think. The money's going to be marked, or the numbers taken, so it's going to be years before he can spend it — if ever. You or I would probably regard it as fool's ransom.'

Realisation suddenly dawned on Ashworth. 'I think I'm with you — it's the fact that he can take it from under my nose—'

'You're getting there, Jim. You see, that would force you to acknowledge just how clever he is. For this man the 'Police Baffled' headlines would be worth more than money.'

'So it's a game?'

'You could look at it that way, but a pretty dangerous one. Always remember you're dealing with an unbalanced mind.'

Ashworth frowned. 'You said he sees it as a game between himself and the police, and yet he's warned against us being called in.'

'But he means the exact opposite,' Gwen said earnestly. 'And it's not between him and the police. Sooner, rather than later, he'll personalise it. You against him.'

'And what form will this take?'

'Now there, Jim, you have his weak point. He'll taunt you . . . all the time finding it impossible to leave you alone . . . will point out how stupid you are. He's really saying, 'Look at me . . . aren't I clever?' Egotism is this man's Achilles' heel.'

'So, we'll catch him?'

'Oh yes, be certain of that.' She raised her eyebrows questioningly. 'It's just a matter of when.'

'Why do I feel you're about to tell me some bad news?' Ashworth said pensively.

'Don't base any police operations on this,' she said hesitantly, 'it's pure conjecture, but I'd guess the first two runs with the money will be dummies. Your man will be there watching, but only because he wants to prove how superior he is. The third run will be the important one.'

'And if he gets the money?'

'Then you've entered the really dangerous area, because then he's faced with a choice. Which would be the best way to demonstrate his cleverness? Release his hostage, who could undoubtedly give some clue to his identity, where he had been held, and countless other things . . .' She looked pointedly at Ashworth.

'Or kill him,' he said flatly.

Gwen shrugged. 'That's about it.'

'So what can I do?'

'Maintain a media black-out . . . even if he gets the money. That way you'll be robbing him of the one thing he craves — attention.'

'But if he murders the victim, he'll be sure of the publicity.'

'Quite. You're walking a tightrope, Jim. When you reach that point, there's no knowing which way he'll jump.'

Ashworth sighed heavily, then asked, 'What's the man like? How does he look?'

'Not much help there, I'm afraid. To the ordinary person he probably seems perfectly normal . . . a little reserved, perhaps.'

'So, I'm looking for a psychopathic genius who appears normal. And I thought this was going to be difficult,' Ashworth said drily.

'There's one thing that may help you enormously — remember, this man sees you not as an enemy, more as an opponent, and if he finds you to be a worthy opponent, that will influence his behaviour quite a lot.'

'What do you mean?'

'Make it difficult for him, but at the same time, feed his ego so that he feels he's really achieving something. But, I warn you, a lot is going to depend on your own judgement.'

All of a sudden Ashworth could feel responsibility weighing heavily on his shoulders. He slowly rose to his feet. 'Well, I won't take up any more of your time.'

'Don't be silly. It's nice to see you . . . and it's getting to be a rare event nowadays.' She smiled suggestively, moving to his side. 'I sometimes think you're avoiding me.'

'That's nonsense, Gwen,' Ashworth protested, feebly.

'No, it isn't.' Her eyes sparkled. 'I can't decide whether it's because you don't like me . . .' A pause. '. . . or you can't trust yourself when you're with me. I like to think it's the latter.'

'Well, it's definitely not the former,' Ashworth confirmed, realising that she was unashamedly flirting, and that he was responding.

Gwen pounced on that immediately. 'Ah, now you've made a statement — you can't trust yourself in my company. Anyway, I shall be finding out in the very near future.'

Catching his puzzled expression, she explained. 'Ken Savage telephoned me. He's fixing something up with the Home Office. You'll be representing the police, and I'll be there in my capacity as a pathologist.' She laughed lightly. 'We'll be staying at the same hotel, Jim. You'll have to buy me dinner.'

'I'll look forward to it,' Ashworth said with a grin.

'Oh, so shall I, Jim. I really shall.'

For a few breath-stopping seconds it seemed that a kiss would be inevitable, but then the front door slammed, and the old stairs creaked as someone started to climb them.

'Drat,' Gwen muttered, glancing at her watch. 'That's my husband, come to prepare for evening surgery.'

She moved back to her desk and Ashworth breathed easily once more.

CHAPTER 8

Holly shunned the office telephone. The call was likely to be difficult enough without Alistair and Mike interjecting at every opportunity, so she used the payphone in the busy main corridor.

'Come on,' she muttered, as the ringing tone sounded for what seemed like an age.

The connection was made and Emily's 'Hello?' thundered down the line.

Holly winced. Her mother-in-law was not fond of the telephone, would only answer if the ringing persisted for too long, and then her response would be bellowed impatiently into the mouthpiece.

'Hello, mum. It's Holly.'

'Yes?' she said, her voice heavy with suspicion.

'I'll be late home tonight.'

After a pause steeped in malice, Emily managed, 'Why?'

Two uniformed constables were now waiting to use the telephone. Holly felt like an errant schoolgirl as she whispered, 'Because I've got to work late.'

There was another silence. Then Emily said, 'There was a programme on telly last week, and they said the most common excuse people committing adultery use is working late.'

How was it possible to commit adultery against one's mother-in-law? Holly thought, sourly. But she let it go and ventured on, 'So I don't know what time I'll be home.'

'You want to be careful, my girl—'

'I've got to go, mum. 'Bye.'

Holly replaced the receiver with relief, thankful that she had at least managed to avoid Emily's latest bulletin on the spread of the Aids epidemic.

* * *

The atmosphere in the Edwardses' house was laden with tension. The heating was full on and, despite the arctic conditions outside, its rooms were oppressively hot.

An aura of expectancy lay heavily in the air. All present were restless and edgy, silently willing something to happen, yet dreading that moment when it came.

Josh Abraham sat with Holly in the lounge. Neither spoke; they sat staring at the telephone and recording equipment which occupied the coffee table in front of them.

Ashworth had surprised them both by gently taking Barbara Edwards under his wing. Holly had assumed that would be her role.

But Ashworth's show of kindness hid an ulterior motive: he needed to gain Barbara's confidence in order to extract as much information about her husband as was possible. To gain a full picture of the man, Ashworth needed to become familiar with the state of their marriage, his movements, his enemies — if any — and the million and one other details that made up a life.

They were, at present, ensconced in the kitchen, and the predominant sound in the lounge was the ominous ticking of the clock.

The lack of dialogue between Holly and Josh was due not so much to inhibitions or shyness, but to a feeling that frivolous small talk would appear irreverent.

However, Holly's demure appearance masked her true feelings of bubbly effervescence caused by Josh's close presence.

Earlier on, due to Ashworth's distrust of her dilapidated Mini, Josh had been instructed to drive her to the Edwardses' house.

During the journey, Josh had proved himself to be stimulating company. They had discussed many things, including music, and had been thrilled to discover that they shared an obsession for the classics — a fact that neither would have admitted to back in the office for fear of ridicule.

When Josh had expertly brought his Nissan Sunny to a halt at a red traffic light, he had casually mentioned that there was to be a performance of Henryk Górecki's Third Symphony at Bridgenorton the following week, and had asked if Holly would like to go with him. She had said that she would love to, and a sudden surge of adrenalin had caused her stomach to flutter deliciously.

Despite the seriousness of the situation, the thought of that date was never far from Holly's mind, and she was happier now than she had been for a long time.

Even so, time marched on, and as seven p.m. became eight p.m., the tension mounted in all of them.

Having left Barbara in the kitchen, Ashworth had taken to prowling around the house. Josh had loosened his tie and undone the top button of his shirt, and Holly's inner mood had become more serious as the minutes ticked away.

Terrifying howls of pain and anger rent the night air as two cats fought out a territorial dispute, somewhere on the snowy landscape. The sounds only added to the feelings of suspense and unease inside the house.

Ashworth was highly susceptible to atmospheres and felt that this one was thick with malevolence, but, he reasoned, it was all part of the kidnapper's ploy to unnerve him.

At nine p.m., when all were convinced that nothing was going to happen, the telephone rang.

Barbara's anguished cry came from the kitchen. Then everything was reaction. Josh was on his feet, activating the recording equipment.

Holly fetched Barbara, whose face was drawn and pale, and led her to the telephone in the hall. 'All right, Barbara, answer it,' she said gently.

Barbara did not move, so Holly picked up the receiver and placed it into her trembling hand. She heard a slight click on the line — Ashworth must have picked up the receiver in the lounge.

'Hello?' Barbara whispered, her tone tremulous.

The acid note in the muffled, distorted voice made her gasp out loud. 'You've told the police . . . bitch! Now, this is what I want you to do. The police will want proof that I've got your husband. Tell them to go to the disused barn on Parker's Farm. Then you'll have to wait for my further instructions in the post.'

The line went dead.

In a state of near-collapse, Barbara repeatedly muttered, 'Oh, my God. Oh, my God,' as the full impact of the situation finally hit her. Then, as Holly slowly steered her back to the kitchen, she let out a series of shrieking wails which Holly's soothing utterances failed to stem.

In the lounge, Ashworth could only listen, impotently. 'Damn!' he cursed, as the sounds became muffled by the closing of the kitchen door.

The call had been too short, too rushed for him to glean anything from it, the voice too distorted to catch even a hint of dialect or accent.

He cast a frustrated glance at Josh. 'Not much to go on, was there?'

'There was a sound on the line, sir.'

'Yes, I heard it. Sounded like metal hitting metal.' He walked to the window, pulled the curtain back and looked outside. 'Fine night for tramping about all over Parker's Farm.'

'Do you want me to look into it, sir?' Josh asked eagerly.

'No, give it to uniform. You'd better ring Pain-in-the-backside — let him know what's happened.'

Ashworth, unwilling to risk another confrontation with Paine within Barbara's earshot, waited outside. By the time the undipped headlights of Paine's Jaguar illuminated the long drive, he was cold, dispirited, and in no mood for tantrums.

The car skidded slightly as it drew to a stop. Paine hurriedly climbed out. 'Is my sister all right?'

'She's upset, obviously, but one of my officers is with her. My DC told you what was said on the phone, I take it?'

'Yes.'

Paine moved to enter the house but Ashworth blocked him, making it plain that he intended to talk outside. Their breath fogged the night air.

Paine hesitated, then blurted, 'Look, Ashworth, about this morning . . . I was out of my mind with worry. Still am, in fact . . .'

And that was it, as close as Paine would ever come to an apology.

Nevertheless, Ashworth began to feel some compassion for the man. He said, easily, 'That's all right, Mr Paine, I understand.'

During the evening, Ashworth had debated about how much of Gwen Anthony's theories he should divulge to Paine. Now he took the decision to pass on all relevant details, in the hope that this would go some way to alleviating the stress, which lay ahead.

Paine listened thoughtfully. 'I see,' he said. 'So, you anticipate a long wait before Simon is released?'

Ashworth nodded. 'We'll maintain a media black-out in the hope of forcing the kidnapper's hand.' He had wisely left out what could happen should the kidnapper have second thoughts about releasing Simon Edwards.

'How much danger is Simon in?' Paine asked, hesitantly.

'Considerable, I'm afraid.'

'God.' Paine's face was beginning to show signs of strain. 'If anything happens to him, it will finish Babs.' He shivered. 'Can we go inside?'

'There's just one thing I'd like to discuss with you . . .'

'Well, can we discuss it inside, Ashworth?' Paine was growing irritable.

Ashworth answered in kind. 'No, we can't, Paine. I feel there are certain aspects of this that are best kept from your sister.'

'Very well. What is it?' Paine snapped.

'The ransom money. The demand is likely to be for a substantial amount. It's unlikely the kidnapper will get—'

'Are you asking if I can raise the money?' Paine asked shortly.

'I was leading up to that, yes.'

'Well, I can. Now, I want to see my sister.'

He stamped towards the house. Ashworth followed, hoping his association with this abrupt man would not be a lengthy one.

* * *

Emily Bedford's routine rarely varied. Always one hour before Holly's return, the central heating was switched off, and windows opened all over the house. These, of course, were always firmly closed as soon as the indoor temperature became low enough to allow Emily to wallow in her martyrdom.

Such behaviour did not appear strange in the old woman's twisted mind. A guilty daughter-in-law was a loyal daughter-in-law.

Tonight was different though. She did not know when Holly would be home, and this had ruined her timing. She had been sitting in the freezing house for over an hour now, and still no sign of her.

Emily, who disliked the cold, wrapped a thick green cardigan around herself and sat, mentally picking at the scab of animosity she felt towards the girl.

She had never been able to come to terms with relationships. Her husband had been a provider — pure and simple. Her son, she had seen as a buffer against the rigours of old age.

When Holly had first come into her life, Emily had viewed her as a threat; someone who had lured her beloved, innocent son away with forbidden fruits.

Holly and Jason had not been many weeks into their courtship when Emily, an avid searcher of pockets, had discovered a packet of contraceptives in the breast pocket of her son's best suit. And Holly's intimate letter — which Emily had read, shocked and horrified — describing the pleasure derived from a sweet encounter in the back of Jason's car.

Sex, to Emily's mind, was an irksome duty expected of a wife and, over the years as she grew more and more self-centred, it became an obligation she refused to fulfil.

Emily's dogma allowed for two distinct categories of women: those who were pure and chaste and — in the spiritual sense, at least — remained virginal throughout life; and those strumpets who used sex to lure sons away from their mothers — the fact that these women actually enjoyed it seemed, to Emily, to beggar belief.

When Jason had died, she had felt a mother's grief; at her husband's death she had felt a wife's sorrow. But neither of these occasions had been allowed to interfere with the obsessional pursuit of her own well-being.

The move to Bridgetown, not to mention Holly's new job, had caused her considerable worry. Being tied to a grave had kept Holly from straying. Now, in a new place, at a police station crawling with men, a girl such as she, so lacking in moral fibre, could soon form a sexual liaison, and the last thing any man wanted was a mother-in-law from a previous marriage queering the pitch.

Emily had no intention of being forced to exist in a council flat on her meagre state pension. No, Holly had responsibilities and Emily would make sure she abided by them.

The deafness of which she so often complained temporarily deserted her as she listened to a car turning into the cul-de-sac. Her limp was strangely absent too as she switched off the light and scuttled to the window, pulling the curtain back a chink.

On seeing that the car was not Holly's Mini, Emily was about to turn away, but it stopped outside the house and her interest was fired. A young man got out and skirted round to open the passenger door.

Emily gave an indignant snort as Holly appeared, laughing at something the young man was saying, then kissing him before running towards the front door. She was almost certain that Holly had waited on the step and waved as the man drove off.

Holly let herself in quietly. Emily — even though there was no one in the darkened room to see her performance — limped across to her chair and painfully lowered herself into it.

She groaned slightly as Holly opened the door and flicked on the light switch.

'Mum, what are you doing in here, with the light off and no heat on?'

'I couldn't go to bed till you got in, and I didn't want to waste money,' she mumbled weakly.

'Oh mum, I wish I'd never mentioned bloody money,' she said with exasperation. 'I just meant we've got to be careful. I didn't mean for you to freeze to death. I'll make us a hot drink.'

Emily sat for a while, listening to the sounds coming from the kitchen, then, spurred on by her moral victory, she hobbled through to Holly. 'If my leg gets much worse,' she said, through teeth gritted against imaginary pain, 'I'll have to use a stick.'

Holly, spooning Horlicks into mugs, smiled weakly. She knew full well that Emily's knee was a ruse with which to gain sympathy and was about to oblige, when Emily said, 'Who was that man who brought you home?'

Holly stiffened. 'Just a colleague,' she answered lightly.

Emily sniffed. 'I hope you don't kiss all your colleagues. They might get the wrong impression.'

Speaking firmly, Holly said, 'Don't be silly, mum. Josh is a friend — and it was only a peck on the cheek. That doesn't mean anything nowadays.'

'Your skirt looks creased,' Emily observed tartly.

The kettle boiled, filling the small room with steam. Holly turned it off and rounded on her mother-in-law. 'What do you mean by that?'

'Nothing, just that it looks like you've been sitting down with it pushed up—'

'Mother!'

Emily changed tack. 'Where's your car then?'

'I left it at the station car park because—'

'Then went off with that man in his.'

Holly banged the Horlicks jar onto the table. 'Look I know what you're trying to say and I resent it. Contrary to what you think, I don't take my knickers off every time somebody wants me to.'

'What a terrible thing to say,' Emily said, in a voice now clear and strong. 'If my Jason could hear you talking like that—'

'Let it go, mother!' Holly cautioned.

If Emily had possessed one small degree of sensitivity she would have realised she was encroaching on sacred ground. As it was, she simply squared up for another attack. 'Jason—'

'Leave Jason out of this,' Holly ordered.

'I will not. He was my son and I loved him,' Emily retorted. 'And if you had, you'd have a bit more respect for his memory.'

At that moment, years of resentment and pain surfaced in Holly. 'You evil bastard!' she shrieked, sweeping the mugs from the table.

So violent was the movement that Emily cringed against the wall as the mugs shattered on the floor.

Tears were streaming down Holly's colourless face. 'I loved Jason,' she cried, her slight body convulsed by sobs. 'It broke my heart when he died. I don't think I'll ever get over it . . . but I can't spend the rest of my life . . .' She stopped abruptly and fled from the kitchen.

Emily sat down slowly as she listened to the angry slam of Holly's bedroom door.

* * *

Prior to leaving the Edwardses' house, Ashworth had been informed by uniformed branch that they had found Simon Edwards's car, hidden in the disused barn on a remote part of Parker's Farm. Bad conditions and lack of lighting meant that Forensic would not be able to look at it until tomorrow. Meanwhile, a patrol car would stay on watch.

He had ordered Holly to report to the house in the morning and spend the day with Barbara Edwards. Josh was to take over in the evening, until ten p.m., when Dennis Paine would arrive from late shift at the factory. He had also arranged with the post office for the Edwardses' mail to be diverted to Bridgetown Police Station.

As Ashworth started his journey home, he mused that this find had destroyed all possibility that the telephone calls had been the work of a crank.

The drive was proving to be far easier than he had anticipated: a snow plough had cleared all major roads and gritting ensured ice-free surfaces. The lane in which his house stood was treacherous, however, and his car skidded badly as he turned into it. Selecting a low gear he crawled up the hill, looking forward to sharing a drink with Sarah in front of a cosy fire.

Turning into his drive he was warmed by the cheerful glow emanating from the curtained lounge window, and, eager to get inside, he wasted no time in garaging the car.

But when he opened the front door, the house was strangely silent: no television noise, no barking dog, and — more worrying — no Sarah coming out to meet him.

With trepidation he hurried to the kitchen, and as he switched on the light a sleepy puppy looked up from her bed and greeted him with a prolonged yawn.

In the dog's mind, her only duty was to protect her owners and, when either of them was at home, she would bark at the slightest disturbance. An empty house was a different matter altogether: with no one to look out for, she could curl up and sleep. Ashworth sometimes wondered whether burglars would be met with furious barks or affectionate licks.

She stood up, wagging her tail with little enthusiasm, then curled up again and closed her eyes.

Ashworth chuckled at the sight of her plump body in the bed. Then he noticed a sheet of writing-paper propped up against the teapot. The message read: 'Jim, I've gone to a meeting of the Samaritans with Jean Tebbit. They're recruiting counsellors. I shouldn't be too late. There are sandwiches in the fridge. Love, Sarah.'

He sighed, but realised it was selfish of him to be irritated by her absence. After all, it was past ten p.m.; it was unreasonable to expect her to spend the whole evening waiting for him to return and discuss his day with her — even though he had been looking forward to doing just that.

The corned beef sandwiches looked cold and unappetising, so he left them and fetched a large whisky and soda from the lounge.

Sitting at the kitchen table he thought about his day as the scotch spread its warmth inside him.

Gwen Anthony's assumption that the kidnapper was of high intelligence was proving to be an accurate assessment, the man having chosen a period when weather conditions would hamper a police investigation, and would make swift movement an impossibility.

Actually, Gwen Anthony had occupied his thoughts far too much during the long evening. Was he simply flattered by her attentions, or did it go deeper than that? Had he reached a point beyond his middle years when he longed to experience again the unique bliss associated with the start of a relationship?

He finished his drink and fetched a refill, chastising himself as he did so — here he was, in the middle of a dangerous case, thinking about Gwen's body!

A stanza of verse came to him:

The gods created women, shaped their forms,
Each promised joy, to drive all thoughts
From the minds of men.

Well, that was true enough. But then Sarah's key in the lock, her cheery 'Hello', made him put aside this reverie. He finished his drink and went to her.

* * *

Emily realised she had overstepped the mark but — unaccustomed as she was to being confronted like that — was unsure of how to put things right.

Her late husband had always been kept firmly at heel by a combination of bullying and nagging. The fact that the poor man would have done almost anything for a quiet life had probably given Emily a totally false impression of her powers.

Having always regarded Holly as a wilful, spoilt girl, bent on making her life a misery, Emily now realised that she must change her ways, or be in danger of bringing about the very set of circumstances that she had worked so hard to avoid.

She made herself a hot drink and swept up the broken mugs as it cooled. Taking her time over the drink, Emily then washed the mug and put it away, wanting Holly to get up to a nice clean kitchen the next morning.

She then trundled upstairs and politely knocked on Holly's door before opening it. 'I'm sorry, Holly,' she called softly into the darkened room. 'It's just that I worry about you.'

When there was no response, she gave a resigned sigh, muttering, 'I never thought I'd live to become a burden. Never mind, I'll be dead and gone soon . . . out of everybody's way.'

Holly waited for the door to close, then sobbed into her pillow, 'Die then . . . die. Just bloody die!'

CHAPTER 9

Two youths strolled aimlessly along a road on Bridgetown's council estate. Their black leather jackets, dark torn jeans, and expensive trainers stood out menacingly against the snowy background.

They were both fourteen years old and adjusting well to puberty. Although often absent from school, they never missed a sex education lesson and were, therefore, aware of the changes taking place within themselves, and — devoid of any guidance or discipline from parents or teachers — were eager to demonstrate their new sexual abilities.

Although little more than children, they possessed the drives, instincts and appetites of adults. These, coupled with an adolescent belief that the authorities were powerless to act against them, produced a dangerous combination, and both viewed crime as an easy game.

Damon Cain was the taller of the pair; his bored face showed signs of mild acne, and his blond hair was shaved off, apart from a lank, greasy strip on top of his head.

The other boy, Delvin Bennett, had the face of a choir-boy, dark perfect skin, and black hair which shone with health.

'We'll go up to Cherry Tree Estate tomorrow,' Damon informed his friend. 'I've got this old bird sussed out.'

Delvin was apprehensive. He said, 'I dunno. We nearly got caught today. I reckon we should stick to Kirsty. She lets us have it—'

'Yah . . . Kirsty,' Damon jeered, digging into the pocket of his jacket, and pulling out a knife with a six-inch blade. 'I'm fed up with her — she lets everybody. And we only nearly got caught 'cause we was doing it wrong.'

He plunged the knife into a refuse sack which was standing at the end of someone's drive, then pulled it sharply upwards until noxious rubbish tumbled from the gaping split.

'How do you mean, we were doing it wrong?'

Damon had moved on to the next drive and was working on another bag of rubbish. 'We was trying to break in with the birds already inside.'

'Yeah.' Delvin agreed.

'That gives 'em plenty of time to ring the police — yeah?'

'Oh, right.'

Damon, spreading refuse all over the garden, said, 'This woman up on Cherry Tree goes shopping most days, and when she comes back she uses the side gate — yeah?' He kicked an empty cat food tin towards the front door of the house, but it veered off, missing the ground-floor window by inches.

'So we break in while she's out?' Delvin enquired.

An upstairs window of the house was thrown open, and a man's voice called, 'Here, what do you think you're doing?'

'Piss off,' Damon shouted back, with indifference. Then turning to his friend, 'Yeah, and we grab her when she comes in. Easy — see?'

'I'll give you, piss off,' the man shouted angrily.

The boys stood and watched as the bedroom light came on, to be quickly followed by the one in the hall.

Unconcerned, Delvin asked, 'What's this bird like then?'

'About thirty.'

The front door was flung open. A man, wearing pyjamas and dressing-gown, carrying what appeared to be a baseball bat, came striding down the drive. Several dogs were barking and a woman called to him, warningly, from inside the house.

The boys made no move. 'As old as that?' Delvin gasped.

'Yeah, but she'll be a good screw.'

They waited until the man was half-way down the drive before running away, not stopping until they had covered thirty yards. Glancing back, they saw him standing at the end of his drive, shaking his fist, and looking around at the mess all over his garden.

The boys jeered, middle fingers aimed crudely at the man. When he still did not approach them, Delvin made a masturbatory movement with his hand until, bored with the episode, they turned their backs and started walking.

'Let's go nick a car,' Damon suggested.

'Yeah,' Delvin replied with boyish enthusiasm. 'Then torch it.'

'Yeah. Come on, then.'

CHAPTER 10

The morning arrived, grey and dismal.

Ashworth hardly uttered two words during breakfast, and was decidedly gruff with Sarah as he left the house.

She was mulling this over while rolling pastry for a batch of steak and kidney pies she was preparing for the freezer, when the reason for his antisocial behaviour suddenly struck her: she had returned home the night before, full of her own news about being taken on as a counsellor for the Samaritans, and had not asked one single question about the kidnap. No wonder he was in a mood.

She was thrilled with her new role, though. The organiser had described her as perfect for the job: caring, mature, sympathetic, and intelligent. Although not overjoyed with 'mature' — that was a word Sarah always associated with Cheddar cheese — she had, nevertheless, felt quite elated.

She was charitable by nature, and the thought of involving herself in the lives and problems of others appealed greatly. She had reached a time in her life when she needed to feel useful, wanted something to fill the huge vacuum left by her children when they fled the coop.

Her powerful maternal instincts needed to be given a focal point; not her husband, though — he always strongly resented what he described as 'fussing'. Nevertheless, she must be careful not to neglect him.

'And I mustn't be sharp with him either,' she told the pastry, remembering his look of annoyance the previous evening when, noticing his empty glass, she had pointedly asked him how many drinks he'd had.

* * *

Ashworth, however, sitting scowling at his new desk, had failed to connect Sarah with his foul mood. He believed its cause lay in the frustrating realisation that today would see little done.

Logic dictated that the kidnapper would not be in touch for at least twenty-four hours, and his first job on arriving at the station, had confirmed this assumption.

He had telephoned the post office, only to be told that there was no mail for Mr and Mrs Edwards. This had deepened his mood, but then hope had been rekindled when the helpful clerk mentioned that, as the post was sorted as soon as it arrived at the depot, anything posted today could be passed to him immediately.

Cheered by this, he set about reorganising the office while waiting for Forensic to contact him with their findings on Simon Edwards's car.

* * *

Jane Taylor's happiness was so complete, not even the atrocious weather could dampen her spirits.

Today was her husband's thirty-fourth birthday, and his first since their marriage, so Jane wanted it to be special.

She trod gingerly along the high street, her black boots slipping in the trampled slush; stopping now and then to brush aside her mass of blonde curls, blown about by a trenchant wind.

Peter had said he fancied a Chinese take-away for his birthday dinner, and Jane was now shopping for the wine to go with it.

With the ease of a woman who had been beautiful all her life, she shrugged off the admiring glances and occasional wolf-whistles from appreciative males and started, once more, for the wine shop.

She thought back to when they had met, five years ago — and how those years had flown. Peter had been her boss — her married boss — at the insurance brokers for whom he still worked.

Jane had been hesitant about becoming involved at first, but their attraction had been too strong to deny, and finally she had bowed to its inevitability.

Three hard years later, embroiled in guilt, frequently depressed, they agreed to end the affair. Jane gave up her job but found she could not forget him. Then, after weeks of anguish, he turned up at her flat, suitcases and all — he had left his wife.

A very bitter divorce followed, and with the small amount of money left over after the settlement, they were able to put down a deposit on number 22 Lea Road, on the Cherry Tree Estate.

They had been living there now for nine months, and Jane was determined to make this birthday perfect.

With two carefully chosen bottles of white wine in her shopping bag, she called into the Chinese restaurant, arranged for their meal to be delivered at eight p.m., then caught the bus.

Thankful to be home, she let herself into the garden by the side entrance, humming the tune from a recent television commercial — an old '70s song which had just shot to number one in the record charts.

In the kitchen, Jane popped the wine into the fridge. Later, she would recall a slight feeling of unease as she did so. But for now, happy and excited, she hurried into the hall and took off her bulky coat.

It was while she was removing her boots, standing there on one leg, that the feeling came again, stronger this time — some primeval instinct warning her of danger — but she shrugged it off as her mind focused on a cup of tea.

She did not hear the noise behind her until it was too late. Suddenly, a gloved hand was clamped over her mouth, stifling her scream of terror. She struggled to get free, but lost her balance and went sprawling.

The two assailants followed her down, roughly turning Jane on to her back, and holding her firmly by the shoulders. Something cold touched her throat and she glimpsed a shining knife blade.

The one behind kept out of her line of vision, but she could see the second youth, kneeling at her legs, well enough. Through her tears she saw he was wearing a black leather jacket, blue jeans, and grey sweatshirt. His balaclava revealed wild eyes, a grinning mouth with dirty teeth.

She felt her skirt being pushed up, a hand viciously probing between her legs, as she thrashed about impotently.

'Get her knickers off,' said the youth holding her down, his foul breath wafting over her face.

'I can't. She won't lift her back up.'

Again Jane could smell the breath. 'Lift your back off the floor, you cow.' These words were coupled with pressure from the knife, digging deeper into her throat. As it was pulled away she felt a line of blood trickle down to her collarbone.

'Don't hurt me,' she whispered. 'Please, don't hurt me.'

'Get your back off the floor then,' the voice commanded savagely.

Terrified, she obeyed, and her pants were pulled off.

She tried to kick out at the youth, but he simply laughed and gripped her ankles, hurting her needlessly.

'Don't. Please, don't,' she pleaded. 'I'll give you anything . . . just leave me alone.'

Her legs were freed as the figure stood up to unfasten his jeans.

'Hurry up . . . fuck her.'

With shocking brutality, her legs were pushed apart.

'No. No.' She tried to scream, but pressure from the knife stifled the sound.

Then the youth's dead weight was upon her, and there was a dreadful pain between her legs.

* * *

Ashworth sat back, contentedly viewing his empire from his rightful position; he was back in his old spot. It was like visiting a familiar place that he had not seen for years.

The old dark wood desk, scratched and stained, was far more to his liking than that modern monstrosity he had just relinquished.

He had moved Stimpson and Whitworth into the new office, thankful for the wall now between himself and Whitworth's infernal cigarette smoke. Holly's unoccupied desk was facing his own, and Josh was in the corner, bent over his computer.

Ashworth wondered how long it would be before Josh's posture was affected by his constant slouching over the machine, and was about to make a comment when a knock came at the door.

'Come,' Ashworth barked.

Any confidence PC Bobby Adams may have gained shrivelled at the tone of Ashworth's voice. But as he entered the office, he determined to keep his voice steady. 'Sorry to disturb you, sir, but we've had word from Forensic on Mr Edwards's car.'

'Yes?'

'It was clean, sir. Nothing on it at all. They said the car was locked when they found it, and the keys appear to be missing.'

The telephone buzzed. Josh picked it up. 'CID. DC Abraham.'

Still with his hand on the door handle, Bobby said, 'That's all, sir. They'll be reporting to you, but I thought you'd want to know as soon as possible.'

'Thank you, Bobby.'

As the door closed, Josh called, 'Suspected rape, sir. Lea Road, Cherry Tree Estate. Uniformed are in attendance. Forensic on their way.'

'Right,' Ashworth said. 'We need Holly for this.'

Josh was already slipping into his leather jacket. 'Shall I relieve her at the Edwards's house, sir?'

'Good man.'

'One complication though, sir. Her car's still in the car park. I gave her a lift this morning.'

The telephone buzzed again.

'CID. DC Abraham.' He looked across to Ashworth. 'It's the post office sorting depot, sir.'

'Right. Get Whitworth to follow you in his car. He can bring Holly back.'

'Yes, sir.'

Ashworth grabbed the receiver. 'Chief Inspector Ashworth here. What have you got for me?'

'A letter's turned up,' the voice informed him. 'Addressed to Mrs B. Edwards.'

'Good. I'll send someone over to collect it.' The ensuing chaos almost made him forget his manners. He added hastily, 'And many thanks.'

Josh and Whitworth were leaving the office as Stimpson came over, a self-satisfied grin on his face. 'Looks like I was right about the rape, sir.'

If he was expecting praise, some acknowledgement of his cleverness, then he was disappointed for all he got from Ashworth was a grunted 'Yes.' Then without looking at the Detective Sergeant, he said shortly, 'I want you to go down to the post office and collect what appears to be the ransom note.'

* * *

In another part of Bridgetown Police Station, Dr Gwen Anthony was washing her hands as sounds from a running shower came from an adjacent room. She was filled with an overwhelming pity as she imagined the vigour with which Jane Taylor would be scrubbing her body, vainly attempting to wash away the feelings of desecration and humiliation.

The examination — even for someone as experienced in the profession as Gwen — had been harrowing. Her findings had proved beyond doubt, though, that the woman had been raped.

After despatching Jane to the shower, she had passed her notes on to the two policewomen in the counselling room, and was now preparing to leave.

Feeling more than a little saddened, she donned her brown sheepskin coat, picked up her black bag, and left the room.

In the corridor outside, Ashworth was restlessly prowling. His presence, despite the severity of the occasion, brought a glowing smile to Gwen's face. 'Jim,' she said warmly.

'Gwen, what's the verdict?'

'She's been raped all right.' Her tone was briskly professional. 'Bruising to the inner thighs — some of it quite severe. Bruising also to the vagina, shoulders and back. There's a cut across her throat.' She indicated where by touching the spot on Ashworth's neck. 'Not deep, but if a little more pressure had been exerted, it would have been. No evidence of any semen present. Either the little darlings didn't ejaculate — which is very unlikely — or they wore condoms. So, Jim, you won't get any help with identity from that source. It was a very nasty attack. What kind of animal could do that to a woman?'

'I don't know,' Ashworth replied heavily. 'But I'm beginning to believe there are a lot of them out there.'

Gwen glanced at her watch. 'Walk with me, Jim. I've left my husband with the surgery — I'll have to get back straightaway.'

Ashworth realised that he had never heard Gwen refer to her husband by name and was curious about their relationship, if indeed they still had one.

She fell in beside him and they started along the corridor. Ashworth said, 'I probably shouldn't be telling you this—'

'Oh, you can trust me with your secrets,' Gwen interrupted cheekily.

Ashworth gave her a smile, then said, 'The kidnapper's been in touch.'

'Oh? When?'

'Last night, by telephone, and today, by post — or so I believe.'

'What's he asking for?'

'I don't know yet. I haven't seen the letter. One of my officers is collecting it.'

They stopped at the lift and were silent as they waited for the doors to open.

Once inside, Gwen said, 'It doesn't fit, Jim. It's too soon. He should be making you sweat.'

'He is,' Ashworth replied darkly. 'I could have done without a rape on my hands.'

'Mrs Taylor could have done without it too, Jim,' Gwen rebuked lightly.

'Sorry . . . that was insensitive.'

'I know what you meant,' she said. 'Actually, this could be something to bring up with the Home Secretary's lot.'

Ashworth let out a scornful laugh, saying, 'Yes, I think I may well invite the Right Honourable Minister and his team to come here for a month and try running things.'

Gwen chuckled merrily. 'Oh, Jim, with your 'straight from the shoulder' approach, I think I'm going to enjoy this conference. Do you know when it is?'

'No, I've heard nothing. Please God, not yet.'

Gwen's eyes sparkled wickedly as she whispered, 'When we're there, I'm going to make you an offer you can't refuse.' It was meant as a light-hearted joke, to draw a response.

But Ashworth was serious when he replied, 'I don't think you realise how tempted I am, Gwen.'

'Then why wait for some conference?' she asked earnestly.

A look of annoyance clouded her face as the lift came to a halt before Ashworth could respond. The doors slid open to reveal a bustling reception. Uniformed officers stood respect-fully to one side as they came out.

Sergeant Dutton was behind the front desk. He called to the Chief Inspector, putting an end to their conversation.

'Sorry, Gwen, I've got to go.'

'Ring me — but not with any more rapes or madmen.'

'I will. Drive carefully.'

CHAPTER 11

The rape counselling room, unlike normal interview rooms, was comfortable and informal. A flower-patterned lounge suite dominated with a cheerfulness that took attention away from the clinically white walls. A coffee table, with large ash-tray, completed the sparse furnishings.

Holly sat in one armchair, and WPC Jill Thompson — a pretty, dark-haired girl of twenty-five — occupied the other. Both were facing the settee.

Holly watched carefully as Jane Taylor, dressed in a plain white bathrobe, mechanically crossed the room to sit in front of them.

She still appeared dazed, deep in shock, and when Holly spoke, she jumped, as if unaware of another presence in the room.

Speaking very softly, Holly said, 'Jane, I'm DC Holly Bedford, and this is WPC Jill Thompson.'

'My husband . . . Peter, where is he?'

'He's been told what's happened,' Holly said gently. 'He's on his way here now. Do you feel like talking, Jane?'

'What about?'

Holly shot a glance at Jill who looked back glumly. 'About what happened to you. Can you talk about it?'

'Yes.'

'Good. When you're ready then. We're in no hurry. Just take your time.'

Jane turned vacant eyes towards Holly. 'They must have been inside the house when I got back,' she began, cautiously. 'I went into the hall to take my boots off . . . and they jumped on me.'

'How many were there?'

'Two.'

Jill asked, 'Did you see their faces?'

Jane shook her head. 'No, they were wearing those things over their faces . . . I don't know . . . balaclavas, I think they're called.'

Holly wanted to extract as much information from Jane as was possible before they actually got on to the rape itself. So, channelling her questions in that direction, she asked, 'Can you tell us anything about the two men?'

'They were boys, not men.'

'What made you think they were boys?' Jill asked.

Jane sat considering for a while, then said, 'I don't know . . . they just seemed like boys . . . their voices. And their clothes . . .'

When she did not go on, Holly prompted with, 'What were they wearing?'

Jane frowned, shuddering violently at the memories. 'Black leather jackets, blue denim jeans. And one of them had a grey sweatshirt with 'Mean Man' in big letters on the front. That's all I can remember . . . I'm sorry . . .' She faltered as her tears fell unchecked.

Holly moved to comfort her and Jill took over the questioning. 'What happened after they jumped on you in the hall, Jane?'

Holly supplied a handkerchief and Jane mopped at her eyes. 'They got me on to the floor. One of them was behind me, kneeling on my shoulders . . . he had a knife pressed against my throat . . .'

An hysterical tremor had crept into her voice but she fought to control it. She went on, 'The other one pushed my skirt up and pulled my pants off. Then he took his jeans down and . . . he just stood there, showing it to me. He'd got a contraceptive on, and I remember thinking, at least I won't get pregnant or catch Aids or anything. Isn't that ridiculous?'

The hysteria finally took hold. With Holly's arms around her, Jane wept quietly and gave herself up to an aguish trembling.

'It's okay, Jane, you cry. Let it out,' Holly soothed. 'We have to ask these questions, though — you do understand, don't you? We have to know.'

'I know,' Jane said finally, as the tears subsided.

'What did they do then?'

'The other one was urging him on to do it to me. Then he . . .' Her voice broke completely.

'Raped you,' Jill said softly.

'Yes, yes, yes.'

'The other boy . . . did he rape you too?'

'Yes, yes, they both did it,' Jane screamed, before burying her head into Holly's chest.

Holly looked despairingly at Jill, who said, 'Did they leave the house then?'

'Yes. They were laughing as they went through the kitchen and out of the back door. I stood up. I was so frightened I wet myself. Please don't ask me anymore . . . please. I can't stand it. Leave me alone now.'

Holly hugged her closer. Jane looked at the two officers pleadingly as she said, 'What will Peter say? What will he think? Oh God, what will he think?'

Holly consoled her as best she could, realising that her feeble platitudes would bring little comfort. Then, leaving Jill with the task of getting Jane dressed, she made her way to CID.

The fact that Jane's information held few real clues to the identities of the rapists helped fuel the well of anger inside her. This wanton, calculated destruction of a person's whole life was beyond her comprehension.

By the time she reached the office, tears of frustration were in her eyes. Walking through the door, she was vaguely aware that the office had been rearranged, and it registered that Ashworth had moved into the main office.

She stopped in front of his desk. 'Notes of the interview with the rape victim, sir.'

On seeing Holly's forlorn expression, Ashworth diverted his eyes to study the notes. 'She hasn't made a formal statement yet?'

'No, sir, she's far too upset for that.'

'I see.' He looked up, still avoiding her eyes. 'Forensics are at the house now and we may have a breakthrough there. They've found a perfect shoe print outside the garden gate — a type of trainer. The angle of it suggests the wearer was about to enter the garden.'

He bundled the notes together briskly. 'Here, give these to Stimpson and Whitworth. Tell them to read through them, then come out here to me.'

Holly hesitated, not knowing where the officers were.

'Oh, they're through there,' Ashworth said, pointing to the new office.

Their mindless banter, which was fast becoming an unbearable irritant to Ashworth, started as soon as Holly entered the office.

Stimpson, so assured of his attractiveness that he regarded any female resistance as merely token, gushed, 'Holly, you've come in to brighten my day . . .'

'No,' Holly snapped. 'The Chief Inspector wants you to read this and report to him.'

'You're so uptight, Holly. Did you know that an orgasm is the best thing to relieve tension? Now, I can help you . . .'

Ashworth was about to go in there and insist that they conduct themselves with a little more decorum when he heard the sounds of a scuffle, a loud slap, and an exclamation of surprise from Stimpson.

'Leave it, Alistair, I'm not available,' Holly said forcefully.

'I was only joking,' Stimpson mumbled through his bruised pride.

'Well, I'm fed up with it. The next time you put your hands on me, I'll break your bloody arm. Is that clear?'

'Yes, yes, now back off. Christ!'

Ashworth just about had time to wipe the smile off his face before Holly returned to her desk, bristling with rage.

When the men emerged from their office, Stimpson pointedly ignored her, making straight for Ashworth's desk. 'What do you want us to do on the rape, sir?'

'Door-to-door,' Ashworth replied shortly. 'Those two lads would have stuck out like sore thumbs on Cherry Tree Estate. Someone must have seen them.'

'Yes, sir.'

Whitworth remained silent, fixing Ashworth with his insubordinate gaze, which was fast becoming a permanent feature.

Ashworth, returning it, said, 'Go,' in a stony dismissive tone.

When the officers had gone, he sat studying Holly's bent head as she busied herself writing a report. Her pen strokes were heavy and aggressive, denoting her still-seething anger.

Casually, Ashworth crossed to her desk where he sat on its edge. 'Holly,' he said gently, 'I think it's wise not to get too involved with a case.'

Holly stood up to face him. 'Sir,' she said, fighting her tears. 'I have just interviewed a woman whose marriage is likely to break up because of what happened. Her emotional and mental health have probably been destroyed, if not permanently, then for some time to come. Now I find it very difficult to remain detached in those circumstances. I'm sorry if that meets with your disapproval.'

Once again, Ashworth felt that he had been put, very firmly, in his place. He changed the subject quickly. 'Would you like me to have a word with Stimpson about sexual harassment?'

'No, sir. It would look as if I'd run to teacher. I can handle it.'

'I'm sure you can,' he said, grinning. 'I'm just a little concerned about how many arms you break in the process.'

'I have a right to . . .' She stopped, then smiled. 'I'm being silly, aren't I?'

'You're being human. Sometimes the two are very similar.'

Easing himself off the desk he reached across for Holly's arm, pleased to find that she did not recoil from this fatherly gesture. 'Come on, young lady, let's go and see Pain-in-the-bum. I'll fill you in about the ransom demand on the way.'

CHAPTER 12

Although the traffic was light, Whitworth's aggressive driving had already enraged several motorists and was slightly unnerving Stimpson, who dreaded the next junction, as Whitworth seemed to regard slowing to take a corner as an act of cowardice.

'Slow down a bit, Mike,' he cautioned. 'You'll get us nicked.'

When Whitworth eased back on the accelerator, he breathed more easily and studied the map spread across his knees. 'You should have taken a right back there.'

Whitworth shook his head.

Stimpson consulted the map again. 'Cherry Tree Estate — yes, it was a right turn back there.'

'We're not going to Cherry Tree Estate,' Whitworth grunted. 'I thought we'd call in the amusement arcade. Have a chat with some of our friends.'

'Mike,' Stimpson protested. 'Ashworth ordered us to carry out house-to-house—'

'Ashworth,' Whitworth snorted. 'He's an old woman. We can have this cleared up today.'

'He does things by the book.'

'Book?' Whitworth gazed at him, his face a mask of innocence. 'What book?'

'Keep your eyes on the bloody road. Whatever you think of him, he's our commanding officer.'

'Not mine, he's not.'

Whitworth took a left off the high street, then a sharp right. With tyres screaming, the car entered a narrow road where small warehouse units stood on land which had originally been gardens of the shops flanking the high street.

Here, the snow had become blackened. Lorries, continually loading and unloading, had melted most of it, leaving water and sludge — unable to escape due to blocked drains — lying across the road like a dirty lake.

Whitworth's car splashed through it — the spray from its wheels three feet high — and stopped outside a warehouse half-way along.

Its conversion into an amusement arcade had been scant: cheap cord carpet covered the concrete flooring; a buffet counter and vending machines had been installed at minimal expense; the residual space was packed almost solid with pinball and fruit machines.

Stimpson was still disturbed by their detour. 'Mike, I think we should do the house-to-house,' he said uneasily.

'Relax, Alistair. Look, half an hour and I can get us a couple of names, then we'll play knocking-on-doors. I want this cleared up. Like the man said — it's not the taking part, it's the winning that counts.'

Reluctantly, Stimpson followed his swaggering partner across the litter-strewn pavement and through grimy swing doors into the arcade.

The high-ceilinged interior was windowless, the only pools of light created by fluorescent strips housed in cheap metal holders, suspended from beams. The place smelt of stale cigarette smoke and damp.

Of the twenty or so youths inside, most were in the coffee area, sprawled on chairs, engaged in noisy discourse.

As the officers entered, one of them looked up and nudged the youth sitting next to him. In a matter of seconds an almost eerie silence had descended, punctuated by the metallic pings of a pinball machine.

The corners of Whitworth's mouth flicked upwards in acknowledgement of the respect that was being shown to him.

This arcade — along with a few other establishments frequented by the more rowdy youths — was fast becoming a no-go area for the police. Not that they feared attack from these teenagers; most simply felt heartily sick of the barrage of abuse hurled at them, enraged that they were powerless to respond in kind, and therefore only entered such situations when absolutely necessary.

Whitworth held no such reservations. Leaving Stimpson at the door he worked his way through the rows of machines to the lone pinball player. 'Wayne Spencer?' he demanded, reaching the denim-clad youth.

'Yeah, I'm Wayne Spencer.' He did not look up, but continued to work the machine which bleeped, rattled and emitted an electronic tune as the player score mounted.

Whitworth moved to the side of the table. 'Do you know who I am?'

Spencer smirked, but still kept his attention on the game. 'Yeah, you're King Shit.'

Whitworth's laugh was a humourless sound as he reached beneath the machine, slowly lifting it from the floor until 'Tilt' appeared on the screen.

'What the friggin' hell you doing?' Like a caricature of a hard man, Wayne Spencer sprang round, adopting a crouch, hands bunched into fists.

'I'm removing any distractions, Wayne, because I want you to pay attention,' Whitworth replied, laconically.

Spencer's arrogant eyes looked towards his friends at the coffee bar but no one came to his assistance.

The expression on that face, which had not yet lost the fullness of youth, was one of perplexity. He had made his play, but without any back-up he now had to make a choice: put up or shut up.

Lowering his hands, he said grudgingly, 'What you want then?'

'That's better,' Whitworth responded easily. 'Someone's told me you're carrying illegal substances.'

'What? I'm not carrying. I'm clean, man.'

'I'll still have to take you to the station. Just to make sure.'

Spencer's bravado resurfaced. 'You won't get me outta here,' he shouted, looking pleadingly towards the other youths.

Unimpressed, Whitworth said, 'I'm arresting you, Wayne, but I won't bother to read you your rights because as far as I'm concerned, you don't have any.'

'My mates won't let you walk outta here with me.'

'Your gang is it, Wayne?' Whitworth allowed his heavy-lidded dark eyes to sweep over the silent, hostile group. 'They look as if a good fart would deck most of them.'

Stimpson was tense as he watched the incident build, certain that his colleague was mishandling a potentially volatile situation. But Whitworth possessed far more shrewdness than people realised; he knew just how far a display of fearlessness could take him. More importantly, he understood the psychology of the mob.

Quietly but firmly, he said, 'Now, if your mates tried to stop us taking you out, there'd be a ruck and someone would get hurt. I promise you, Wayne, if that happens, I'll see to it you get badly damaged.'

He saw some of the fight go out of Spencer's eyes. 'Walk, Wayne. Don't look or speak to anybody. Just walk out the door and get into the car.'

For a few seconds it hung in the balance. If just one boy came forward to help Spencer, the rest would follow, and Whitworth, instead of enjoying this uneasy peace, would be faced with a near riot. Even he exhaled with some relief when Spencer turned on his heel and walked towards the door.

Outside, Stimpson ushered the boy into the rear of the vehicle. As Whitworth sauntered to the driver's seat he looked back to where the other youths were spilling out of the arcade, no doubt contemplating their loss of face for having passively stood by and done nothing to help one of their own.

He took his time getting into the car, then drove back up the high street, turning right as if heading for the police station, but then taking a first left which led into a network of narrow lanes.

Stimpson was noticeably alarmed. 'Where are you going, Mike?'

'Wayne wants to talk to us somewhere quiet before we take him in. Isn't that right, son?'

'No, it ain't.' He looked imploringly at Stimpson. 'Make him take me in, man.'

Stimpson was strongly debating whether he should pull rank when Whitworth slowed the car, bringing it to a halt on a snow-covered grass verge.

Turning to confront the youth, he said flatly, 'Right, Wayne, the word is, you're dealing grass, LSD, crack—'

'Here, what you on? I've got enough on me for a couple of smokes — that's all. There's no crack in this dump anyway.'

With a wolfish grin, Whitworth said, 'There will be if I get some and put it with your things at the station.'

'I want to talk to you, Mike,' Stimpson ordered, climbing angrily out of the car.

'Think about it, Wayne,' Whitworth cautioned, before following.

Keeping the boy in view, Stimpson led Whitworth a few feet away from the car before rounding on him. 'What the fucking hell are you doing? You're fitting the kid up — I can't go along with this.'

'Stay cool, Alistair—'

'We have to take the kid to the station, Mike. I don't want to make that an order, but you're way out of line.'

Whitworth scratched his head, then lit a cigarette. 'Give me two minutes with that kid and I'll have the names of the rapists,' he said persuasively.

'I can't stand by while you plant evidence—'

'I'm not asking you to. I'm not going to fit the kid up. Just let me get the names. You can claim the credit. A rape case cleared up in a day — think how that would look on your record.'

Stimpson hesitated. 'You're not going to do anything that could bounce back on me?'

'It won't bounce back on you or me. I know what I'm doing, Alistair.'

'All right,' Stimpson said, reluctantly. 'But I'll wait out here.'

Whitworth climbed into the back beside Spencer. 'Right, son, you could save yourself a lot of grief, you know.'

'How?'

Whitworth drew on the cigarette. 'You heard about the woman who got raped?'

'Yeah.'

'Give me a couple of names.'

'No way,' Spencer protested. 'You'll get me knifed.'

'That's good, Wayne. So you know who did it.'

'I'm telling you—'

'You don't tell me, kid . . . I tell you. Give me those names and I'll just book you for possession. You'll be out of the station and back granny-bashing before you know it.'

'I'm—'

'Don't interrupt me,' Whitworth spat viciously. 'If you don't give me the names I'll plant enough stuff to get you five to seven years. I've looked at your record, son: car-thieving, possession, breaking and entering . . .' He pulled on the cigarette and exhaled slowly, watching the smoke waft around inside the car. 'Now, there's a thought — breaking and entering,' he said, almost to himself. 'If I found a balaclava at your house you'd be in the frame for rape.'

Spencer began to panic. He reached for the door handle.

'You get out of this car and I'll break your legs,' Whitworth said with cold malice.

Spencer looked at him; his startled eyes, his trembling hands, told Whitworth that the tide was turning in his favour.

'I want my social worker,' Spencer whined.

'Your sexual fantasies don't interest me,' Whitworth laughed, mockingly. 'By the time you get to that lady, I'll have enough to put you away for fifteen years.'

'You're a bastard,' Spencer said, tears brimming in his eyes.

'You'd better believe it — and this is a good day. You're eighteen now, Wayne. It's the big boys' holiday camp for you this time. Nice place — you'll find yourself locked up with a couple of old lags for twenty-three hours a day, and when they've been banged up for a few years, they develop a liking for young boys. You'd be fresh meat.'

He let this sink in for a few seconds, then, with an air of finality, he said, 'Last chance, son . . . give or you've got grief.'

'You can't do this.'

'I can do anything I like. That's what you little toe-rags don't understand.' He reached for the door handle. 'Right, I'll tell my partner you don't feel like cooperating.'

Spencer muttered something, then stared moodily out of the side window.

'I didn't catch that, Wayne.'

'I said, Damon Cain and Delvin Bennett.'

Whitworth leapt out of the car. 'We're in business, Alistair.' He threw away his cigarette end which hissed as it sank into the snow.

A look of relief stole across Stimpson's face. Stamping his feet against the cold, and digging his hands deep into his overcoat pockets, he approached Whitworth boldly. 'Mike, your methods frighten me. You sail too close to the wind.'

'I get results.'

'Yes, well, just calm down when you're with me. Remember, I want to stay here and work my way up the ladder.' He studied Whitworth's impassive face. 'What would you have done if I'd pulled rank and made you take that kid in?'

'I'd have done it, of course.'

'That's good.'

Stimpson looked smugly confident until Whitworth added, 'Then I'd have phoned your wife and told her about the little WPC who's dropping her knickers for you.'

Although Whitworth had been smiling during this, there was little doubt in Stimpson's mind that he meant it.

'You are a bastard, Mike.'

'So everybody tells me. But like my old dad always said — nice guys lose.'

Stimpson had already decided that, for the sake of his future, Whitworth would have to be sacrificed.

CHAPTER 13

Their footsteps rang out as Holly followed Ashworth up the perilously steep metal stairs to the causeway leading to Dennis Paine's office. At the top, Ashworth paused to peer over the rail containing the platform. The cloying odour of leather permeated the air.

From this vantage point the layout of the factory could easily be seen. Machines which cut out the belts and handbags gave way to the closing department, where female staff nimbly ran the products through heavy duty sewing machines. Further along were partitioned offices, housing various types of machinery — the uses of which Ashworth could only wonder at — and then there was the despatch department, where the finished products were boxed and sent off.

Holly could see that Ashworth was fascinated with the scene below. 'What are you thinking, sir?' she asked.

'Just that from his office, Paine can overlook his whole operation. I bet that's by choice, rather than by accident.'

'None of the staff look very happy, do they?'

'No,' Ashworth agreed. 'From what I've heard about the place, it's hard work for low wages. They earn decent money, but they have to work all the hours God sends for it.'

Something had been bothering Ashworth since entering the building. Suddenly he realised what it was. 'That sound, Holly, where's it coming from?'

As there were so many sounds coming from different parts of the factory, Holly was puzzled as to which one he meant.

'That one . . . metal on metal,' Ashworth said, listening intently. 'There it is again.' He looked around, hoping to synchronise a machine with the sound. Then he had it. 'The cutting room.'

'I'm not with you, sir.'

'That sound was on the tape.'

'You think the phone call was made from here?'

'It's beginning to look like it.'

'But how could it have been?'

'Why not? Come on, let's go and talk to Paine.'

They continued along the platform to Paine's glass-fronted office. He was seated at his desk, behind a clutter of papers, and belt and bag samples, talking earnestly into the telephone.

On seeing the officers, he gesticulated for them to come in and sit down, all the while continuing his one-sided conversation. 'I don't care what problems you're having. Get them here by this time next week or consider the order cancelled.' The receiver was slammed down. 'Bloody suppliers. You'd think in this recession they'd be falling over themselves, but all I get is a tale of woe.'

'We've received the ransom demand, Mr Paine,' Ashworth informed him.

'I gathered that from your phone call,' Paine said abruptly. 'Well? How much?'

'One hundred and eighty thousand. Can you raise that by tomorrow?'

'Yes. I've had a word with Babs. We can get it together.'

'Right, the drop is tomorrow night, at a place called Poacher's Wood. That's—'

113

'I know where it is,' Paine stated, sharply.

'Let me finish,' Ashworth said, with forced patience. 'The kidnapper has asked that you act as courier. You're to take the money to Poacher's Wood at 11 p.m. and leave it on the small stone bridge over the stream, then drive back home.'

'That's all the letter said?'

Ashworth shook his head. 'No, it went on at some length. The money has to be in used banknotes, no consecutive numbers. And if we mark it in any way, our friend will know.'

'What do you advise on that?'

Slightly taken aback that Paine should request advice, Ashworth said, 'Normally we'd mark the money, but at the end of the day it's up to you.'

Paine contemplated this, then shook his head. 'No, don't mark the money. I'm not taking any chances. You'll be in place in the wood, I take it?'

'I think the less you know about the police operation the better,' Ashworth replied, curtly. He looked at Holly, who took her cue.

'What's that sound, Mr Paine?' she asked, pleasantly.

'What sound? Does this have anything to do—'

'There it is — metal hitting metal,' Holly broke in.

With an impatient sigh, Paine said, 'That is a clicking press, young lady. The operative places a knife on the leather, the press comes down and cuts out the belt.' Then, with heavy sarcasm, 'Is there anything else you'd like to know? Perhaps I could show you round the factory—'

'That sound is on the tape of the call your sister took from the kidnapper,' Ashworth interjected.

Paine's mouth gaped open. 'Are you suggesting the call was made from this factory?'

'The tape suggests it, I don't.'

'That's impossible, Ashworth.'

'Is it? Would any of your staff have access to a telephone during the evening?'

'Well, yes, the offices downstairs aren't locked. But why should anyone here want to kidnap Simon? It's ridiculous.'

'Does Mr Edwards have any enemies here?'

'Ashworth, when you're in business, enemies crawl out of the woodwork.'

'Actually, Mr Paine, I'd have thought that in this particular business, if anyone had made enemies—'

'It would be me,' Paine said wryly.

'You took the words right out of my mouth.'

Paine, with a rare display of civility, said, 'Chief Inspector, up until three years ago, Simon was managing director, and I was technical director. And — not to put too fine a point on it — Simon wasn't good at the job. Too damned soft. Let people walk all over him. As we were equal partners, I put my foot down and took over as managing director, which meant that I, and I alone, took the day-to-day decisions in the running of the factory.'

'This is all very interesting, but—'

'If you'll listen, I'll explain,' Paine said, brusquely. 'There were a lot of difficult decisions to be taken; decisions affecting the lives of many. As Simon has a way with people . . . a certain amount of charm, which I seem to lack . . .'

Ashworth smiled but remained silent.

'. . . I thought it best for Simon to have the job of informing the staff of those changes.'

'Oh, I see. So, who did he have to upset for you?' Ashworth asked, bluntly.

Paine glared at him. 'There were the workers we had to lay off.'

'Have any of them been reinstated since?'

'Some, but I'd have to check the personnel records before I could come up with names.'

'Is there anyone else who could have a grudge?' Holly asked.

After a moment's thought, Paine said, 'There's Len Warren.'

A mental image of Warren surfaced in Ashworth's mind. 'What could he have against your brother-in-law?'

'He was shop steward, until I decided that the union had to go. I gave my workers a choice: leave the union, or find other jobs. They fell into line.'

'Did Warren take that badly?'

'Well, of course he did. You know what these people are like — little Hitlers, the lot of them. He was forever complaining about minimum wages, or the factory being too hot or too cold.' Paine gave a scornful laugh.

Ashworth said, 'Len Warren has a birthmark on his face, doesn't he?'

'I don't know if it's a birthmark but, yes, he has a large red mark on one of his cheeks. What's that got to do with anything?' Then it registered. 'You're not thinking about what that doctor told you?' he scoffed. 'Warren? Highly intelligent? The man's a cretin.'

'Maybe, maybe not,' Ashworth intoned. 'What's he like?'

'As a shop steward, when he thought he had some power, he was bolshie. Now that's been taken away from him, you'd hardly know he exists.'

Sensing that Ashworth had finished this particular line of questioning, Holly asked, 'Can you think of anyone else who might dislike Mr Edwards enough to want to harm him?'

Paine was silent, thoughtful. Holly was certain he was keeping something to himself. 'Mr Paine, may I remind you that it's an offence to withhold information from the police—'

'Don't you threaten me, young lady,' Paine flared. 'I'm a law-abiding citizen. Save your bully tactics for the yobs who go around stealing cars.'

'Paine, will you please stop being discourteous to my officers,' Ashworth retorted. 'DC Bedford is perfectly correct in saying that withholding information is an offence, as is taking a vehicle without the owner's consent. Neither offence is committed by law-abiding citizens.'

Paine conceded that point, and Ashworth said firmly, 'Now answer the question, please.'

'It's very delicate.'

'We're very discreet.'

Paine leant forward confidentially. 'It's about Julie, our secretary,' he whispered. 'She and Simon were . . . friendly.'

'Your secretary and Mr Edwards—'

'Keep your voice down, for God's sake, she's in the next office.'

Ashworth looked towards the stud partition and lowered his voice. 'So, why would she have a grudge against Mr Edwards?'

'Not Julie . . . her husband.'

'How was this affair conducted?'

'That's the point. Julie's husband, Alan French, works here. He's on permanent two-till-ten shift. Julie finishes work at five p.m., so Simon can tell Babs he's going to the factory in the evenings, when in fact . . .' He shrugged. 'It's convenient.'

'Very,' Ashworth commented. 'And if the husband found out . . .' He got to his feet abruptly. 'Right, Mr Paine, there's nothing we can do about this while the news blackout is in place. When will you collect the money?'

'First thing in the morning.'

'One of my officers will accompany you to the bank and take the money back to the station.'

'You're not going to mark the money, Ashworth,' Paine barked, back to his old form. 'I will not allow it.'

Ashworth smiled. 'I preferred you when you were whispering,' he said, heading for the door. 'I just want that amount of money in a safe place. We'll bring it to the house tomorrow night, at ten p.m.'

Ashworth caught Paine's look of relief as he ushered Holly out of the office.

Outside, a thaw was well under way: icicles, hanging from the gutterings were diminishing rapidly; snow, still lingering around the periphery of the car park, was turning a slushy yellow.

Holly lengthened her stride to keep up with Ashworth. 'I can see the line of enquiry you're following, sir,' she said, 'but would someone who actually worked at the factory, someone who knew Mr Edwards, be stupid enough to abduct him, and then demand a ransom?'

When they reached the Sierra, Ashworth turned to look back at the L-shaped building, over whose main entrance a disgruntled worker had chalked the word 'ALCATRAZ' in bold letters.

'Holly, if the kidnapper is in that building, then I just pray to God that Simon Edwards isn't already dead.'

* * *

Stimpson, with an exasperated Whitworth in tow, was executing house-to-house enquiries in the immediate vicinity of Jane Taylor's house. It was laborious work and, so far, had achieved nothing — no one, it seemed, had seen anything or anyone suspicious at the time of the crime.

They now knew the identities of the perpetrators of the rape, but without concrete proof, this knowledge was of little use.

Whitworth longed to search their homes for incriminating evidence, but knew that no magistrate would sign a search warrant on such scant informaton — hence his mood of irritation.

As Stimpson knocked at a house three doors down the road from Mrs Taylor's, he muttered, 'I'd sell my body to get a result,' just as the door was opened by a pretty blonde of around thirty.

Although her face, framed by thick fluffy hair, was attractive, the focal point was her body: a perfectly proportioned five feet nine, which seemed to have been poured into blue jeans and white blouse; garments which showed off her delicious shape to its best advantage.

'Hello,' she smiled.

'Hello, I'm DS Stimpson, and this is DC Whitworth.' He showed her his warrant card. 'We're making enquiries in the area, and I wondered if we could ask you a few questions.'

She glanced at the warrant card, then looked more intently at Stimpson's handsome face.

'This is nice,' Stimpson exclaimed as they entered the living room. 'A country cottage in the middle of town.'

Whitworth viewed the plastic ceiling beams, the cottage-style lounge suite, the rustic coal-effect gas fire, with anything but enchantment.

'Thank you,' the woman answered shyly. 'That's the effect we've tried to create. Please sit down.'

They sat on the sofa which had been wedged into the bay window recess.

'Mind if I smoke, love?' Whitworth asked.

'No, of course not,' she said, reaching for an ashtray on the hearth and placing it on the occasional table in front of the officers. Whitworth lit a cigarette.

'We're sorry to bother you—' Stimpson began.

'It's no bother at all.' She was obviously attracted to the good-looking policeman, and flattered by his attentions. 'What can I do to help?'

Stimpson did not want to mention rape at this juncture, for fear of compounding Jane Taylor's ordeal by making her the subject of curiosity amongst her neighbours; such victims had been known to withdraw their complaints when events became too traumatic.

He said, 'We're making enquiries about a burglary in the area. We're asking people if they've seen anything suspicious recently.'

'I don't think so. I mean, I haven't seen anything suspicious that I can think of.' She smiled at Stimpson. 'Can I offer you a cup of tea?'

He smiled back. 'Thank you, that would be nice.'

'That would be nice,' Whitworth mimicked after she had left the room. 'What are you playing at?'

'Getting the information we need,' Stimpson grinned. 'You just wait here.'

He quietly let himself into the large kitchen. The woman was filling a kettle at the stainless steel sink. Stimpson's sudden appearance startled her. 'God, you made me jump,' she cried, placing hand over heart.

'Sorry,' Stimpson said, earnestly. 'I thought I'd give you a hand.' He glanced around the room at the oak units. 'I really do admire your taste.'

'Thank you, kind sir.'

'Right, where's the teapot?' he said cheerfully, busying himself with the tea-bag container. 'I'd better have your name . . . just for the record.'

'Clare Johnson.'

'And are you married, Clare? You don't mind if I call you Clare, do you?'

'Not at all and, yes, I am married.'

'I knew it,' he said, with feigned disappointment. 'Anyone as beautiful as you would have to be.'

'I can see I'll have to watch you,' she giggled, carrying the steaming kettle to the teapot. 'My husband works on the oil rigs. He's away for months at a time.'

'That must be very lonely for you.'

She looked into his eyes. 'Sometimes it is, yes.'

'And dangerous — an attractive woman like you on her own. I may have to keep an eye on you.'

'What would the neighbours think about that?' she countered.

'Ah, they need never know.'

'Stop it,' she reproved gaily, replacing the kettle on the worktop beside the sink. 'I'm a respectable married woman.'

'You're right, I must stop it. But your looks just drive everything else out of my head. I'd almost forgotten why I'm here.'

Giggling again, she said, 'Oh, you are a fool.'

'Clare,' Stimpson said seriously as he joined her at the sink. 'We have to be very careful when asking questions. We mustn't be seen to be leading people.'

'How do you mean?' Clare asked, obviously disappointed by this change in conversation.

'Well, why we're here is, we're trying to find out if anyone saw two young boys on the estate this morning. They're about fifteen years old.'

After a moment's thought, Clare said, 'Hold on, I think I did. Yes, they looked rough — out of place.'

'Good, Clare. What time was this?'

Her brow furrowed as she concentrated.

'Could it have been around eleven a.m.?' Stimpson prompted.

'Yes, it must have been, because the news had just been on the radio. I always switch it on at ten thirty and it must have been on for about half an hour.'

'Even better, Clare. Now, can you show me where you saw them?'

'You'll have to come upstairs with me . . .'

'Can't that wait until after the questioning?'

Clare shrieked with laughter. 'You really are terrible. Stop it.'

They went upstairs to the front bedroom. Stimpson noted the double bed and, with an effort, brought his mind back to the case.

Clare Johnson eased herself round the corner of the dressing table which stood in the bay window. Stimpson squeezed in beside her; their bodies touching in the confined space. 'There.' She pointed out of the side window. 'The house on the corner — they were outside that.'

Stimpson found himself looking at Jane Taylor's house. 'They were definitely standing outside that house?'

'No, not standing. I was making the bed and I stopped to look out of the window. They walked past here and stared at the corner house, then they came back.'

'How were they behaving?'

'I don't know really,' she said vaguely.

'Think carefully, Clare, because that's the house we're interested in. Would you say they were behaving suspiciously? Walking backwards and forwards, sort of staking out the property?'

'Now you come to mention it, yes, I suppose they were.'

'And you must have got a good look at them.'

'Not really, I wasn't taking that much notice.'

'But you've some idea of what they looked like? Just think, take your time . . . I'm quite enjoying having your leg pressed against mine.'

'I bet you're a devil on the quiet,' she said, smiling shyly, dimples appearing in her cheeks.

'The boys,' Stimpson persisted. 'What did they look like? Start with their clothes.'

'Leather jackets and jeans, I think — and, hold on, one of them wore white trainers . . . I remember thinking how bulky they looked. Yes, and they both had woolly hats on.'

'You see how much comes back when you really try,' Stimpson encouraged. 'Was one of them a really nice-looking boy?'

'I don't know. I don't really look at boys.'

'Think, Clare.'

'Well, I suppose one was better-looking than the other.'

'So, one of them was good-looking, and the other wasn't?'

'Yes,' Claire stated definitely.

Stimpson reached into his inside pocket, making sure his forearm brushed against Clare's ample breast as he did so.

He brought out two photographs. 'Thanks to your powers of observation, you've confirmed what we already know. These are the lads we're after.' He showed her the photographs. 'You're making a positive identification, then?'

Clare studied the faces. 'Well, it looks a bit like them.' She sounded doubtful.

Stimpson moved away from the window. 'You're saying these are the boys, then?'

'Yes,' she stated, following him to the side of the bed. 'Yes, that's what I'm saying.'

'Thank you, Clare, you've been a great help.' He returned the photographs to his pocket. 'You really have been a great help, you know,' he murmured, brushing his hand across her cheek and into her hair.

'Stop it,' Clare protested weakly. 'You shouldn't be coming on to me like this.' She lowered her eyes. 'Not with your friend downstairs, anyway.'

The message was unmistakable; Stimpson seized upon it immediately. 'I shall have to come back this evening to take a full statement, I'm afraid, Clare. In fact, I could make it out at the station, then all you'll have to do is sign it. Okay?'

Alarmed now to find herself officially caught up in a police investigation, Clare said timidly, 'All right, but it won't involve me in anything, will it?'

'You'll only be involved with me,' he said, suggestively. 'There'll be no comeback on you, I promise. No one outside the police will see or even know about it.'

'So, I'll see you tonight then?' Her smile was back.

'Yes, and I'll look forward to it.'

Whitworth strutted towards the car; Stimpson lagged behind, waving to Clare at the door.

Inside the vehicle, he said cheerfully, 'How's that for mixing business with pleasure? I can write out a statement — saying anything I want — and this evening I get to sample that very sexy body.'

Whitworth, about to remark that Stimpson's methods were as devious as his own, merely grumbled, 'I didn't get my cup of tea.'

CHAPTER 14

Ashworth found it hard to delegate, especially as he had only been working with his officers for a matter of days and was, therefore, unsure of their abilities; nevertheless, even he could not cope with two serious crimes at the same time, so felt forced to hand over the Jane Taylor case to Alistair Stimpson.

Although he personally disliked the man, there was nothing to suggest that he was not up to the job; indeed, all evidence pointed to the contrary. Even so, Ashworth, true to character, could not totally relinquish his authority.

He was in the new office, listening to Stimpson's account of their findings. Whitworth was perched on the edge of his desk, cigarette clamped between his teeth, looking for all the world like a Mafia hit man.

'So, what have you got that you can pull these two lads in with?' Ashworth asked, dubiously.

'We had a tip-off, sir,' Stimpson lied smoothly, 'and door-to-door turned up a positive sighting of the two suspects outside Mrs Taylor's house at about the time of the rape.'

'That's good work,' Ashworth conceded, 'very good work.'

He slowly wandered over to the glass wall and stared out; the thaw had come earlier than predicted, he thought, as more and more red pantiles and thatch began to show on the roofs below him. 'Any previous?'

Whitworth made his only contribution to the discussion then: a sound midway between a laugh and a snort.

Stimpson shot him a warning glance. 'As long as your arm, sir: taking without consent; possession of drugs; vandalism, sex with a minor. They've been in and out of juvenile court for years, but have never had more than a slapped wrist.'

'Right, bring them in.'

'With respect, sir, you realise the paraphernalia that entails: their parents and social workers present at all interviews; as many breaks in questioning as they want—'

'Yes, I do realise — what's your point?'

'Well, sir, I think these kids, aided by their social workers, are going to refuse to answer questions . . .'

Ashworth nodded. 'Yes, go on.'

'And if they do that, we've got very little to go on. So, sir, with that in mind, I'd like search warrants for their homes, and an order to hold them in secure accommodation — at least over the weekend.'

'Yes, all right, I'll authorise both of those moves. Apply to a magistrate as and when you need.'

'Thank you, sir,' Stimpson said, with obvious relief.

'Good, is that all?'

'Yes, sir.'

'Right, let me bring you up to date with the kidnap case. The ransom demand is calling for a drop to be made at a local wood at 11 p.m. tomorrow. I'd like you to be with me, DC Whitworth.'

Such was Whitworth's surprise, he almost toppled off the desk; cigarette ash fell on to his shabby shirt as he slid to his feet. 'Yes, sir,' he said, hastily brushing himself down.

'You won't be requiring me?' Stimpson asked stiffly, annoyed at being excluded.

'Yes, I shall, but I'd like to discuss it with you in private,' Ashworth said, looking pointedly at Whitworth.

The Detective Constable returned the stare before say-ing, with much sarcasm, 'I've just remembered something I've got to do, so if you gentlemen will excuse me . . .'

When he had gone, Ashworth turned to Stimpson. 'As you're the only member of the team — apart from myself — who's married, I've decided not to include you in the first ransom drop, in case things go wrong.'

'The first?' Stimpson queried.

'That's a long story. What I want you to do is go with Paine to the bank in the morning, collect the money, and bring it back here.'

'Yes, sir.'

'How certain are you of the case against the two juveniles?'

'One hundred per cent.'

'Well, just tread carefully. You know what the Crown Prosecution Service is like — make it watertight.'

* * *

It was five thirty before the officers were able to detain Damon Cain and Delvin Bennett. Calls to their homes had proved fruitless. So, working on the assumption that, sooner or later, the boys would turn up at the amusement arcade, they parked some thirty yards away from it, and waited.

Sure enough, after an hour, they were rewarded with the sight of the youngsters walking towards them.

As soon as they drew level with the car, Whitworth got out and blocked their way. The boys' first reaction was one of flight, which Whitworth's fleetness of foot quickly thwarted. He grabbed the boys by the collars of their leather jackets and, such was his strength, he was able to lift their slight frames clear of the ground as he bundled them into the back of the car.

Grinning wildly, he climbed in beside them. 'Hi, guys, I'm your friendly community policeman.'

As they had not been arrested, but were merely being brought in for questioning, Whitworth had no right to search them, but he did, nevertheless, on the pretext that they might be carrying concealed weapons. The search, however, carried out discreetly in the back of the car, revealed nothing more sinister than loose change and latch keys.

It was at the station when the problems really began: they could not interview the boys until their parents and social workers were present, and locating them was proving difficult.

Uniformed officers sent to find the parents had drawn a blank. The social worker, Ms Jenny Rolands, was not available, and word had been left for her to contact the station as soon as possible — whenever that was likely to be.

In the meantime, Cain and Bennett were shown to separate interview rooms where uniformed officers watched over them.

Both officers were greatly frustrated by the loss of momentum caused by this delay.

As he paced the corridor, Whitworth glanced yet again at his watch. 'The little toe-rags are getting plenty of time to make up stories, create alibis,' he muttered resentfully.

'There's nothing we can do about it, Mike.'

Whitworth, sick to death of Stimpson stating the obvious, ignored him and carried on pacing and muttering.

Sergeant Dutton appeared then; as always, his ambling gait suggested that there was nothing in life demanding any degree of urgency, and, being far too good-natured to hold a grudge against the men for their past misdemeanours, he wore a smile on his face as he reached them. 'Ms Rolands is here, and aren't you two lucky?'

'How do you mean?' Stimpson asked.

'Well, she's a radical, even by social worker standards. She really does believe that if the police could be kept off the streets there'd be no problems.'

'Where the hell is she?' Whitworth snapped.

'She went to the loo,' Dutton told him. 'If I could offer you a word of advice . . . I'd go carefully — she's got quite a lot of influence with the Police Committee.'

'We'll sort her out,' Whitworth said, with a firmness which brought a nervous look to Stimpson's eyes.

Jenny Rolands strode purposefully along the corridor. She was perhaps early thirties, a large, big-boned woman, with dark blonde hair pulled back and secured with an elastic band. Her features were harsh, masculine; her expression was fierce. She was wearing a white polo-necked sweater, ill-fitting navy-blue trousers, and a long afghan coat which looked as if it had seen the inside of several charity shops before settling with its present owner.

Whitworth's eyes widened at the sight of the gargantuan figure marching towards them. 'Christ,' he whispered, incredulously, 'where did she take a leak — the ladies or the gents?'

'This is DS Stimpson, and this is DC Whitworth, madam,' Dutton said diplomatically, as she stopped before the group.

'Hello,' she said brusquely. 'I believe you're holding Damon Cain and Delvin Bennett.'

'That's right,' Stimpson said.

'Why?'

'We're hoping to talk to them about a rape which took place earlier today.'

Jenny Rolands shook her head in disbelief, uttering a sound of scornful derision.

Stimpson went on, 'We're having some difficulty in contacting their parents.'

'Neither of the boys has a father—'

'Surprise, surprise,' Whitworth interjected.

'. . . living at home,' she finished, glaring pointedly at the detective.

Sergeant Dutton, sensing that a confrontation was imminent, melted away.

'What about their mothers then?' Stimpson pressed.

'I'm not one to beat around the bush — Delvin's mother is a prostitute; rarely, if ever, at home. In my opinion, the lack of a stable home environment is the cause of the boy's problems.'

'Shame,' Whitworth sneered.

'I don't like your attitude,' Rolands flared.

'It'll grow on you,' Whitworth assured her, pleasantly.

Stimpson stepped in to defuse the situation. 'And Cain's mother?'

'Much the same story.' She was studying Whitworth with curiosity; usually her reputation and bluster — not to mention connections that went right up to the Chief Constable — were enough to guarantee a greater respect than her position or manner deserved; however, in Whitworth, she saw a man who deviated somewhat from the norm. 'I want to see the boys,' she ordered.

Stimpson said, 'We're going to talk to Bennett first.'

'He's a very sensitive lad, so I don't want you mentioning his mother. I shall be there to see that he's treated properly. Is that understood?'

'Very clearly,' Stimpson stated smoothly.

Delvin Bennett, totally unconcerned, was seated at the interview table. His angelic young face lit up when he saw the social worker. 'Why am I here, Jenny? I haven't done anything — honest.'

'It's all right, Delvin, I'm here to sort things out.' She fetched a chair and sat next to the boy.

Whitworth winked at the uniformed officer to the left of the door, then crossed to the tape recorder. Switching it on, he intoned, 'DS Stimpson and DC Whitworth interviewing Delvin Bennett at . . .' He glanced at the wall clock. '. . . 7.05 p.m. on 8 January. Also present, Ms Jenny Rolands, social worker.'

With much concern, Rolands looked the boy up and down. 'Have they treated you well, Delvin?'

'No, Jenny,' he blurted, 'they've taken my trainers, and that one . . .' He pointed to Whitworth. '. . . hit me on the head.'

'Is this true?' Rolands demanded.

'That's a very serious allegation, Delvin,' Whitworth said, sitting beside Stimpson to face the boy. 'Where are you claiming the assault took place?'

'You know,' Bennett accused.

'Where are you claiming it took place?' Whitworth asked demurely; indeed, since switching on the recorder, his whole personality seemed to have changed; he had become quiet, polite; his tone, one of fatherly concern.

'In the car — you banged my head when you pushed me into the car.'

'I think the best way to resolve this is to call in the police doctor, don't you, Ms Rolands? A vicious assault of the type Delvin is alleging would undoubtedly leave marks.'

Jenny Rolands stood up and ran her hands through Bennett's hair, fingering his scalp.

'Would you like the doctor to take a look, Ms Rolands?' Whitworth asked politely.

Sitting down again, she spat, 'No, leave it.'

'Am I to take it, Ms Rolands, that you have examined Delvin, and you have found no evidence to support his claim? You see no reason to call in the doctor? Is that correct?'

'That's correct,' she replied tetchily.

'Good. Now Delvin, we're trying to find your mother—'

'I protest,' Rolands said, jumping to her feet. 'I told you—'

Remaining moderate, Whitworth said, 'I can see no reason for you to protest. Someone in your position must be aware of the guidelines that apply to the police questioning of minors. Let me remind you — we must make every effort to ensure that their parents are present. I'm sure you'll want me to adhere to regulations.' Whitworth flashed her a wicked grin.

Seething inside, Jenny Rolands returned to her seat, realising that this scruffy, tough-looking individual was aiming to outmanoeuvre her.

The boy was beginning to show signs of confusion and concern; years of watching the bombastic manners and strident tones of his mentors turning police officers into jelly had reinforced in him a belief that the authorities could do little to control this behaviour — but now, doubts were creeping into his mind.

Whitworth lit a cigarette. 'Have you any idea where your mum is?'

'No.'

'Is she working? Does she have a job?'

'No.'

'So where is she?'

'Out walking.'

'Walking? In this weather?'

Bennett looked imploringly at his social worker, who simply smiled sadly and nodded her head for him to speak. Morosely, he turned his attention back to Whitworth. 'She's on the game.'

'I see, and do you know where she works? The area? It's very important she's given a chance to be here.'

'I don't want her here,' Bennett yelled stridently. 'She couldn't care less about me.'

'All right, son, stay calm,' Whitworth said, exchanging a glance with Stimpson.

Stimpson asked, 'Did you know a woman was raped on the Cherry Tree Estate this morning?'

'No. Why should I?'

'Where were you this morning, Delvin?' Whitworth jumped in.

'Don't know.'

'Were you on the Cherry Tree Estate?' Whitworth persisted.

'No, I wasn't.' His tone was petulant but the panic was clear in his eyes.

'Someone left a shoe print at the scene of the rape, Delvin. That's why we took your trainers, to see if they match.' This was Stimpson, and as he spoke, fear flashed across the boy's face.

Whitworth followed quickly. 'And we've got a witness who saw you there. You're in trouble, son.'

The boy began to cry. 'Make them leave me alone, Jenny. I haven't done anything. Tell them to stop frightening me.' He bowed his head, sobbing dramatically.

Jenny Rolands's voice cut through the tense atmosphere. 'You really must stop bullying Delvin. I won't allow you to wear him down till he admits to something he hasn't done. I demand we break for hot food and a drink.'

Unseen by Rolands, Bennett lifted his head to smirk at Whitworth, who smiled back, saying, 'Yes, of course you can have a break. We have other enquiries to make, connected with this case. We'll send someone in to take your order.' He sauntered over to the tape recorder, stated the time and reason for termination of interview, then switched off the machine.

'How long do you intend to keep Delvin and Damon here?' Rolands demanded shrilly.

Her brusqueness was beginning to ruffle even Stimpson's usually impeccable manners, and he retorted, 'You want time to eat your hot meal, don't you?'

Whitworth was far more forthcoming. 'You'll be here for a while yet, lady.' His customary contemptuous tone had returned now that the tape recorder could no longer bear witness to it.

'Don't address me as 'lady',' Rolands snarled.

Whitworth shrugged indifferently. 'We're applying for a warrant to search the homes of these two little treasures of yours,' he told her, 'then, depending on what we find there, we could be asking for a secure accommodation order.'

'They can't do that, can they, Jenny?' the boy squealed. 'They can't search our houses?'

Whitworth spread his hands on the tabletop and leant forward menacingly. 'Yes, we can, son,' he said quietly, 'and when we find the knife, the sweatshirt and the balaclavas . . . we're going to do you for rape.'

'I'm reporting you to the Chief Constable,' Rolands blustered. Whitworth studied her disdainfully. 'Your privilege . . . lady.'

CHAPTER 15

During the drive home, Ashworth was positively gloating over the inaccuracy of the weather forecast. The evening air was extremely mild for January and swiftly melting snow formed babbling rivulets of dirty water gushing towards the drains.

Chuckling merrily, he turned the car into his drive, relishing the prospect of pointing out this glaring error.

Unfortunately, Sarah was not there to listen and his good humour died on seeing yet another note waiting for him in the kitchen. It told him that she had gone to a Samaritans' meeting, would be home at eight fifteen, and would prepare a meal then.

With an angry flourish, Ashworth crumpled the note and deposited it in the pedal bin. He looked down at the dog circling his feet, tail wagging hesitantly, slightly perplexed by her master's lack-lustre welcome. 'Come on, Peanuts, let's go into the garden.'

Moodily, he strolled around the lawn. The wind was soft, and although spring was still a long way off, the promise of it was in the air, but this did little to brighten his disposition.

Inside once more, he checked the kitchen clock; eight fifteen had already come and gone. It was, in fact, eight fifty when he heard Sarah's key in the lock.

The dog, fearing an invasion, bounded to the front door, coat bristling, a growl deep in her throat, but the sight of Sarah set her tail wagging furiously and, barking with enthusiasm now, she scurried back to impart the good news to Ashworth.

Sarah bustled into the kitchen. 'Sorry, Jim,' she said, smiling, 'I got held up. There's so much to learn about counselling.' She noticed his fixed, angry expression, but carried on brightly. 'I'll do us something out of the freezer, shall I? Is there anything you fancy?'

'No,' he replied shortly. 'It's too late to eat now. I won't sleep properly.' His stomach chose that moment to let out a prolonged rumble.

Sarah exhaled sharply. 'What's wrong, dear?'

'Nothing.'

'It's because I'm late home, isn't it?' She walked to where he was sitting at the breakfast bar. 'Look, I'm sorry, Jim, but this Samaritan thing is something I really want to do,' she stated firmly. 'I'll try not to let it interfere with us, but it's important to me.'

Still his face remained stony.

'I'll make it up to you tomorrow,' she offered as conciliation. 'Just tell me the meal you fancy, and I'll prepare it.'

'I'm out tomorrow night. It's to do with the kidnapping.'

'I think you're being a little bit unfair, Jim,' Sarah said, trying to sound reasonable. 'I'm expected to sit here all evening by myself whenever you're out working.'

Ashworth, fearing he was losing the argument, stubbornly refused to look at her, and to make matters worse, his stomach gave another hollow rumble. He brooded for a moment, then suggested morosely, 'I suppose a few slices of cheese on toast would be all right.'

Later on, wholly cheered by three good measures of best Highland malt, he was in the bathroom, preparing for bed. With much vigour he brushed his teeth, all the while admiring his reflection in the mirror. He could easily pass for a man ten years younger, and his body — particularly since his weight loss — would not shame a man twenty years his junior. But, more importantly, he did not feel his age; in neither appearance nor outlook could he perceive the approach of his autumn years.

Jauntily replacing his toothbrush in its glass, he rinsed his mouth. The landing floorboards creaked beneath his light step as he made his way to the bedroom.

Sarah was already in bed, absorbed in a book. She smiled absently as he climbed in beside her, then, carefully marking her place, she lodged the book on the bedside table. 'Goodnight, dear,' she said, planting a lukewarm kiss on his lips.

But Ashworth startled her by slipping his arms around her shoulders, making it difficult for her to withdraw from him.

After many seconds he released her. 'What are you doing, Jim?' she laughed.

He slipped his hand down on to her breast, asking softly, 'Do you feel sleepy?'

Sarah frowned, saying, 'Jim, I'm bushed . . . really.'

Stung by the rejection, Ashworth released her and leant back against the headboard. Their sex life, over the years, had settled into a cosy routine, lacking excitement but worthwhile, nevertheless; this was the first time that Sarah had refused him.

He felt her hand on his arm. 'Don't you think we're getting a little bit past that sort of thing, dear?'

Leaning over to switch off his bedside lamp, he said sadly, 'Yes, I suppose we are.'

As he drifted fitfully between veils of light sleep and drowsy consciousness, images of Gwen Anthony's inviting nakedness repeatedly enticed him, but each time he reached out to touch her warm flesh, she vanished, leaving him to come awake with a start.

He found himself with a solid erection, which was comforting, for it assured him that — whatever Sarah might think — he was far from past that sort of thing.

* * *

Ashworth's Saturday got off to a bad start, and continued to spiral downwards throughout the day.

Waking early, he exercised the dog in the fanciful half-light of dawn. This was usually his favourite time of the day, one which augured new beginnings; a time when yesterday's seemingly insurmountable problems could be seen in a more positive light.

But this morning a gloomy air of disenchantment clung to him; invisible to the eye, but as real as the light swirling mist which partially concealed the cheerless landscape. Today, he felt dissatisfied, cheated somehow, as if an important part of him had been laid to rest prematurely.

'Walk,' he snapped, turning into his drive, even though the dog was trotting obediently by his side.

He glanced at his Sierra, sitting waiting on the gravel. There was heavy condensation inside and he cursed himself for not having put it into the garage the previous evening.

Inside the house, he was relieved to find that Sarah was still sleeping as from the stairs, he could hear her soft rhythmic snores. The dog was yapping for breakfast, and as Ashworth tossed a handful of mixer biscuits into her dish, the thought came to him that it had been years since he had noticed his wife's habit of snoring.

Opening the bread bin, he took out a sliced wholemeal loaf but, being without much appetite, he returned it, unopened, and made himself a cup of tea.

The dog retreated to her bed and, as if aware of her master's unhappiness, fixed him with a doleful stare.

Ashworth was tempted to finish the tea and leave for work, but at some time between pouring and drinking it, he relented and filled a mug for Sarah.

She was still asleep when he entered the bedroom, and she started when he lightly shook her shoulder. 'What?' Her eyes opened; she blinked rapidly. 'What time is it?'

'Half-past eight,' Ashworth mumbled. 'I'll put your tea on the bedside table.'

Sarah sat up in bed. 'Thank you, dear. Are you off?'

'Yes,' he grunted, already heading for the door.

'Jim?' Her voice stopped him. Deep inside, he was hoping for some sensitively worded suggestion that they talk over any problems they might have. But all she said was, 'Be careful, dear.'

'I will.'

As he walked downstairs, he could hear the dog crying from the confines of the kitchen; the clamorous sound did nothing to soothe his rankled nerves so, with much haste, he grabbed his coat and left the house.

The car would not start. Ashworth swore repeatedly under his breath, turning the key again and again until giving up and getting out to dry off the spark plugs. That cured it; at the next turn the engine roared into life. He headed for the station, and by the time he arrived — fifteen minutes late — he was in his 'you upset me and God help you' mood.

It was a widely held notion that police stations were quiet places at weekends, but this was a fallacy. Friday and Saturday nights were probably the busiest of the week as far as the police force was concerned, with revellers, vandals, car thieves, and opportunistic burglars filling the cells to overflowing. Special courts were asked to convene, so clearing the cells for the next influx.

This particular Saturday proved to be no exception. The front reception area was a mass of moving bodies. Uniformed officers led bleary-eyed prisoners out to the courts for reasons unknown to them, now that the alcohol had been slept off. An infuriated member of the public stood at the desk, loudly demanding to know if his car had turned up — and if not, why not? An entire cross-section of society, from punks to pensioners, waited to be seen.

Ashworth pushed his way through to the stairs, glad to leave the cacophony behind him. Josh Abraham, the sole occupant in CID this morning, looked up as the Chief Inspector entered the office. 'Good morning, sir,' he said brightly.

'Morning,' Ashworth barked back.

Subdued by this fierce entrance, Josh stammered, 'Alistair escorted Mr Paine to the bank. The money's over there, sir.' He indicated an expensive briefcase which stood on Ashworth's desk. 'Mr Paine left a set of instructions for you, sir . . .' Josh continued, until he became aware of Ashworth's sharp stare.

'Did he now? And what, pray, are they?' he asked, tartly.

Josh glanced at a piece of paper on his desk. 'He reiterates that the money is not to be marked in any way. He wants an officer at his sister's house tonight, and you're to phone him during the day.'

Ashworth eased into his chair, swivelling it round to look out over the rooftops of the town. He was glad he had missed Paine; his present mood would have made a confrontation inevitable. 'And where is DS Stimpson now?'

'He and DC Whitworth are interviewing the juveniles about the rape, sir.' He picked up a second piece of paper from his desk. 'They searched the boys' homes last night and came up with balaclavas, a knife, which could quite easily be the one used in the attack, and a sweatshirt which matches the victim's description. Also, the footprint matches trainers worn by one of the boys. So they feel they've got enough to send to the Crown Prosecution Service.'

'Mmm, so do I,' mused Ashworth.

Josh went back to his computer.

Ashworth studied the back of the man's head, and attempted to pin-point what it was about Josh which irritated him so much. His strict attention to detail, the endless lists he insisted on making, should have smacked of efficiency, but somehow those self-same attributes lent him a rather prissy air. Also, that damned computer he tapped away at all day — what did it actually produce? At the end of any given period, what could be seen for all that feverish typing? Ashworth, always keen to get the best value from resources, made a mental note to look into this.

Perhaps what bothered him more than anything were the whispered rumours, concerning Josh, circulating discreetly around the station; they, undoubtedly, were the crux of this matter.

Ashworth — probably because his own daughter lived so far away — was developing an almost parental concern for Holly's well-being, and he felt sure that any attachment she formed with young Abraham would only bring further unhappiness into an already troubled life.

However, being mature enough to realise that, at present, his view of things was somewhat distorted, Ashworth decided to postpone, for the time being, the taking of any definite decisions on any matters, professional or personal.

He stood up. 'See the money's put into the Chief Constable's safe,' he ordered as he strode to the door.

* * *

Meanwhile, Holly was suffering no such reservations about Joshua Abraham. Since their bitter row, Emily had maintained a polite near-silence — a situation which Holly found highly pleasing, for it gave her time to think, and daydream about Josh.

She had spent hours trying to put her feelings into perspective. He was always kind, courteous, and — whenever they were alone — extremely good company.

Holly knew from experience that many men could behave indelicately; could, within the space of a few days — by the use of sexual innuendo, wandering hands, and other such ploys — assess their chances of success, and adjust their attitudes accordingly.

Josh was a refreshing change. He seemed to be totally honest and appeared to genuinely enjoy her company.

But he never tried anything! Was she glad? She remembered seeing a film once, in which the hero — or villain, whichever way you looked at it — had perfected a technique whereby he feigned sexual indifference to each beautiful woman he found desirable. This novel approach unleashed something inside the women, bringing about a complete reversal of roles — in short, the women became the peacocks, and actively set out to catch this man.

The fact that Holly was travelling to Bridgenorton to have her hair cut and restyled said much for the validity of this hypothesis.

Deep within herself, Holly's emotional scars were beginning to fade; subconsciously, she was preparing to close the door to the past, take a chance on life, and live for the present.

CHAPTER 16

The dank scent of rotting vegetation hung heavily over the brooding wood, and the sounds of nocturnal creatures working their way stealthily through the undergrowth made an eerie overture.

Ashworth's knee creaked painfully as he shifted position amongst the thickets, attempting to alleviate his discomfort; he had been crouched on the wooded slope for almost an hour now, and numbing cramp was working up his legs.

Directly below him was the small stone bridge on which, some ten minutes earlier, Paine had deposited the briefcase containing the ransom money. He had not lingered — for this was an unfriendly place after dark — but had returned immediately to his car, stalling it at first in his eagerness to be gone.

Long after the car had disappeared along the track, Ashworth's eyes remained firmly fixed on the briefcase; he feared that if he averted them for a second, the money would be spirited away.

There came an ominous crashing sound close by, as a night predator — perhaps a fox — closed in on its prey.

The hackles rose on Ashworth's neck, and his forehead was covered with sweat, even though he felt numb with cold.

He shot a feverish glance down the steep slope and was reassured by the sight of Whitworth's upturned face, white in the grey blackness of night.

Although he had never considered himself to be of a nervous disposition, Ashworth was glad to be keeping this vigil in the company of Whitworth, together with Josh, and six uniformed officers, all of whom were scattered around at various vantage points.

Unable to tolerate his discomfort any longer, he began to work his way carefully down the declivity, conscious of how the stillness distorted and amplified his movements. By the time he reached Whitworth he was slightly breathless, and his limbs ached as the blood began to circulate once more.

'I could use a cigarette,' Whitworth grunted, as Ashworth settled in beside him.

'You won't get one for some time yet,' Ashworth replied shortly.

They sat there in silence for a while, then in a hoarse whisper, Whitworth said, 'I've been thinking — if someone cared to work their way up that stream with a bike or moped, they could have the money off the bridge and be in open countryside in minutes. We wouldn't stand a chance.'

'I know, I've been having much the same thoughts myself,' Ashworth admitted miserably, eyes straining to catch any slight movement that the dark might throw up.

Fifteen long, unproductive minutes passed, and then there was action.

'There's a car coming up, guv,' Whitworth said, pointing to his left.

Ashworth looked to where the car was slowly easing along a dirt tract leading to the bridge; its headlights were switched off, the driver picking out his route with just the benefit of sidelights. It was perhaps a quarter of a mile away.

'Could be just passing through,' Whitworth ventured.

'Doubt it,' Ashworth threw back. 'That track doesn't lead anywhere; it ends at a cattle grid a mile up the road.'

'It's stopping,' Whitworth whispered, his voice alive with excitement. 'I think it's one of the large Vauxhalls — recent, by the shape.'

They watched, hardly daring to breathe, as the car pulled onto the picnic area beside the bridge, its sidelights now extinguished. Then they lost sight of it as huge laurel bushes blocked the view.

Sounds of a car door opening and the slamming of the boot, reached their straining ears.

'That's it, guv, we've got to go in,' Whitworth urged. 'That could be a bike coming out of the boot.'

'Don't be ridiculous,' Ashworth hissed. 'He wouldn't leave the car there.'

'It could be stolen, guv. Come on, we've got to go in.'

Ashworth did not want to be too hasty. He prayed that this was the kidnapper and fervently hoped that this operation would be a success. Simon Edwards was out there somewhere, and Ashworth wanted him back in one piece.

As Whitworth fidgeted restlessly beside him, he came to a decision; fighting to keep his breath steady he reached into his pocket for the radio. 'All officers apprehend occupant of car parked in picnic area. Go carefully.'

Whitworth was already snaking his way down the steep embankment, with an agility which Ashworth envied; close to the bottom he stumbled, falling heavily, but rolled over and came to his feet running, crossing the road with the speed of an unleashed greyhound.

Ashworth made a slower, more cautious descent — his shaky legs still seeming to have a life of their own — and by the time he reached the road, all officers were in the picnic area.

Whitworth was walking towards him, arms waving to imply negation. 'No, guv. Courting couple — they were at it by the time I got to the car.'

'Damn,' Ashworth muttered angrily. 'Damn.'

Whitworth lit a cigarette; the other officers chatted amongst themselves. The tension which had built up over the last hour or so was quickly evaporating.

Ashworth, clutching at straws, asked, 'There's no chance it's a cover?'

'I don't think so. When I wrenched the car door open, neither of them knew whether they were coming or going.'

This remark, uttered by a poker-faced Whitworth, brought considerable sniggering from the uniformed officers.

'All right, calm down,' Ashworth commanded impatiently. The noises stopped abruptly.

Ashworth's gaze took in the parapet of the bridge, and panic gripped him — the briefcase was gone.

'I've put the money in the boot of my car, sir,' Josh's calm voice assured him.

Ashworth swallowed hard, and said, 'Good man.' Then, turning to Whitworth, 'Are the couple all right?'

'The lad's shaken up, and the girl went into near hysterics when she realised half of Bridgetown nick had had a good look at her pussy.'

Another outburst of boyish merriment threatened, but Ashworth's stern gaze soon quelled it. 'I'd better have a word with them,' he said.

The young man, no more than twenty years old, was standing by the driver's door, his face pale and shaken. By his side, sobbing into an already sodden paper tissue, was his blonde girlfriend. Ashworth's formidable appearance only served to bring fresh squeals of distress to her lips.

'We weren't doing anything, Mr Ashworth,' the young man protested.

'That's not how it looked from where I was standing,' Whitworth quietly quipped, causing the girl to wail with renewed vigour.

'Mike,' Ashworth chastised. He took Whitworth's arm and led him round to the other side of the car. 'Have some sensitivity, will you? This might be a joke to you, but for these youngsters, it's pretty traumatic.'

'Right, guv,' Whitworth said, with barely concealed mirth.

Ashworth returned to the couple, cutting short the young man's explanations. 'It's all right, Jamie, you haven't done anything the police are interested in—'

'We are getting engaged,' the girl blurted out.

'Oh, good,' Ashworth replied lamely. 'Anyway, you just stumbled into a police operation, that's all.'

'So my dad won't have to know?' Jamie asked hopefully.

'Ah.' Ashworth's pregnant pause did little to help the girl's emotional state. 'We shall have to eliminate you from our enquiries, I'm afraid.'

'Oh, God,' Jamie moaned, in a tone which implied that his whole world had just come to an end.

'There's no need to worry, though,' Ashworth reassured him. 'I'll leave it as long as possible, and I won't go into details. Can't you tell your dad you stopped for a kiss and a cuddle? Even he couldn't object to that.'

'I suppose not,' Jamie said doubtfully.

'It'll be all right, don't worry. Now, your young lady's distressed — why don't you take her home?'

'Yes.'

'Oh, Jamie, tell me, what did you take out of the boot?'

The question brought on a fresh outburst of crying from the girl.

'It's my dad's car, you see, and . . .'

'Yes?'

'Well . . . I needed the car rug . . . the stains on the upholstery . . .'

Whitworth's shoulders were shaking with suppressed laughter.

'Yes, all right, Jamie, off you go then,' Ashworth said hastily, mentally kicking himself.

The still-sniffing girl walked around the car, her eyes fixed firmly on the ground. Whitworth gallantly stepped forward to open the door for her. Once settled in the seat, she was aware that Whitworth had not straightened up, nor had he closed the car door. Hesitantly, she glanced at him and followed his gaze to the tiny frilly white garment nestling behind the gear stick.

'Don't catch cold, love,' he whispered.

The girl took one look at his wicked grin, and burst into tears again. 'Take me home, Jamie,' she sobbed.

Whitworth's face was a picture of innocence as he closed the door. They all watched the car pull away.

'You know the lad, guv?' Whitworth asked, above the sound of crashing gears.

'Very observant,' Ashworth commented drily. 'Yes, his father's the local bank manager . . . and a lay preacher.' He chuckled. 'A few years ago he was on some council committee, always beefing on about used condoms being all over the town. As long as I don't drop the lad in it too much, this little incident could be very useful if I ever need information about someone's bank account.'

A surprised Whitworth glanced at Josh. 'That's not very ethical,' he said, cynically.

'All right, lads,' Ashworth called out. 'It's all over here. Those of you still on duty report back to the station, the rest of you go home. Josh, leave the money with me and go to the Edwardses' house.'

Their cars were parked some thirty yards away, behind a bank of dense undergrowth. As they walked towards them, Ashworth remarked, 'Talking of ethics, I've been hearing complaints about your behaviour.'

'The social worker,' Whitworth scoffed. 'I know what she needs, but I just can't find anybody hard up enough to give it to her.'

Ashworth, still on the adrenalin high, laughed loudly; he was beginning to appreciate Whitworth's rather base sense of humour.

The roar of car engines disturbed the quiet of the night. Above the noise, Ashworth said, 'She has complained, yes — but so has someone a little closer to home.'

'Alistair Stimpson.'

'You don't sound worried.'

'I'm not, guv. When Alistair wants to come at me from the front, I'll explain my actions.'

Ashworth was surprised by the lack of animosity displayed by the man; he found it refreshing.

They rounded the bushes. Josh was waiting to hand over the briefcase.

'Thanks, Josh. Wait in your car, I'll be with you in a minute.'

Ashworth locked the money in the boot of his car as Whitworth asked, 'Have you got any complaints, guv?'

'If I had you'd have heard them by now,' Ashworth assured him. 'I'll offer you some advice though.'

'Oh yes?'

'Next time you decide to shave off corners, don't do it with Stimpson around.'

The moon came from behind a bank of low cloud and lit up the grateful smile on Whitworth's face. He said, 'Do you want me to clear things up at the Edwardses' house? I've heard Paine gets up your nose.'

'And he wouldn't get up yours, I suppose?'

'Water off a duck's back,' Whitworth shrugged amiably. 'I'll just keep calling him "sir", and agreeing with him — make him mad as hell.'

Ashworth found the thought most appealing. 'Yes, all right, I'd like you to. I'm in no mood for Paine, anyway. I'll take the money back to the station.'

'Right.' Whitworth began to stride off.

'Oh, and Mike . . .'

'Yes, guv?'

'Thanks.'

Whitworth, grinning, touched his forehead in a salute and sauntered over to Josh, who was belting up in his car. Banging on the roof, he shouted, 'Okay, Funny Guy, you and me are going to see the man, Paine.'

Josh pulled his car in behind Whitworth's souped-up Cortina, and as they drove out of the field, Ashworth could hear Whitworth's strangled voice declaring, above the beat of heavy metal music, that he would never see his baby again.

CHAPTER 17

Ashworth spent Sunday morning holed up in his study. The gravity, the enormity of the case, enthralled him. Something about it was not right, but he could not put his finger on it. Various concatenations filtered through his mind, to be dissected, examined; every minute detail searched to find the part which did not ring true.

Sarah, well used to her husband's total absorption in his work, was blissfully unaware of any worries he might be having away from the job. She had failed to observe his sour expression at breakfast when she had listened to his narrative of the ransom drop, but had not extended the conversation, wishing instead to tell him about the wonderful television film he had missed.

To Sarah's mind, diets had no place at Sunday lunch, so — eager to placate her petulant spouse — she served up lashings of his favourite roast beef and potatoes, fresh vegetables, and Yorkshire pudding.

She smiled indulgently as he tucked in with obvious relish; he deserved a good meal. His recent self-imposed adherence to the strict diet pleased her immensely, and it would seem that he had, once again, taken up his long-abandoned fitness programme: press-ups, knee-bends, and even those dreadful sit-ups.

There was still one area of her husband's intake which Sarah would have loved to tackle — his consumption of scotch whisky. She did make the occasional sortie, reducing his nightly drinks from three to two, but could not claim any consistent results and the subject remained taboo.

After lunch, with most of the snow gone, Ashworth set about edging the flowerbeds, and generally pottering about.

In the evening they watched a television play, or rather, Sarah watched; Ashworth's mind kept drifting over various subjects and, as it wandered yet again, he came to the conclusion that the plot — if indeed there was one — had been very carefully camouflaged.

Nine thirty, and ritual dictated a sherry for Sarah, a scotch and soda for himself. He was pouring these when the telephone rang. 'I'll get it,' he said, passing the sherry to Sarah on his way to the hall.

He took a sip of his drink, then picked up the receiver. 'Ashworth.'

'Hello, Jim.' It was the weary voice of Don Facer, head of the Forensic department. 'I've got you to thank for being dragged out of the pub.'

'What's happened?'

'The second ransom note's turned up. Posted this morning at Bridgetown main post office.'

Ashworth's glass jarred as it was set down. 'Go on,' he urged tensely.

'Same paper as the first — cheap. Written in biro. No finger-prints—'

'What does it say?' Ashworth cut in, impatiently.

Facer snorted. 'Well, although it was addressed to Mrs Edwards, it's definitely meant for you. Goes on at great length about your shortcomings. Chummy claims he was in the wood last night, and actually touched the briefcase containing the money. He's quite pleased with himself. Anyway, then it gets on to the real nitty-gritty . . .'

Ashworth sighed loudly. 'Go on.'

'It says: 'These are my instructions. On Monday, 11 January, at 6 p.m. Dennis Paine is to take the money to the public telephone box by the stone cross. He is to wait for me to call him. I will then give him further instructions. If these instructions are not complied with, I shall kill Simon Edwards.' That's it, Jim.'

'All right, Don, thanks. I'll let you get back to the pub.' He put down the receiver and stood for a while, sipping his drink, contemplating the message. It struck him that the wording of it suggested an educated man, or at least a man used to letter-writing who liked to show off his skill. Ashworth fervently hoped that tomorrow night would not prove to be yet another wild-goose chase.

He returned to the lounge where Sarah was still engrossed in the play. 'That was the station,' he remarked. 'There's another ransom drop tomorrow evening.'

She glanced up. 'That's good, dear — I'll be out tomorrow, as well,' she said, turning her attention back to the television.

Ashworth longed to talk about the case, and Sarah's apparent indifference rankled him. 'I'm going to make a phone call. I'll do it in the study . . . I'd hate to disturb you,' he said pointedly.

'Yes, dear.'

Now, far more supple and energetic than he had been for some years, Ashworth positively bounded up the stairs. In the study, he sat behind his desk and took a long drink, relishing its taste and fiery effect.

Picking up the receiver, he frowned as he searched his memory for the number; silently mouthing the digits, he tapped it out.

The telephone rang perhaps half a dozen times before being picked up. 'Hello, Holly, it's Jim Ashworth.'

'Hello, sir,' Holly said with surprise.

'Sorry to disturb you at this time of night, but the kidnapper's made contact.'

'That's quick.'

'Yes, that was my first thought.' After making her familiar with the letter's contents, he said, 'Why I'm ringing — I want you to follow Paine tomorrow evening.'

'Me, sir?'

'Yes. I do have good reasons: firstly, your car is fairly nondescript—'

'It's a banger, you mean,' she joked.

'It is,' Ashworth laughingly agreed, 'which means it won't stand out as a police vehicle. Secondly, I don't think our man's going to be expecting a woman.'

'And I'll be out of contact for the whole time?'

'You'll have a mobile phone, but that's all. We can't afford to take risks, Holly. This drop could be the real one.'

'Okay, sir.' She gave a nervous laugh. 'I just wish you'd waited till the morning before telling me.'

'I didn't, for one very good reason — I want you to take your car into the police garage in the morning for a thorough service. I don't want you having to call out the AA . . . they might not know a man who can help with a kidnapping.'

'Right, sir,' she laughed.

'How did Barbara Edwards take the news last night?'

'Paine's been pestering the doctor to put her on stronger tranquillisers. I wouldn't say she's out of it, but she's damned close to it most of the time.'

'Probably the best thing.'

'Perhaps,' she said, sounding far from sure, 'but the man really is a pig.'

'How did he get on with Whitworth?'

Holly giggled. 'It was so funny — you know how scruffy Mike is, well, Paine kept looking him up and down, turning his nose up, and raving on about police incompetence. Mike just stood there, taking it all, saying 'Yes, sir,' and 'No, sir,' until Paine had finished, then he asked him if he'd like to come out for a Chinese. It doesn't sound funny now, but it was at the time.'

'Paine declined the offer, I take it?' Ashworth laughed.

'Yes. Mike took Josh and me out for a meal though. Behind that big macho bit, he's quite nice.'

'He grows on you, I suppose.' Ashworth paused. 'About you and Josh . . .'

'Yes, sir?'

Ashworth caught the defensive note in Holly's voice; realising that he was about to seriously overstep the mark, he checked himself, and said brightly. 'You'll both be in tomorrow morning?'

'Yes, of course.'

'Well, I'll see you then,' he concluded heartily. ''Bye.'

The receiver had hardly settled in the cradle when, impulsively, he picked it up again to tap out another number.

As he listened to the ringing tone, he wondered what he would do if a male voice answered. For a few seconds he considered putting the receiver down, but then it was too late, the connection was made and Gwen Anthony's 'Yes?' came down the line.

'Gwen, it's Jim Ashworth,' he said, unaware of the fact that he had lowered his voice.

'Jim, how lovely. You've caught me when I'm a bit tiddly, I'm afraid.'

'I wasn't aware doctors indulged,' he reproached her teasingly.

'This one most certainly does.' She fully emphasised the *double entendre*.

With reluctance, Ashworth brought his mind back to the matter in hand. He said, gravely, 'We've had a second ransom demand. It's for tomorrow.'

'And when was the first?'

'Of course, you don't know, do you? It was yesterday.'

'This doesn't sound right, Jim. The whole thing is too rushed.'

'I know, that's what I thought. In some ways the man conforms to type, but his eagerness to get the money just doesn't ring true.'

There was an ominous pause. 'There's one possibility you'll have to consider . . . it could be that Simon Edwards is already dead, and the kidnapper wants to get his hands on the money before the corpse is discovered.'

Ashworth's voice was strained as he said, 'That's the conclusion I'd reached. I just wanted it confirmed. Sorry to have disturbed you, Gwen.'

'You haven't, but you are being a bit naughty . . .'

Her brightness cast aside the previous tension, and Ashworth smiled as he said, 'Why?'

'Do you know how much I charge for consultations? I really do feel you should offer to buy me a drink.'

Ashworth heard a floorboard creak beyond the study door. Quickly, he said, 'As soon as this is all over, I shall.'

'Is that a promise?'

'A firm one.'

Gwen's laugh was delightful as she said, 'Good, I'll let you go then. 'Bye.'

He replaced the receiver hastily as Sarah came into the room. 'Who were you talking to, Jim?'

'Holly Bedford, my DC,' he lied easily. 'Just arranging things for tomorrow.'

'You'll miss the end of the play, dear.'

That would be a blessing, he thought, draining his drink. He sat for a moment, staring into the empty glass, striving to ignore the stab of guilt in his chest, then he followed Sarah downstairs.

CHAPTER 18

Next morning, Ashworth found front reception strangely quiet as he strode through the station doors at nine a.m. sharp.

Martin Dutton — seated behind the enquiries desk, and wearing his 'have I got bad news for you?' expression — signalled for Ashworth to join him.

'What's the matter, Martin?' Ashworth asked, while struggling out of his jacket.

'Have you got your handcuffs with you, Jim?'

'I'm not following.'

'You'll need them . . . to chain young Whitworth to the radiator.' As Ashworth's eyebrows lifted questioningly, Dutton went on, 'The Crown Prosecution Service, in its wisdom, has deemed it unsafe to proceed with the rape case against the two lads—'

'But the case is watertight,' Ashworth declared angrily.

'You know the CPS, Jim,' Dutton replied, with more than a trace of bitterness. 'My lads call it the Can't Prosecute Service. They all say if they had a pound—'

Ashworth cut him short. 'Whitworth has taken it badly?'

'He's not one to hide his feelings, is he? Young Bobby didn't know the meaning of most of the words he used.'

Ashworth approached the office with trepidation. He felt concerned for Whitworth. How badly would he react to this injustice? And how could Ashworth best calm the situation?

The first of these questions was answered quite forcibly when Ashworth opened the door to his office, and was greeted by a long string of lewd expletives, delivered in Whitworth's Manchester/London twang.

'Give me a break, Alistair, it's fuck—'

'Quiet now, Mike,' Ashworth ordered gently.

Whitworth, his usually swarthy complexion now drained of colour, turned to face him. 'The CPS threw out the rape case, guv.'

'Yes, I heard.' Ashworth sat at his desk. 'Did they give reasons?'

Stimpson, who was greatly disturbed by the Chief Inspector's use of Whitworth's first name, tried to take control. 'They say the shoe print in the snow doesn't mean anything. It was made by a very popular brand of trainers. The only thing it proves is that the rapist takes the same size as Delvin Bennett. Same goes for the sweatshirt logo — half the kids in Bridgetown wear it.'

'What about the eyewitness?'

Whitworth snorted. 'The fucking—'

'Now stop it, Mike,' Ashworth thundered from behind a pointing finger. 'I won't tolerate that sort of language in this nick. Do you understand?'

Subdued, but still smouldering, Whitworth went and sat on Holly's desk.

Stimpson said, 'They say the witness was too far away from the lads to give a positive identification. As for the balaclavas and the knife — well, the lads weren't carrying them when we picked them up, and they swore they only used them for fishing. I've been trying to impress on Mike that we'll get them. They've got a taste for it now — it's only a matter of time before they do it again.'

'Not with the CPS, we won't,' Whitworth interjected, angrily. 'I bet if we caught them on top of a woman, they'd say there's no evidence to suggest that she hadn't invited them to do it.'

'Can you give us a minute, Stimpson,' Ashworth asked, nodding towards the door.

Stimpson was most put out by this obvious dismissal and he strode haughtily out of the office without comment.

Ashworth sympathised with the despairing look on Whitworth's face. 'Mike, it's done,' he said. 'Water under the bridge.'

'Yobs, one — Bridgetown nick, nil.'

'That's how it looks now, certainly, but Stimpson's right — we will get them.'

Whitworth's dark eyes blazed hostility. 'You don't see it, do you, guv? This bloody stupid system prevents us from doing the job. The more these kids get away with, the more convinced they'll become that we can't do anything to them.'

Ashworth did see, only too clearly. 'Where are the boys being held?'

'Clifton House.'

'Right. Would you like me to go and tell them they're not being charged?'

'No, guv, win or lose, I clear up my own cases.'

* * *

The relaxation room at Clifton House was more in keeping with a quality hotel than a secure holding place for young offenders. Its plush blue carpet was expensive. Luxurious chairs and sofas were dotted about, providing seating for up to fifty inmates.

Numerous pursuits were catered for here, ranging from television — Stimpson had noticed a huge satellite dish on the way in — and video games, to table tennis and snooker. There were books and magazines aplenty; the magazines well-thumbed, the obviously unused books in pristine condition.

Today, a tense atmosphere hung over the room. Jenny Rolands sat with Bennett and Cain on a huge four-seater settee; the boys dwarfed by the large plump cushions. Stimpson and Whitworth stood before them.

Whitworth stared out of the window overlooking the gardens and playing fields, trying to distance himself from this extremely unpalatable situation.

Stimpson said, 'Delvin, Damon, I'm here to tell you that the police will not be bringing any charges against you.'

Jenny Rolands smiled and squeezed the boys' hands reassuringly. Cain, running fingers across his spotty face, looked bewildered. Bennett smiled triumphantly as he stared at Whitworth's profile.

'So, you're free to go,' Stimpson finished on a strained note.

'You've had these boys imprisoned in this place for no good reason,' Rolands's austere tone proclaimed. 'I'll be complaining about this.'

Bennett, his eyes still fixed on Whitworth, sneered. 'We did it, King Shit, and you can't do nothing about it.'

Whitworth's head came round sharply. He pointed at the social worker. 'Now, you heard that little toe-rag just admit that they raped the woman.'

'I heard no such thing,' Rolands flared. 'You antagonise the youths of this town. There was never any trouble before you came here.'

Whitworth turned to Stimpson for support. 'He's just admitted it, Alistair.'

'I know, Mike,' Stimpson whispered harshly, 'but there's nothing we can do. Let's go.'

But Whitworth was reluctant to leave it there. 'If another woman gets raped,' he hissed, shaking his fist at Rolands, 'it'll be on your conscience, lady.'

'If you do your job properly and catch the rapist, there won't be another one,' Rolands responded jubilantly. 'You're too busy trying to pin all crimes on innocent youngsters.'

'Let's go, Mike,' Stimpson urged.

'Do me a favour, lady — have a crap life.' It was a hollow victory, but he was determined to have the last word.

Rolands' fleshy face flushed at the insult.

'Leave it now, Mike,' Stimpson insisted, taking Whitworth's arm and jerking him away.

Bennett's high-pitched laughter mocked them on the long walk to the door.

'Stop it, Delvin,' Rolands lightly chided. 'You mustn't laugh at the police.'

In the corridor, Stimpson said, 'We'd better go and sign the release order.'

'You do it,' Whitworth said, staring morosely towards the floor. 'I can't stand this place. I'll wait outside.'

He wandered off along the wide, white-walled corridor towards the front door. But he did not go outside; instead, he paused by a table on which lay piles of mail for the inmates.

He studied the colourful 'No Smoking' sign as he lit a cigarette, clamping the cork tip between his teeth and narrowing his eyes against the smoke.

He stood there smoking for a while, and then backed into an open doorway as he caught sight of Delvin Bennett strutting along the corridor. The boy disappeared into a room some twenty yards away.

Smiling grimly, Whitworth moved swiftly. He pushed open the door and was met by an overpowering smell of disinfectant.

Bennett was standing a few yards away, with his back towards him. Whitworth deftly flicked his lighted cigarette between the boy's open legs; it hit the white enamelled urinal, and dropped into the flooded trough.

Bennett turned and gave an imperceptible cry of fear when he saw the churlish expression on Whitworth's face.

'Just you and me now, toe-rag,' Whitworth muttered coldly.

CHAPTER 19

The news that Delvin Bennett had sustained a head injury, needing sixteen stitches, reached Bridgetown Police Station before the detectives returned. By and large, it was greeted with numb disbelief.

This, however, was not a feeling shared by Chief Constable Savage, as he paced Ashworth's office. 'This is serious, Jim. The press will crucify us with it,' he growled. 'I've had that terrible Rolands woman on the phone, claiming Whitworth was behaving like a psychopath prior to the assault.'

'Alleged assault,' Ashworth calmly corrected from behind his desk. 'Let's give our own lads the same rights as everybody else, shall we?'

'It's obvious he did it.' Savage stood still long enough to light a cigarette. 'The man's all wrong for the job — anybody could have spotted that from day one.'

'Why didn't you then, when you were describing him as the backbone of the team?'

'That's not fair, Jim. Christ, I don't need this, you know — I've got Police Committee meetings coming up, not to mention meetings with community leaders and the civil liberties wallahs.'

'And I don't need it either,' Ashworth said sharply. 'I'm in the middle of a kidnap case, or had you forgotten?'

Josh, as always, was lost in his computer program, but Holly was acutely embarrassed at being privy to such a frank exchange of words between two high-ranking officers.

Then, as if that embarrassment had conveyed itself to Savage, he stubbed out his cigarette, saying, 'Shall we continue this on the way to reception, Jim?'

'Surely.'

As they walked along the corridor, Savage said, 'He shouldn't have been sent out on such a sensitive job.'

'Let me have a word with him,' Ashworth said patiently.

'You'd better. He'll have to be suspended, you realise.'

They began to descend the stone steps.

'Ken, you're over-reacting — Stimpson and Whitworth were together, and I can't see Stimpson being involved in something like this.'

'Oh, but you can see Whitworth—'

'I didn't say that,' Ashworth declared smartly.

'Whitworth has got a violent temper, Jim.'

'Mike does have a volatile nature, I'll grant you that, but the fact that he's been in the force for ten years suggests that he knows how to control it.'

Ashworth was almost skipping down the steps. Savage, wheezing badly behind him, said, 'I need this sorted quickly.'

'Ken, we can't do anything until they get back.'

'You don't seem to understand how serious this is,' Savage puffed. 'You've had no experience of it. If there's just a hint of suspicion, the man will have to go; anything less and we'll be accused of a cover-up.'

When they reached the bottom of the steps, Ashworth turned on Savage. 'Stop panicking, Ken, it's probably no more than the kid making mischief.'

'Mischief? Sixteen stitches?' Savage wearily rested his back against the wall. 'I'm the one who gets the flak, you know. I've got social workers screaming at me; Dennis Paine

ranting down the phone about his bloody brother-in-law . . .
and County Hall shouting about our wages bill.'

'And I'm off enjoying myself, solving all these crimes,'
Ashworth caustically remarked.

'Don't be sarcastic. All I'm saying is, you've got to look
at CID overtime.'

Ashworth, close to using up his quota of patience for the
day, scathingly replied, 'If I knew the kidnapper's address, I'd
take the damned ransom money to him in my lunch hour.'

'Don't go too far, Jim,' Savage warned. They had
reached the reception lobby. 'Right, I want to see Stimpson
in my office the minute he comes in.'

Ashworth shook his head despondently as he watched
Savage career down the corridor towards his office. As he
gloomily surveyed the car park, Whitworth's car pulled in.

If the DC had been given advance information of the
storm awaiting him, it was not betrayed in his bearing.
Ashworth watched as he arrogantly climbed out of the car,
slamming the door behind him and throwing his keys into
the air, to catch them behind his back. The immaculately
dressed Stimpson appeared equally unperturbed.

Once they were inside, Ashworth's expression alerted
them immediately to the fact that all was far from well.

'Guv?' Whitworth said, in an unusually tentative tone.

'Stimpson — the Chief Constable's office, right away,'
Ashworth ordered. 'Mike, come with me.'

He led Whitworth to a locker room, and his voice still
had a cutting edge to it as he snapped, 'In here.'

He held the door open for Whitworth, who flicked the
light switch as he entered, bathing the windowless room in
a harsh, unflattering glow. There was a slight trace of foot
odour in the air.

Ashworth closed the door, and stood with his back
against it. 'Right, what happened at Clifton House?' he
asked, secretly reassured by Whitworth's puzzled expression.
So far, everything about the DC's behaviour suggested he
was innocent.

'Nothing happened, guv. We told the two kids and their minder there'd be no charges made, signed the release papers, and came back here. What is this?'

'Delvin Bennett claims you followed him into the toilets and hit him twice. He's got sixteen stitches in his face to prove it,' Ashworth told him bluntly, watching his face closely for a reaction.

Whitworth closed his eyes. 'Oh, God,' he said, 'I've been fitted up.' He turned sharply and hit out at one of the metal lockers. The sound reverberated loudly around the confined space.

'Did you follow Bennett into the toilets?'

'Yes, guv — I warned him I was still on his case, and told him, if he even breathed too loud, I'd nick him . . . but I didn't thump him.'

'So how did his face get cut?'

'Oldest trick in the book — they injure themselves, or get somebody else to do it, then blame it on the police.'

'If it is such an old trick, you've shown an appalling lack of judgement, putting yourself into such a compromising situation.'

'I never thought it would happen in a place like this, guv. Manchester, the Smoke, yes . . . but not Bridgetown.'

'Did you have an argument with the social worker?'

'I had a ruck with her, yes. She was there when Bennett admitted he and Cain raped the woman.'

Ashworth seized on this. 'Did Stimpson hear that?'

Whitworth pulled a rueful face. 'Yes, but I'm not expecting any help from that direction.'

'No,' Ashworth agreed, 'but I'll give you all I can. We'll interview the social worker, the boys . . .' He paused. 'You know what this means, Mike?'

'Yes. Yobs, two — Bridgetown nick, nil . . . and Mike Whitworth gets sent off the pitch.'

He dug his hand into his pocket, brought out his warrant card, and passed it to Ashworth.

'We'll get to the truth, Mike.'

162

'Yes, that's what scares me.'

'Why should it scare you?' Ashworth asked suspiciously.

'Well, you know what's got to happen if I'm to have the remotest chance of clearing my name — those kids have got to get juiced up on whatever it is they take, then go out and hurt another woman.'

For a fleeting second, Ashworth glimpsed the humanitarian behind Whitworth's tough, uncaring facade; then it was gone. 'Like the man said, guv — life's a bitch, and then you die.'

'You really ought to see the Chief Constable before you go.'

'I'll give that a miss, if you don't mind.'

'All right, I won't make it an order.'

'No, don't, guv — not today.'

Ashworth stood aside to allow Whitworth to leave the room, then he watched as he made his way to the car park, most of the arrogance gone from his walk.

Ashworth was in a quandary: on the evidence available, it looked increasingly likely that Whitworth had struck the youth. And if that was indeed the case, he could not condone the action, but he could at least understand it. There had been a number of occasions during his career when he had come close to doing something similar himself.

Throughout his years in the police force, no one had ever referred to him as 'guv' — he was beginning to like the ring it had.

Ashworth continued to watch as Whitworth's car pulled out on to the road. Even the roar of the Cortina's powerful engine seemed subdued, he thought, before turning and heading back to his office.

CHAPTER 20

By three p.m., Ashworth's mental energies were beginning to dissipate, and he was having to close his mind to the thought that a lot more blackness lay ahead on this dark day.

Holly and Josh had taken the news about Whitworth badly; this had surprised him somewhat, but it would seem that, although Mike Whitworth could initially appear unpalatable, he was a taste which could be acquired.

Stimpson had not helped his colleague's case one bit, when he stated that Whitworth, in his opinion, had been spoiling for a fight at Clifton House, and that Delvin Bennett's outburst had not constituted an admission of guilt.

Ashworth had packed him off to take Bennett's statement, and was glad to see the back of him.

Ken Savage had continued to rant and rave about anything and everything — from Whitworth leaving the station without seeing him, to the amount of overtime being booked by CID — until finally his congested throat, further aggravated by his chain-smoking habit, would allow no more than a hoarse, croaking whisper to pass his lips.

Ashworth was at his desk, trying to take stock of the day, when Holly marched into the office, balancing two plates, and tea in plastic cups.

'Ham rolls, sir. You missed lunch,' she declared, in a matronly sort of way, setting down a cup and a plate in front of him.

'Thanks,' he muttered, glancing at her own plate, which was laden with two ham rolls, a Mars bar, and some chocolate biscuits. 'You're eating a lot today,' he remarked, sipping his drink.

'Nerves about tonight,' she admitted sheepishly.

Ashworth almost dropped his tea. 'Oh, my God — tonight,' he exclaimed. 'I've forgotten to tell Paine about the drop.'

'I took care of it, sir,' Holly said efficiently. 'I went to see him at the factory. He's got the money, and he knows about the drop.'

Ashworth smiled at her gratefully. 'Has anyone ever told you, you're the most wonderful woman in the world?'

'Not for a good many years, sir, no,' she replied truthfully.

* * *

Dennis Paine's Continental-style villa sat high on a hillside, overlooking Bridgetown.

As Holly waited in her car, on the lane outside, she had plenty of time to regret her excessive eating habits earlier in the day, for now stress was slowing down the workings of her digestive tract, leaving an uncomfortable knotted feeling in her middle.

The fact that the mobile telephone, which lay on the passenger seat, was her only link with the station, and that Paine would soon be driving about with one hundred and eighty thousand pounds in his car, only heightened her feelings of dread.

A little before six p.m., the undipped headlights cruising along Paine's sweeping driveway heralded his departure. Holly allowed him to turn into the lane, then followed at a discreet forty yards.

The stone cross was a medieval monument which stood at the foot of a short hill leading into the high street. Paine parked outside the telephone booth, and Holly shortened the distance between them to twenty yards.

She was more than a little worried that when Paine drove off, she could lose him at the traffic lights on the crest of the hill.

Paine, pacing back and forth, casting surreptitious glances at his wristwatch, suddenly dashed towards the telephone and grabbed the receiver.

Holly started the Mini's engine and kept one eye on Paine as she checked that the road behind was clear.

Paine flew out of the booth and into his Jaguar. Holly pulled out, but slowed when his car remained stationary.

'Come on,' she breathed, as motorists behind her honked their disapproval at the Mini's crawling pace.

Then Paine's car moved off. Holly accelerated, watching the traffic lights ahead. She exhaled with relief when they turned from green to amber, then to red as she tucked the Mini in behind Paine's Jaguar. When the lights turned to green again, Paine steered left into the high street.

Two gruelling hours later, after an extensive tour of Bridgetown, Bridgenorton, and surrounding countryside — during which time Paine had stopped at no fewer than nine telephone boxes — they were, once more, back at the stone cross.

Holly's eyes were sore from driving in the dark, and her nerves were jangled. By now, though, there was far less traffic on the road, which calmed her a little.

Paine came out of the booth, looked around, then climbed into his Jaguar. Not wishing to make the same mistake twice, Holly, holding the car on its clutch, hung back. She sensed something was wrong when Paine did not move off, and instinctively looked around for anyone approaching the car.

There was a small slight man, wearing a long brown rain-coat, standing opposite the telephone box, waiting to cross the road. So intently was Holly watching him that Paine's car had been moving for a couple of seconds before she realised.

'Shit,' she exclaimed viciously, letting the clutch out, and swinging the car into the road, not seeing a Ford Fiesta coming up behind; a collision was avoided only by the driver being quick to bring it to a halt amidst the sounds of screeching tyres.

Two cars were now between Holly and Paine's Jaguar as she dashed off in pursuit. She seemed to have lost the ability to salivate, and her stomach cramped as she watched Paine approach the amber light.

Stop . . . please! she silently pleaded, but the Jaguar turned left into the high street just as the lights turned to red.

She slammed on the brakes, coming to a halt only inches from the car in front. Grabbing the mobile telephone, she frantically tapped out the number.

'Yes?' Ashworth's terse voice jumped from the earpiece.

'I've lost him, sir,' Holly moaned breathlessly. 'I'm at the traffic lights at the stone cross. Paine turned into the high street on a red light.'

'Keep calm, Holly,' a dejected Ashworth said. 'Pursue as soon as possible. I'll get all available cars into the area.'

* * *

At ten p.m., back in the CID office, an air of despondency clung to them all. The hint of prettiness which had been brought to Holly's face by her new swept-back, fluffed-up hairstyle was now marred by her dull eyes, her tight-lipped, fixed expression.

Josh's blank look gave away no hint of what he might have been thinking or feeling. For once his chair was turned away from the VDU, and only his slight restlessness as he gazed around the room betrayed his unease.

Stimpson, perched on the edge of Holly's desk, was unusually quiet. Every now and then, he stole a glance at his reflection in the glass outer wall.

The pungent smell of Whitworth's stale cigarette smoke still lingered in the room. The throb of traffic from the expressway was a distant mournful wail.

Ashworth appeared in the doorway, his rugged features gaunt and strained. 'Nothing,' he muttered, shaking his head slowly.

'Oh, God,' Holly said softly.

'Don't feel too badly, Holly,' Ashworth slumped into his chair. 'This man's clever — his last instructions to Paine at the stone cross were to time it so that he left you behind at the red light. He knew you were there — God knows how.'

Holly frowned and sighed deeply. Josh asked, 'Where did Paine drop the money?'

'He had to throw it over the gate at Low Meadow Farm.'

Josh thought through the geography. 'So he doubled back on himself?'

'That's right,' Ashworth said. 'First left after the lights, down the hill, and then left again. My guess is, the kidnapper was in the field. After collecting the money, he could just stroll across country to where his car was parked.'

'But why didn't Paine contact us after he dropped the money?' Holly asked.

'Because', Ashworth began, wearily, 'he was instructed to drive to Bridgenorton and park outside the Robin Hood pub where he was told his brother-in-law would be released soon after eight thirty. When Simon Edwards still hadn't turned up at nine p.m., Paine got in touch with us.' He thumped the desktop despairingly with his fist. 'If only the damned fool had rung us just after the drop, we could have had the kidnapper in custody by now.'

'It must have been a bit of an ordeal for him, though, sir,' Holly ventured. 'It was bad enough for me. How's he taking it?'

'Badly,' Ashworth replied flatly. 'The man looks worn out. Ken Savage and I have just spent half an hour with him and, true to character, he's threatening to sue the police for negligence. Mind you, if Simon Edwards turns up as a corpse

— what with the unmarked money and everything else — I'm not certain he wouldn't have a good case.'

'The money's not unmarked, sir,' Josh said quietly. No one spoke, but all eyes pivoted towards him. Shyly, he stammered, 'I spent Saturday feeding the serial numbers into the computer.'

Ashworth felt a huge surge of gratitude. 'Well, at least that's something. Good work, Josh.'

Blood rushed to Josh's face as he said, 'At least the press won't be able to make us look quite so silly.'

'Hold on,' Ashworth said, almost to himself. 'This may be a time when looking silly is the clever thing to do.'

'How do you mean, sir?' Holly asked, puzzled.

'If we stick to our original story, that the money's unmarked and we didn't take the serial numbers, in the short term we're going to look foolish, but the kidnapper is going to feel free to use the money, and when he does . . .' He left the sentence unfinished. 'Right, you three go home and get some sleep. I'm spending the night here in case Simon Edwards turns up.'

Tired, dispirited, and hungry, no one challenged his decision.

'Did you contact my wife?' Ashworth asked Holly a little while later, as she was getting into her coat.

'Yes, sir. She said she didn't get in herself until quarter to ten. I told her you'd not be home tonight.'

'Did she give any message?'

'No, sir.'

'Right. Goodnight then.'

'Goodnight, sir.'

Holly left Ashworth staring into space.

There were occasions, during that long, lonely, uneventful night, when Ashworth craved for the comfort only a cigarette could bring.

CHAPTER 21

Tuesday morning's newspapers carried the story of Whitworth's suspension for allegedly assaulting a juvenile.

This did nothing for morale at the station, which sank still further when Simon Edwards failed to materialise during the day, and finally hit rock bottom when the evening newspapers carried the news of the kidnap, and the botched ransom drop.

* * *

By Wednesday morning, Bridgetown CID was in a deep state of melancholy.

It lifted for a second when Ashworth received a call from Central Control. 'We've found Simon Edwards for you,' the officer told him.

Ashworth, with heart pounding, rested the receiver between ear and shoulder, and grabbing pen and paper, said, 'Thank God. Where?'

'In the river,' he replied, with insensitive cheerfulness, 'just on the bend of Beggars Meadow. Bobby Adams is attending officer. He's summoned half the nick to seal off the area.' The officer sniggered. 'Probably felt lonely with only a body for company—'

'Cut the patter,' Ashworth snapped harshly. 'This is a murder investigation, not the Des O'Connor Show.'

Holly exchanged a doleful glance with Josh at the mention of the word 'murder'.

The officer continued soberly. 'The police surgeon is in attendance, and Dr Anthony's been informed.'

'Right.' Ashworth replaced the receiver. 'Simon Edwards's body has just turned up in the river,' he announced sombrely. 'Holly, you come with me.'

As he reached for his waxed jacket, he said, 'Where's Stimpson?'

'I think he's taking a statement from Mike Whitworth,' Holly said, zipping up her anorak.

'Why doesn't anybody ask me, before they go charging off?' Ashworth demanded, as he stormed out of the office.

Holly took in a deep breath, gave Josh a wan smile, then hurried after him.

Beggars Meadow had been bequeathed to the town by the Lord of the Manor in late Norman times, for the purposes of sport and recreation. It had derived its name from the fact that, in the Middle Ages, it became a meeting place for beggars and vagrants. The netless goal posts, standing on the five-acre site, bore evidence that the English were staunch sticklers for tradition.

Ashworth dismally noted the thirty or so uniformed officers forming a large semicircle around a small off-white tent, pitched near to the river's edge.

He parked the car on a gravelled area, close to the road, as a rather embarrassed Martin Dutton strode across to meet him, the gravel crunching loudly beneath his shiny black boots.

'Morning, Jim. Dr Anthony's with the body now.' He looked towards the river. 'Bobby Adams answered the call. A local angler hooked the corpse. It was tangled in a submerged tree in the eddy there. Lucky it was, too — with the flood flow on that river, it could have been out to sea by now.'

Ashworth nodded grimly.

'Young Bobby's handled things really well, all things considered . . .' His eyes moved to the multitude of officers. '. . . but I'm afraid he rather misinterpreted securing the site. I plan to have a word with him later.'

'Get most of them back to the nick, Martin,' Ashworth scowled. 'If there's a major incident in town, we'll be in trouble.' Then he almost smiled, saying, 'And tell Bobby I didn't seem to notice.'

As Dutton shouted orders, Ashworth and Holly began the trek towards the tent. The ground was wet, spongy, and the light wind sweeping across the meadow carried with it sounds of the rushing river, and — Ashworth imagined — the decaying smell of death.

Inside the tent the smell was strong, no longer imagined. Gwen Anthony was crouching beside the corpse as they entered. 'Jim,' she said solemnly, reaching for him as she stood up.

Ashworth took the proffered hand, giving the fingers a gentle squeeze. Holly was startled by the intimacy of the gesture and looked away quickly.

'Procedure, procedure,' Gwen complained. 'As if I need a police surgeon to tell me Edwards is dead.'

Ashworth reluctantly looked at the body lying on a clean sheet. The face and neck were discoloured, swollen to such an extent that the eyes had all but vanished behind mounds of puffy purple flesh; the mouth was horribly distorted.

Much of the skin had begun to peel, and some of Edwards's hair which had come adrift from the scalp was now plastered around his face and neck.

Around the nostrils and lips hung a fine white foam; the hands were chalky white and heavily wrinkled. Edwards's expensive suit was tattered, with most of the dye washed out of it in places.

Holly had the taste of acid vomit in her mouth, and she could not help noticing Ashworth's Adam's apple bounce as he too had to swallow hard.

'Cause?' he managed to ask in a steady voice.

'Drowning,' Gwen replied. 'See the foam around the mouth and nostrils? That's a mixture of air, water and mucus — it's one of the few external signs of drowning. I'm certain the post-mortem will confirm that.'

Ashworth forced himself to lean closer to the remains of Simon Edwards. 'There are a lot of injuries to the body.'

'Yes,' Gwen agreed, 'but don't get your hopes up. Don't forget, it's been buffeted about in the river for a number of days, so it's hit a few things. Then there are the pike — they're not averse to taking a chunk of flesh out of a human body.'

The thought made Ashworth visibly shudder. 'How many days had he been in there?'

Gwen glanced at Holly's ashen face. 'Do you think we could continue this outside, Jim? The Scene of Crime boys want to come in with the cameras.'

'Of course,' Ashworth said with relief.

They all three gulped in fresh clean air as they emerged outside.

'Wait here, Holly,' Ashworth ordered.

He wandered with Gwen along the riverbank, relieved to be out of the makeshift tent. 'I'm glad that's over,' he remarked.

'We're supposed to be immune to it, Jim.'

'Yes, I know. Are you?'

Gwen's expression was desolate as she replied, 'No — and I've got the job of cutting him up.'

They stopped, and Gwen rested her black bag on the ground. The river was a swirling, ugly mass of dark brown water. Ashworth watched as the complete branch of a tree was propelled downstream faster than a man could run.

'How many days has he been dead, Gwen?'

'It's going to be vague, I'm afraid — the low temperatures of late have slowed down putrefaction. I'd say four to ten days.'

'As vague as that?'

'Sorry, Jim, that's all I could put before a coroner.'

'And what could you put before a Chief Inspector?' he asked hopefully.

'Well, for my favourite Chief Inspector, I'd say the peeling skin and loose hair suggest the body has been in the water for about ten days.'

'Since Edwards went missing,' Ashworth mused.

'Off the record, Jim, yes.'

The sun showed itself briefly, lifting Ashworth's spirits as it twinkled and danced on the surging water.

'When will you be doing the post-mortem?'

'I'll have to do it today. I can't put him on ice because that could destroy evidence, and with this mild weather—'

'Don't go into details,' Ashworth said hurriedly. 'Just give me a time.'

Gwen smiled. 'I'll do it first thing this afternoon, so if you call by the hospital at four, I'll give you what I can. Is that a date?'

'Yes, but I can think of more pleasant places.'

'And come alone, Jim,' she said, stooping to pick up her bag.

Ashworth watched her walk away; even hidden under a thick blue anorak, with coarse jeans tucked into green wellington boots, her body looked inviting.

With leaden reluctance he turned away and fixed his eyes on the hostile river. His thoughts were centred on the horrifying fragility of human life as he set off back to the tent.

'All right, Holly,' he said, briskly, 'we're finished here.'

'Anything, sir?' Holly asked, striving to keep pace with his furious march.

'Yes, plenty to go on,' he replied abruptly. 'Now we have to break the news to the family.'

Holly felt quite offended that Ashworth had not shared with her the information gleaned, and her tone was sharp as she said, 'Do you want me to take a couple of WPCs and go to see Barbara Edwards?'

'Yes, and I'll take Paine,' he said without relish. 'And we'd better hurry up before the press get wind of this.'

They reached the Sierra. 'Tell me,' he said gruffly, 'what do Stimpson and Abraham do all day?'

'Maybe you should ask them, sir,' she said, repaying his earlier snub.

* * *

Of the many unpleasant duties a police officer is obliged to perform, the most disturbing by far is having to break the news of an untimely death to the victim's relatives. Holly had had to do this many times in her short career, but it had not become any easier.

As she pulled up outside the Edwardses' house, Barbara's tired pale face was at the window. With her, in the car, were WPC Jill Thompson and WPC Ann Kimble, both of whom were experienced and sympathetic to this part of the job. Before they were even out of the car, Barbara had the front door open.

Holly's heart sank as she viewed the look of hopeful anticipation on the woman's face.

'Have you found Simon?' she asked, her tone excitable, highly strung.

'Can we go inside, Barbara?' Holly said gently.

Barbara looked in alarm from one to the other, trying to decipher their expressions. 'Something's happened, hasn't it?'

'Let's go inside,' Holly urged, more strongly this time.

'What's happened?' There was a tremor of hysteria in the voice now.

Holly firmly took command by gripping the woman's arm and leading her into the house. Barbara, offering no resistance, allowed herself to be escorted into the lounge.

'Barbara, sit down,' Holly coaxed. 'I'm afraid I have some bad news.'

She would not sit down, but remained standing in front of the armchair; her hands were shaking, and a pulse throbbed in her temple. 'It's Simon, isn't it?'

Holly knew of no words with which to make this easier or more bearable; far better to have done with it and allow Barbara to escape into the soothing balm of shock. 'I'm afraid your husband is dead.'

'Dead?' Now she sank heavily into the chair. 'Dead? How?'

'His body was found in the river this morning.'

Holly was ready for tears, a numb silence even, but not the crazed hollow laugh which escaped Barbara's lips as she said, 'The river? God, you don't know how ironic that is. I sometimes think he should have married the river — if he wasn't fishing there, we were forever walking along its banks.' Suddenly her smile faded. 'He lived for that river — and now he's died in it.'

Holly could not tell whether the memories being evoked were happy ones. She had never encountered a response such as this, so moved quickly on to the next safe stage in proceedings. 'Ann — tea, I think. The kitchen's second on the right off the hall.'

WPC Kimble nodded vaguely, then left the room.

'Just sit quietly, Barbara, we're organising some tea.'

'Thank you . . . it's Holly, isn't it? Yes, that's right — I always think of 'The Holly and the Ivy'. It helps me to remember your name.'

Holly smiled, but inwardly she was panicking; this wasn't the Barbara she had come to know.

'Holly, dear, you couldn't get my medication for me, could you? It's in the drawer of Simon's desk.' She waved weakly towards a neat desk standing in a corner of the room.

Its drawers opened with a smoothness that only money could buy. In the third one down, Holly found a bottle containing white tablets. These she immediately identified as barbiturates, or 'downers' as they are more commonly known, because of their ability to relieve stress and bring about a feeling of relaxed well-being.

She handed the bottle to Barbara, who struggled, with shaking unsteady hands, to lift off the 'child-proof' top.

Eventually, she gave up and Holly opened it for her, saying, 'Do you want to wait for your tea?'

'No, I'm all right,' Barbara told her, swallowing three of the tablets with an ease which came with familiarity.

Holly pulled up a pouffe and sat at Barbara's feet.

'I did a little deal with myself, you know,' Barbara said with a strained laugh. 'I said to myself that if I kept off these for today, Simon would be all right. Isn't that stupid?'

Holly shook her head, looking up as Ann came in and placed the tea tray on the coffee table.

Barbara carried on talking against a background of clinking cups. 'I was going to get off these things . . . the tablets, I mean. Simon was going to have me admitted to a clinic — but what does it matter now?'

Ann laid two cups on the tiny table to the side of Barbara's chair.

'Of course it matters,' Holly said eagerly. 'Have you been addicted to pills for long?'

'I'm not addicted,' Barbara responded fiercely. 'Simon used to say that. God, the rows we had about it. I could have killed him . . .' The tears came then; Barbara buried her face in her hands and sobbed. 'They're all prescribed drugs . . . I'm ill. Oh, but when I think I could have killed Simon . . . and now he's dead . . .'

'It's all right, Barbara, you're bound to feel like that — everyone does,' Holly soothed. 'Look, I've got to go now, but I'll leave Ann with you. Who is your doctor?'

'Dr Anthony,' Barbara replied numbly, wiping her eyes with a handkerchief.

'Good, now if you need her, Ann will take care of it. Do you understand me?'

Barbara nodded; her eyes were now blank, both from shock and the effects of the drug filtering through into her bloodstream. 'It's the husband . . . my doctor. I don't like his wife — she's too flirty with the men.'

Holly could not have agreed more, remembering that the sexy doctor seemed to be on very friendly terms with her Chief Inspector.

Outside, as they walked towards the Mini, Jill remarked, 'Thank God that's over. What were those pills she took? Christ, she was flying.'

'They were only downers,' Holly said, getting into her seat and opening the passenger door for Jill. 'Whatever she said about laying off the pills, I think she was high when we got there. I'd like to know just how much junk is flying around her body.'

Once Jill was settled, Holly started back for the station. 'Ann's a bit preoccupied this morning,' she observed.

Jill's giggle was mischievous. 'She thinks she might be preggy.'

'Careless,' Holly remarked.

'Yes, and the might-be father works with you.'

'Oh, who's that?'

'Alistair Stimpson.'

'Alistair?' Holly echoed. She knew there had been a good deal of rivalry among the WPCs for the attentions of the handsome Stimpson and, judging by her uniformed colleague's gloating manner, Holly guessed that perhaps Jill — having been passed over in favour of Ann — was now glad that they were about to get their just deserts.

Jill confided further. 'Yes, he thought she was on the pill, and she thought he was wearing a condom. As if you can't tell the difference.'

'Really,' Holly said. She did not like gossip, so strove to contribute as little as possible.

'Mike Whitworth was the one I fancied. He reminds me of a young Al Pacino.'

'I can't say I've noticed,' Holly said, becoming increasingly bored with the conversation.

'But I suppose we've seen the last of him,' Jill lamented. 'Pity about Josh Abraham — he's quite dishy.'

'What do you mean, a pity?' Holly asked, through a stab of jealousy.

'Don't you know?'

Holly did not know, but she found out as she listened. The words hurt; she felt each one stab her like a knife.

As the car weaved through the traffic on automatic pilot, she could hear herself making inconsequential small talk, but her mind was on what a fool she had made of herself. She thought of the small black pants and bra set she had purchased, which had brought on a bout of self-righteous sniffing from Emily. The way she had stuffed herself with food, trying to put back the stone in weight she had lost since Jason's death. And for what?

You'll never be happy again, Holly, her mind taunted . . . you're always going to be a skinny small-breasted little freak that no man would ever look at, except for one thing — and even then the bag over the head would be compulsory . . .

CHAPTER 22

Ashworth made his way along the metal catwalk, the ring of his shoes on the hard floor competing with the throb of the machinery below.

The door to Paine's office was open, and Ashworth could see him sitting behind his desk, staring at the telephone. He coughed to announce his arrival.

Paine looked up. 'Ah, Ashworth.' He gestured towards the chair in front of his desk.

Feeling awkward, ill at ease, as he always did when in Paine's company, Ashworth sat down.

'Well, you've been spared the job of breaking the bad news,' Paine said gruffly. 'Ken Savage has been on the phone.'

Ashworth was relieved. 'I've sent someone to tell your sister, and—'

Paine cut short the sentence with a wave of his hand. 'Yes, yes, I know, Ken told me.' He stared into the distance, his face devoid of any expression. 'It's funny, you know, but I thought that when this finally happened — we both knew it was on the cards — I'd be shattered. Now it has, I feel relieved, almost happy.'

'I think that's quite natural.' Ashworth had prepared himself for a tirade, so Paine's reasonableness had taken him off guard.

'Is it? My brother-in-law's dead, my sister is on the verge of a breakdown — and this news is likely to push her over the edge — and the person who's caused it all is walking about with one hundred and eighty thousand pounds. Not a great deal to rejoice about there.'

'He hasn't walked away. We'll get him.'

'How?' Some of the frostiness had returned to Paine's manner. 'There's no trace on the money . . .' He stopped and looked at Ashworth. 'Are you telling me there are clues on the body?'

'No . . .'

Ashworth was being evasive; he debated whether to tell Paine that they had the serial numbers of the ransom money but decided against it.

His feel for the case told him that someone connected with the factory was responsible for the abduction and death of Simon Edwards, and for that reason he wanted to keep the investigation as low key as possible.

If the kidnapper could be made to believe that he had got clean away with it, start to spend some of the money, it could then be traced back to its source.

'. . . but we are making enquiries in certain areas.'

'When . . .' Paine hesitated. 'When was Simon murdered?'

'That's proving rather difficult to establish. I'm hoping the post-mortem will come up with something definite, but at the moment I believe your brother-in-law was killed on the day he went missing.'

While Paine seemed to digest this, Ashworth said, 'Tell me about his movements that day.'

'How many more times?'

'As many as are needed,' Ashworth said firmly.

Paine began resignedly. 'He came into my office—'

'No, before that, tell me about earlier in the day.'

'Earlier in the day,' Paine repeated. 'Now there you have me. Wait a minute, I remember now, Simon did one of his vanishing tricks — he was always doing them.' He stopped, his mouth slightly open. 'Oh God, what a thing to say in the circumstances.'

Remorse, however, did not come easily to Paine, and on this occasion it did not linger long. 'But I have to say,' he continued, 'Simon was missing a good deal of the time, and I'm not sure things didn't run more smoothly for that.'

'Do you know where he was that morning?' Ashworth asked, steering Paine back to the matter in hand.

'Yes, the river,' he said with a distasteful sniff. 'He and Alan French went to peg out a stretch of the bank for a fishing match.'

'Alan French?' Ashworth queried. 'The husband of your secretary, who Edwards was so friendly with?'

Paine glanced towards the door of his secretary's office. 'Yes,' he answered in a low voice.

'And you definitely saw Edwards after that?'

'Yes, of course I did, I told you — he asked me to visit his home and collect his overnight bag. That was in the afternoon.'

'So Edwards was having an affair with your secretary, and he was also on good terms with her husband.' Ashworth's tone suggested disbelief.

Paine laughed. 'I can see you're not an adulterer, Ashworth. What better cover than to be a friend of the family, always coming and going? Nothing to make the neighbours suspicious, you see.'

'Yes, I do see. She's in today, I take it? Julie French?'

Paine nodded.

'And does she know about Edwards's death?'

'Yes, I told her. She's been blubbing ever since.'

'Right, I'd like to have a word with her.'

'Help yourself. She's next door. Now, if there's nothing else, Ashworth . . .' He pointedly picked up a pile of invoices from his desk.

Ashworth did not move. 'Well, yes, there is. Edwards's car disturbs me. When it was found, it was locked and the keys were missing. Now, why should the murderer take the keys?'

'Is it so important?'

'Yes, vitally so. If we can find those keys, they'll lead us to the last person to see your brother-in-law alive.'

'Fascinating, I'm sure.' Paine waved the invoices. 'I don't want to appear mercenary, but I do have a heavy workload and Babs needs my support in so many ways.'

Ashworth stood up. 'With a good deal of respect, I must say that you don't seem unduly distressed by your brother-in-law's death.'

Paine seemed to be on the verge of a verbal outburst, but with noticeable effort, he controlled himself. 'Ashworth, this may surprise you, but I just wish all of this would go away. I'm one hundred and eighty thousand pounds out of pocket, but I'd willingly let that money go. What's happened so far has been bad enough for my sister, but you probing about can only worsen the nightmare.'

'Surely apprehending the murderer would go some way towards setting your sister's mind at rest?'

'You think so?' Paine asked tartly. 'If you, as you put it, apprehend someone — what then? A year before the case gets to court. The trial. Can't you appreciate the effect that will have on Babs? She'll be lucky to come through it. So, yes, I'm sorry Simon's dead, but if anything happens to my sister, it will just about finish me. I hope that clarifies my apparent lack of feeling.'

'Admirably so,' Ashworth said. 'Now, if you'll excuse me, I'll have a word with Mrs French.'

'Yes, yes.' Paine had already turned his attention back to the invoices.

As he stood in the doorway of her office, Ashworth had time to study Julie French before she became aware of his presence.

She was seated behind an ancient desk, staring at a mug of cold coffee in front of her. Her shiny black hair was shoulder length, cut in an unfussy style which suited her pretty face. Although her large blue eyes were red and slightly puffy from crying, and her full mouth was set in a solemn line, she was still undeniably attractive.

Her garb — heavy cord jeans, white polo-neck sweater, and thick green quilted body-warmer — was chosen to combat the low temperature inside the factory, rather than to create an impression.

She looked up as Ashworth gave a diplomatic cough. 'Mrs French?' he asked.

'Yes.'

'I'm Chief Inspector Ashworth, Bridgetown CID.' He produced his warrant card as he walked into the room. 'I'm making enquiries into the death of Simon Edwards.'

She barely glanced at the card. 'Oh dear.' There was a tremor in her voice. 'This has come as such a shock. I didn't even know he was missing. We all thought he was on a business trip.'

She took a tissue from a box on her desk and blew her nose as Ashworth pulled up a chair and sat down.

'I'm sorry,' she said, 'but this is upsetting. Can I offer you a cup of coffee?'

'That would be nice.' His eyes twinkled as he glanced back in the direction of Paine's office. 'I've just been next door with your boss, and hospitality seems a little thin on the ground,' he said, making no attempt to lower his voice.

'Like a lot of other things.' Julie French's whispered reply was accompanied by a sad smile. 'I'll make you one.'

She stood up slowly and walked across the office to where a small kitchen was partitioned off. Ashworth followed her, noting that she was taller than he had expected.

The room — equipped with the bare essentials: chipped white sink, dilapidated cooker, and power point — was hardly enough to accommodate four people; he squeezed his way into it and closed the door.

'Do you mind if we talk in here?' he asked. 'I've some very delicate questions to ask and I'd rather we were not overheard.'

'I see, the gossip-mongers have been at work already, have they?' She looked at him pointedly as she filled the kettle and plugged it in.

'You could say that, I suppose. Look, Mrs French, there's no easy way to ask these questions . . .'

'Ask away,' she said resignedly.

'I believe you and Simon Edwards were friends.'

'Yes, we were.'

'And what was the nature of your relationship?'

She avoided his eyes and busied herself, washing two mugs beneath the cold water tap. 'Alan — that's my husband — and Simon went fishing together.'

'Yes, I know that. So you're telling me he was your husband's friend and that was the only contact you had with him?'

'Yes.' She sighed as she turned off the tap. 'No.'

'You were on very intimate terms, I believe,' Ashworth said bluntly.

'Oh, my God, if Alan and I had known this would all come out, we'd never have done it.' She lowered her head and stared into the sink.

'You were on intimate terms?' Ashworth persisted.

'Yes.'

'And was your husband aware of this?'

She turned to face him, the coffee temporarily forgotten. 'Yes, he knew about it.'

'I've been told that your husband was with Edwards on the morning he went missing. They were at the river together.'

'Yes, they were . . . and in the afternoon, too.'

'In the afternoon?' he asked quickly.

'Yes.'

'At what time?'

'About three — they still had a stretch to peg.'

'Now think about this very carefully, Mrs French,' Ashworth cautioned. 'You were having an affair with Edwards, your husband had found out about it, and he was with Edwards around the time that he died.'

The colour drained from the woman's face, and alarm surfaced in her eyes. 'But Simon was kidnapped . . .'

'We believe he died on the day he went missing.'

'Oh God, what a bloody mess,' she said dejectedly, close to tears again. 'Why did I do it?'

'What have you done?'

There was a mixture of fear and embarrassment on her face. 'Not only was Alan aware that I was having sex with Simon . . . he encouraged it.'

Ashworth looked at the boiling kettle. 'I think we'd better turn this off or we'll have a Turkish bath.' He reached for the wall switch and clicked it up. 'So your husband encouraged you?'

Assuming that Julie would perhaps talk more easily if he was not watching, he occupied himself with making the drinks.

'Yes, it started when a group of us had too much to drink one night. Oh God, I'm so embarrassed.'

Ashworth poured boiling water on to the coffee granules and waited.

'I believe it's called . . . having a modern marriage, or swinging. Anyway, Alan and I found we liked it and started doing it on a regular basis.'

'I see.' Ashworth passed her the mug. 'So you had an affair with Edwards. And your husband was doing the same with whom?'

Her look was evasive but Ashworth could not decide if this was simply out of embarrassment, or because she was hiding something.

'Various women,' she said eventually, 'and they were not affairs. We would all be together.'

Ashworth sipped the coffee; the harshness of the cheap brand was not to his liking. 'Your husband will confirm all of this?'

'Yes, I think he will.' She chewed on her bottom lip. 'How much of this will have to come out?'

'As long as none of it has anything to do with Edwards's abduction or murder, it won't have to,' he assured her.

She seemed relieved by this.

'But there is one thing,' he added. 'I shall need to see you and your husband together this evening.'

'I'll ring Alan and tell him, then he can take today off.'

'It will be about seven, or later, and I shall have another detective with me.' He paused. 'Tell me, do you know of anyone who may have wanted to harm Edwards?'

'No,' she said, shaking her head vigorously. 'He really didn't have an enemy in the world.'

Ashworth thought, if the news of your swinging sessions had ever got out, I can think of one he'd have had.

He left Julie French, and was passing Paine's door when the man called, 'Ashworth, can I have a word?'

'Surely,' he said, looking enquiringly into the office.

'Look, I feel that I shall be forever apologising to you,' he said, 'but what I should have said was, I wish it would go away, but I know it won't. So, keep me posted and if there's anything I can do, just let me know.'

'You can rely on that,' Ashworth said.

As he left the factory, the thought which had entered his mind shortly after Simon Edwards's disappearance came back to him, and he knew it would keep on returning until the question it posed was answered.

CHAPTER 23

Gwen Anthony need not have asked Ashworth to come alone for the results of the post-mortem at the hospital; the way events were going, he was guaranteed to do so.

By nature he had always been something of a loner and, when deeply involved in a case, with a collection of intriguing facts waiting to be pieced together, he saw other people as an encumbrance. True, he liked others to act as sounding boards for his ideas, but he resented their own contributions.

Holly and Josh were not aware of this, but very shortly they would be, and both would put the wrong interpretation on his taciturn behaviour.

As he waited for Gwen in the Victorian wing of Bridgetown General Hospital, the lethargy that had been with him over the last few days vanished before a surge of restless energy which pulled him in many differing directions.

He hated this place. Not even the primrose-coloured walls could camouflage the depressing antiquity of the building, nor could the freshly cut flowers that abounded on window sills disguise the clinical ambience which hung in the air.

The sound of Gwen's footsteps, echoing and re-echoing against the high walls and ceilings, broke the silence. She was wearing a smart two-piece black suit; the skirt, long and full, swished around her calves as she walked.

When she reached Ashworth, her usually smiling face was sombre. 'Jim, I hope I haven't kept you waiting.' She managed a tight smile.

'No, Gwen. What have you got for me?'

The double-meaning joke which sprang into her mind was quickly dispelled as she viewed his preoccupied expression.

'Much the same as I told you this morning,' she said.

As she talked, they walked to the visitors' reception area and sat down.

'He died from drowning. Time of death impossible to determine — but you know my views on that. There are countless injuries on the body, but it's impossible to ascertain with any confidence whether these were received before or after death. There is a wound on the back of the head though, which could have been caused by a blow before he went into the river . . .'

Ashworth looked at her hopefully.

'. . . but I need to run some tests to establish whether Edwards was conscious when he entered the water.'

'How long will that take?' he asked, looking at his wristwatch.

'I won't have the results before six, I'm afraid. You could pick me up,' she said cheerfully, 'and take me for that drink you promised.'

'What about your car?' he asked absently.

'My husband dropped me off. Come on, lighten up, Jim,' she cajoled.

'I'm sorry, there are just so many things going around in my mind.'

'Wrong, Jim, what you meant to say was, yes, Gwen, I'd love to take you out for a drink.'

Her infectious personality finally got to him. He laughed. 'Yes, I suppose that was what I meant to say.'

'Good.' She stood up briskly. 'Now I can get back to cutting up bodies. See you at six.'

He watched her walk the length of the corridor; the sway, the shape of her body, the sexuality radiating from her, caused a dull ache of longing inside him. As if aware of his watching eyes, she turned, and as she waved a message passed between them, and Ashworth felt himself beginning to bend towards the inevitable.

He drove back to the station, the light of the day already gone. Holly and Josh were in the office, the computer bleeping as he settled behind his desk.

'Alistair Stimpson's taken sick leave, sir,' Holly informed him.

Ashworth snorted. 'Sick leave — just when everything's starting to happen. Right, that leaves us undermanned. Josh, you'll have to close that thing down for a few days.' He waved dismissively at the VDU.

Josh turned to meet the stern gaze of his superior, as Ashworth said, 'I've been meaning to have a few words with you for some time, young man. You're spending too much time with that damned thing.'

'My job specification does state—' Josh began defensively.

'Your job specification states that you're a policeman,' Ashworth interrupted, 'and that requires powers of deduction and reasoning, not to mention a certain degree of bluff. Now, I want you to demonstrate to me how many of those qualities you possess.'

'Yes, sir,' Josh said, looking rather bewildered.

'Good. Now, you can make a start by interviewing this Rolands social worker woman. Find out if Delvin Bennett did admit to raping Jane Taylor.'

'Yes, sir,' a crestfallen Josh replied. 'Oh, Mike Whitworth phoned in — he said he's been watching Cain and Bennett. They're spending a lot of time on the Ethelvale Estate. He reckons the next rape could be—'

'What the hell's Whitworth doing that for? He's suspended,' Ashworth thundered.

Josh got up, his colour rising. 'I don't know, sir, you'd better ask him. I'm just passing on the message.' He took his coat from the rack and left the room, slamming the door behind him.

Damn, Ashworth thought, I handled that badly — but this office has got to be sorted out.

An awkward silence prevailed for a few minutes, then Holly said, 'Barbara Edwards took the news far better than I thought she would.'

Ashworth grunted in reply and fiddled with the knot of his tie.

'I think she has a drug problem, sir — tranquillisers and other prescribed medication.'

'Oh, yes?' Ashworth said, hardly listening. 'Holly, I want you to meet me tonight at the home of Paine's secretary, Julie French. Her husband was with Edwards shortly before he went missing.'

'Right, sir. What's the address?'

'62 Nene Lane. Be there . . .' He remembered his date with Gwen. '. . . at 8 p.m.'

* * *

Josh sat in the car, still angered by what had just happened. This was the Ashworth they had been told to expect, but had begun to doubt existed. Now it seemed he had emerged as large as legend, and twice as nasty.

Ashworth's dressing-down had completed a circle of isolation which had been forming around him for days. Earlier, Holly had cancelled their date for the following evening on the pretext that her mother-in-law was ill. Josh had realised that this was a lie when his offer to record the concert for her on his pocket tape recorder had been met with nil enthusiasm. What was wrong with these people?

All of this had made him aware that he was homesick. Something inside him yearned for rolling moorland, sweet clean air, familiar places and things, a sense of belonging which he knew would never be found in this place.

As he started the Sunny's engine he felt sure of one thing — he would not tolerate many more of Ashworth's tantrums.

CHAPTER 24

The lounge of the Crofter's Arms was always deserted at six fifteen on a weekday evening, which was the main reason why Ashworth had chosen it for his slightly clandestine meeting with Gwen.

The pub's interior was warm, cheerful; it had not yet been invaded by piped music, pinball machines or jukeboxes, which probably accounted for its lack of patronage.

Ashworth was at the serving hatch to the main bar, ordering a large gin and tonic for Gwen, a non-alcoholic lager for himself. He carried the drinks to where Gwen was sitting at a small corner table, and pulled up a stool to sit facing her.

'Cheers,' she said, sipping the drink. 'Now, after the day I've had, this tastes good.'

Ashworth sampled his lager and, pulling a face, said, 'I wish I could say the same.'

'You're a man who needs the real thing, Jim.' She studied his pensive face. 'I'm sorry I haven't been more help.'

'Mmm.' He sounded distant. 'Gwen, how can you tell that Edwards was conscious when he went into the river? When you explained in the car, I couldn't understand.'

'How can I simplify it then? Death by drowning is caused by asphyxia, meaning that signs of anoxia show up during the post-mortem. Anoxia simply means lack of oxygen. The greater the signs of anoxia, the more the victim struggled in the water. Edwards put up a considerable struggle.'

A thought struck Ashworth then. 'Is it possible he was unconscious when he went in, and the shock of the cold water revived him?'

'Yes, it is, Jim, but it's impossible to reach a conclusion either way.' She drained her glass. 'What is it that bothers you so much about this?'

His earlier detached air had now been replaced by enthusiasm. He said, 'The kidnap — there's something wrong with it. It's almost as if someone added it as an afterthought.'

'A pretty elaborate afterthought. And what would be the point?'

'You may be able to supply the answer to that. Edwards's body is in the river. The killer knows there's a freeze-up on the way, which means the corpse won't turn up for, what — possibly six weeks? But then he gets worried that Edwards could be found before the river freezes over. Now, if that had happened, would it have made any difference to your findings?'

'Oh, I see what you're getting at. Yes, it most certainly would. If I'd had access to the body within, say, two days of death, I could have told you a lot more about the head wound.'

Ashworth leant forward. 'Tell me what you can now.'

'Well, I won't get too technical, but when a body has been immersed in water, the appearance of wounds can become misleading because the water causes the blood to change. The longer the body is in the water, the greater the changes. In Edwards's case — because of the amount of time he'd spent in the water — it was impossible to determine whether the injuries were caused before or after death. But I don't think most lay persons would have that sort of knowledge.'

'So it would have to be someone who knew something about medical science?'

'Or forensic science,' she offered. Then she hesitated, and said, 'Look, Jim, do you mind if I have another drink? It's been a cow of a day.'

'Oh, Gwen, of course. I'm sorry,' he said, reaching for her glass, 'I'm so wrapped up in this case.'

'No, no, I'll get it,' she laughed.

Their hands met around the glass, and Ashworth felt a slight electric charge pass through him.

Since their arrival a few more customers had trickled into the lounge, and as they were both well-known local figures, there was bound to be some speculation as to what the GP and Chief Inspector were doing together in this out-of-the-way country pub. But in no way did their curiosity disturb Ashworth; he found Gwen's company relaxing, and he was enjoying talking about the case.

She squeezed back behind the table with her refill which, he noted, was another double measure. Glass clinked on glass as the tonic water mingled with the gin. 'I shall have to make this the last one. I don't eat lunch on post-mortem days,' she confided. 'I'll end up tipsy.'

As she settled back with her drink, she changed the subject. 'I think you're complicating it too much, Jim. You believe the killer to be a local man?'

'Yes, I'm certain of it.'

'And the motive was some grudge he had against Edwards?'

'That's about it, yes.'

'So why dismiss the red herring theory — get the police hunting nationwide for a kidnapper, and overlooking things closer to home?'

'No.' He shook his head resolutely. 'The kidnap and the ransom drops were ploys to delay us in finding the body — I've made up my mind about that.'

'And I've heard, once you've done that, it's very difficult to get you to change it.'

'So they say.'

Gwen glanced at her watch. 'Jim, we really ought to be going. I'd like to get home before my husband gets back from his surgery . . . and I also want to talk to you somewhere a little more private,' she added confidentially, before finishing her drink in two quick swallows.

In the car park she linked arms with him as they walked towards the Sierra. 'This is the first date I've been on where the main topic of conversation has been *dead* bodies.'

'Sorry, Gwen,' he chuckled. 'Now, there's something I want to ask you about Barbara Edwards.'

'I've a feeling you're going to ask me to divulge information I shouldn't,' she said gravely as Ashworth opened the car door for her.

He did not reply until he had climbed into the driver's seat, then he said, 'How bad is her drug addiction?'

'Jim, this is not fair,' she protested lightly. 'Barbara's my husband's patient, but the confidentiality rule still applies.'

'I wouldn't ask if it wasn't important,' he assured her persuasively.

Ashworth heard her exhale, then, 'It's bad — and, not surprisingly, it's worsening. Simon Edwards wanted her to go into a clinic for treatment.'

Ashworth started the car and eased it into the narrow lane. 'And how did Barbara take that?'

'Badly. Contrary to general belief, most addicts are quite happy with their lot — they're not seeking a cure.'

'And Dennis Paine?'

'I don't know what his reaction was to Barbara having treatment, but after Simon went missing he was on to my husband to increase the strength of her medication. He said she needed it to calm herself down.'

'I see.' Ashworth turned left at the crossroads.

'But I think he's seen the light now because he wants Barbara admitted to hospital for her own safety.'

The lane was becoming narrower; branches from the hedges bordering the road brushed against the car windows.

'Why the interest?' Gwen asked.

'Nothing really, I just like to know everything,' he said, smiling. 'God, Gwen, you do live in the middle of nowhere.'

'It's just round the next bend.'

Ashworth slowed the car and crept around the sharp turn.

'There's a little lay-by set back from the road,' Gwen informed him. 'Pull in there.'

Ashworth almost missed the turn, which was no more than a gap in the hedge, barely wide enough for a car to pass through. The tyres bumped on hard earth as he brought the vehicle to a halt. He turned off the engine, killed the lights, and for a few moments everything was inky blackness.

'Have you thought about us, Jim?' Gwen asked bluntly.

His eyes became adjusted to the dark and he studied her profile. 'Gwen, there are so many things to consider.'

'Such as?'

'Such as your husband and my wife.'

'Your wife? How often do you have sex with her?'

Ashworth opened his mouth to protest.

'No, tell me, Jim.'

'Not frequently,' he grudgingly admitted.

'Not frequently — if ever. Remember, I'm Sarah's doctor. Thank God I'm not yours. There are enough complications in this already. So — would I be taking anything away from your wife? Anything she really wants?'

'No,' he said flatly, 'but what about your husband?'

'Huh, my husband.' She made a sound of exasperation. 'We've been married for twenty years and, well, he just doesn't seem to do anything for me anymore.' She turned to stare out of the window. 'What do I have to do to get you to make love to me?'

'Gwen—'

'Jim, I've spent the day cutting up the corpse of someone who got out of bed one morning, and didn't make it back that night. Believe me, it's an experience that makes you want to grab what you can, while you can.'

Ashworth heard himself ask, 'Where?'

Gwen gave a low throaty chuckle. 'At last,' she breathed, placing her hand on his thigh and leaning towards him. 'Shush,' she said urgently, 'I thought I heard a car.'

Ashworth listened and caught the approaching sound of a revving engine.

'It must be my husband,' Gwen whispered.

As the car crept round the bend, its headlights illuminated the lane. Behind the hedge, Ashworth found he was holding his breath. It passed by and they listened as the sound faded into the distance.

'He won't miss me for an hour,' Gwen said softly.

Far from quelling the driving desire within Ashworth, the incident seemed to have fuelled it, and he said quickly, 'Where can we go, Gwen?'

'Bed doesn't have to be bed, you know,' she said provocatively. 'Just let nature take its course . . . that's doctor's lingo.'

Ashworth felt the years peel away, pulled from him by her demanding lips, the hand that caressed his thigh before slipping between his legs.

His fingers felt enormously large and clumsy as they struggled with the buttons of her jacket.

With her mouth still almost touching his, Gwen murmured, 'Let's get into the back.'

Even in the near darkness Ashworth could see her breasts heaving as her breath quickened.

Hurriedly they got out of the car. Ashworth climbed into the back and pushed the front seats forward.

Through the gloom he could see Gwen standing precariously on one leg. 'What on earth are you doing?' he laughed.

'I'm taking my pants off,' she replied breathlessly. Then with much haste she climbed in beside him.

Any control he had left evaporated when his hands met her firm trembling thighs. He pushed her skirt upwards and at last touched her coarse body hair.

With a panting gasp Gwen reached forward, and Ashworth heard the rasp of his zipper as she pulled it down, then felt the sweet sensation of her cool fingers as they touched him.

* * *

198

He had expected to experience guilt, regret, or at least some sense of sadness after his disloyalty to Sarah, but nothing could push aside the strong surge of euphoria which had overtaken him after his pleasurable encounter with the comely Gwen. Temporarily, he had escaped the shackles of domesticity, had operated as a free spirit, and he had enjoyed it.

Usually a stickler for punctuality, Ashworth was not at all concerned that he was now thirty minutes late for his eight p.m. appointment with Holly.

The expressway, bathed in the yellow glow of overhead lights, stretched before him; the Sierra's speedometer recording seventy miles an hour as it effortlessly cruised along. His side indicator lit up the grass verge as he negotiated the slip road.

At the roundabout, Ashworth took the first left into Nene Lane, part of the Ethelvale Estate. Holly's Mini was parked half-way along the road. His gawky DC and her dilapidated car seemed out of place in such a smart area.

A secretary and a factory worker couldn't afford this sort of place — not on the wages Dennis Paine pays, he thought, parking behind the Mini.

Holly's expression betrayed the fact that she had not appreciated the forty-five-minute wait, but Ashworth was not in an apologetic mood.

'I've been with Dr Anthony,' he explained stiffly, climbing out of the Sierra. 'Getting the post-mortem results.'

Holly noticed the creases in his suit, his slightly dishevelled hair as she said, 'Anything positive from it?'

'No, very little. Edwards was alive and conscious when he went into the water. Apart from that, nothing.'

His offhand reply, together with his untidy appearance and late arrival, only served to confirm Holly's suspicions that there was another body — other than that of Simon Edwards — uppermost in his thoughts.

'A bit expensive for the likes of the Frenches, I'd say,' he remarked, staring at the house.

It matched the others in the lane; not exactly upmarket, more middle-of-the-range. Very little originality had been displayed in its design but, even so, double-bay-fronted houses with four bedrooms carried a mortgage of around seven hundred pounds a month, and Ashworth doubted that the Frenches' total income would amount to much more than that.

'I thought the same, sir,' Holly said, 'but we can't start asking where their money comes from, can we?'

'Not yet,' he replied stoutly, as the garden gate swung shut behind them. 'They were expecting us around seven, so if they've got anything to hide, they should be nicely sweating by now.'

Which is more than can be said for me, Holly thought, sitting in the cold for three-quarters of an hour.

Ashworth ignored the bell and knocked on the door. The hall light was switched on immediately; its glow filtered through the half-glass door.

An apprehensive Alan French opened it. In his late twenties, he was a dark-haired, good-looking man, dressed in a thick fisherman-knit sweater and brown cord trousers.

'I'm Chief Inspector Ashworth, Bridge—'

'Yes, I know who you are,' French said.

'And this is DC Bedford. I believe you are expecting us.'

'You'd better come in.'

French ushered them into the lounge. Ashworth's seemingly casual glance recorded the brown velvet three-piece suite, expensive carpet, large bookcase, and the customary television and video recorder — recent models too, by the look of them.

Julie French was sitting on the settee; the soft glow from the wall lights lent her an almost angelic appearance. She smiled meekly at Ashworth then returned her gaze to the floor.

Although Julie's low-cut blue blouse and short white skirt did not meet with Ashworth's approval, he had to admit that she and her husband looked just like any other attractive young couple.

'Please sit down,' French said. 'Can I offer you a drink, or is it true that you don't, while on duty?' His hale and hearty manner was merely a manifestation of his nervousness.

'We do, sir, but not at the moment, thank you,' Ashworth said solemnly.

French sat beside his wife and they held hands. Holly and Ashworth sat in the armchairs.

'I'll come straight to the point, Mr French. I believe you were one of the last people to see Simon Edwards alive.'

'Yes, so Julie tells me.' French seemed determined to hold Ashworth's stare.

'And what time was that, sir?'

'It would have been about three thirty. We were pegging out the bank for a fishing match.'

'Where would that be, sir?'

'The stretch from the bridge, down to the weir.'

'And he just walked off, I take it?' Ashworth remarked, taking his eyes off French to glance around the room.

'Yes, if my memory serves me right, he said, "I shall have to love you and leave you, Alan. I've got something to take care of".'

'Just that? No mention of his business trip?'

'None, but then Simon never discussed things like that with us.' French shrugged. 'And in any case, I was skiving — I should have been at work at two.'

'I see. Nice place you've got. How long have you lived here?'

Holly saw the sly glance which passed between them, but Ashworth missed it; he was still looking around the room.

'About two years,' French told him.

'And before that?' Ashworth continued in a conversational tone.

Julie French spoke up for the first time. 'Perrybrook Road,' she said. 'That's—'

'Yes, small, terraced houses. I know it well. Quite a step up for you.' He brought his attention back to the husband. 'Tell me, how long have you worked at the factory?'

'I've been there five years, and Julie, two and a half years.'

'Now,' Ashworth said, 'Mrs French told me that she and Simon Edwards had sexual intercourse on a regular basis, and that you were aware of this.'

Julie clung tightly to her husband's hand. Holly could see her knuckles turning white.

'Yes, that's right,' French replied in a subdued voice. 'We want to be open and frank with you because we've got nothing to hide.'

In Ashworth's considerable experience he had found that, when suspects of a crime declared that they had nothing to hide, he could expect the reverse to be true.

'Would you like to tell me about it?'

French cleared his throat, looked at his wife, then launched into his explanation. 'We like to think of ourselves as a modern couple. We've been married for eight years—'

'Nearly nine,' his wife corrected him.

'Yes, nearly nine,' French went on. 'Well, just after Julie started working at the factory, Simon took a fancy to her. She was flattered at first, but didn't think anything of it. You know I was very friendly with Simon?'

Ashworth nodded.

'Well, he was at the house a lot. He helped us move in here, and at the end of the day we had a few drinks. I told him I couldn't thank him enough for all the help he'd given us, and he said, let me go to bed with Julie — that'll be thanks enough. We both thought he was joking. Then he lurched into some half-drunken lecture about American Indians or Eskimos offering their wives to their best friends. We had a few more drinks, then things got silly and . . . well, we all ended up in bed together.' French both sounded and looked rather shamefaced.

'I see. So when did three-in-a-bed graduate to four?' Ashworth asked bluntly.

'Just natural progression, I suppose,' French replied. 'We both found the experience enlightening, once we'd got over thinking of it as just a drunken mistake. We began seeing it as a way to improve our marriage, rather than destroy it.'

'The problem isn't when your partner is having sex with someone else,' Julie chipped in, 'but when they're doing it behind your back . . . deceiving you.'

Ashworth thought how like a mouse championing a cause she looked. 'No doubt you're right in your assumptions,' he said breezily, 'but they're of little interest to us. If you could let us have the names and addresses of the other ladies in your forward-looking group, we can interview them and eliminate you from our enquiries.'

'No,' French said, a little too quickly, 'and in any case, it's one woman, not women.'

'But your wife led me to believe there were a number of women involved.'

'Yes, I know that,' French snapped. 'She panicked when this started to come out into the open. But there's only one woman, and she's married. We won't name her because it would cause too much trouble. That's final.'

'Ah, so her spouse is not forward-looking. How very inconvenient.'

Neither French, nor his wife, seemed stung by Ashworth's sarcasm, and the outburst he had been hoping for did not materialise, so he decided to try cajolery. 'We are very discreet,' he coaxed. 'No one, apart from the lady herself, will know we're looking into it.'

'No,' French said resolutely. 'We haven't done anything illegal. You've no right to hound us.'

'As you wish.' Ashworth stood up with an air of finality. 'But we shall put our own interpretations on your silence.' He purposely directed the remark at the frightened Julie French.

Her husband led them to the front door.

'Goodnight, sir,' Ashworth said abruptly, before opening the door and stepping outside.

Alan French listened to their footsteps retreating down the path. 'Shit,' he muttered, hitting the door lightly with the flat of his hand.

In the lounge, Julie was peeping around the curtains at the front window.

'Get away from there, they'll see you,' French hissed.

She let go of the curtain and shrank back. 'What are we going to do, Alan?'

'Nothing,' he replied forcefully. 'Nothing. Why the hell did you have to tell them about Simon?'

'I just panicked. I thought they knew.'

French grabbed her arms roughly and shook her. 'They don't know anything. Just get that into your head. They don't know.'

'They'll find out about the money, and the car, Alan, I know they will,' she said hopelessly.

'Not if we keep our nerve, they won't.'

Outside, Holly shivered in the cold night air. Inwardly she was seething. Not once during the interview had Ashworth, either by word or gesture, invited her to take part. This, coupled with the fact that his mind did not seem to be on the job, was creating within her an almost irrational anger.

'Interesting,' Ashworth commented as he looked back at the house.

'Yes,' Holly said flatly.

He glanced at her sullen face. 'I'm sorry about being late, Holly, really I am. But my business with Dr Anthony was important . . .' He smiled to himself. '. . . Not to mention pressing.'

'It's not that, sir. I don't mind how late I work.'

'What is it then? I can tell by your attitude you're angry with me.'

For a few moments the bubbling well of frustration inside her threatened to overflow. She wanted to tell him that, yes, she was angry — bloody angry — because she felt excluded from the investigation; felt as if she did not exist. She wanted to tell him that, in her opinion, bunking up the good doctor was taking his mind off the job.

Instead she said in a defeated tone, 'It's Josh. I think you treated him unfairly.'

Ashworth was puzzled. 'Josh?' Then realisation dawned on his face. 'Look, Holly, I've got one officer sick and another suspended. I need every available person out here.'

'I think you're picking on him.'

'Well, I'm sorry, but I can't kid-glove people. Josh Abraham gets the same treatment as everyone else. No better. No worse.' Holly's sour look prompted him to say, 'Oh, this is hopeless. I'd better be going, I need to see Mike Whitworth to tell him to stop following those kids about.'

Realising that she was not addressing the real problem, Holly relented. 'Would you like me to do that?'

Ashworth glanced at his wristwatch. 'But it's half-past nine.'

'I know, sir. I'm not in any hurry to get home.'

'Well, it would help. Just tell him to lay off.' He walked to his car. 'I'll be late in tomorrow. I'm going to see Len Warren.'

'Will you want me to go with you, sir?'

'No, no, no,' he said, shaking his head as he got into the Sierra. 'I don't want to ring too many alarm bells.'

Holly watched the car's tail lights as he drove away. 'No, no, no,' she mimicked, 'if you're there you'll press alarm bells.'

Climbing angrily into the Mini, she muttered to herself, 'I know I'm ugly and skinny but, bloody hell, I didn't realise everybody thinks I'm thick.'

She slammed the door so violently that the handle used for winding down the window promptly fell off and landed with a dull thud on the Mini's threadbare carpet.

CHAPTER 25

Ashworth turned into his drive. For once, classical music had been sidelined, and the melodious message of the Four Tops blared from the car's speakers.

He locked the car and walked to the house, feeling happy, lightheaded, detached from reality almost — feelings usually only experienced by young lovers.

As soon as he opened the front door Peanuts came bounding out of the lounge to greet him, barking wildly as she circled his legs.

'Good girl,' he said, for once devoid of the irritation usually provoked by this ritual. 'Good girl.' He crouched down to stroke the dog. 'Just let me walk about, eh?'

'I'm in here, Jim,' Sarah called from the lounge.

With the dog trotting at his heels, her tail wagging with pleasure, he went to join her.

She was sitting in an armchair, a pile of papers in her hand. On the floor, beside her, was a brand new black executive case.

'She's been out, dear,' Sarah said, indicating the dog. 'I've only been in half an hour myself. Have you eaten?'

'Yes,' he lied. 'I think I'll have a drink. Do you want one?'

'No, it's all right, I've got one.'

He was taking the cap off the whisky bottle when Sarah said, 'Gwen Anthony phoned, and the message was — she thinks she's satisfied, but can you check tomorrow, just to make sure?'

Ashworth felt his colour rise as he poured the drink. 'That's to do with the post-mortem,' he hastily explained, cursing Gwen's impish sense of humour.

'I realised that, dear,' Sarah replied absently. 'How's it going, by the way?'

'Slow, slow,' he said, sipping his drink. 'I'm just waiting for quick, quick.'

Sarah gave a shallow laugh. 'There's another thing, Jim. I've been offered a course with the Samaritans, but it's in London and I'd be away until next Tuesday. If you object, I won't go.'

Ashworth studied his drink as he contemplated five days of freedom. 'No, by all means go, Sarah,' he said generously. 'Just enjoy yourself.'

Sarah put the papers down in a huff. 'I know the work is voluntary, but it's not going to be a holiday, you know,' she said sternly.

'I didn't mean to imply that it was,' he said quickly, eager to avoid a confrontation.

* * *

Mike Whitworth's address was a boarding-house in the Thorprise area of Bridgetown. The streets were littered with drink cans, chocolate bar wrappers, and general refuse.

Holly turned into the grand-sounding Mount Rise and found it depressingly seedy. Victorian houses stood in the broad tree-lined road. Undoubtedly, these five-storey buildings had once represented the full splendour of a gracious age, but they had now fallen into almost irreversible decay. Unpainted masonry was crumbling around windows; slates were missing from most roofs; and the once great oaks — their roots pushing up paving slabs — were now no more than convenient urinals for the area's considerable dog population.

The Mini pulled up outside number 25. Holly got out and set the alarm. Wide stone steps, flanked by two lions at their base, led up to a green front door. Inside was a long dark corridor with doors leading off.

A thick-set man, in his forties and completely bald, was staffing reception, which was little more than a serving hatch in the wall.

He looked up from his newspaper when Holly tapped on the counter. 'Yeah?' he said, impolitely.

'Mike Whitworth — what's his room number?'

'It's at the top. When you run out of stairs, you're there.'

'Thanks,' Holly said.

As she walked away, the man shouted, 'If you leave in the early hours, keep the noise down, will you? And tell that crazy, it says no loud music in our terms.'

There was no carpet on the stairs, just nailed-down pieces of linoleum. The walls were covered with the original varnished wallpaper, which was now pockmarked and grimy. Tobacco smoke, sweat and cooking smells mingled with the dampness of the building.

Holly climbed four flights and found herself on a small landing. There was a payphone on the wall, and nine steps which led to a startlingly blue door. Sometime in the past it must have been beaten down for there was a crack running from top to bottom of it; the glue which had been used to stick it back together bubbled beneath the paint.

Loud rock-and-roll music thumped its way through the wood, at a volume which threatened to disintegrate it once more.

Holly's first knock went unanswered, so she banged harder.

'Leave, before I get mad,' Whitworth's voice commanded above the din.

'It's Holly Bedford, Mike,' she hollered back.

208

The music died and Whitworth opened the door. He looked surprised. 'Hi, Holly,' he said, 'I thought it was that jerk on reception complaining about the music again.'

He was naked apart from a pair of dark blue training trousers, and the dumb-bell he was holding suggested that she had disturbed his work-out. His well-developed chest, arm and stomach muscles glistened beneath a film of perspiration.

Holly felt desire kindling inside, her repressed needs heightening the arousal out of all proportion to the situation.

'Come on in.' His teeth flashed white in his dark face.

She noted, thankfully, that the room was clean — undoubtedly Whitworth was responsible for this — but the furnishings were spartan. The centre of the floor was covered by a large red and brown patterned rug; around its edges the floorboards were stained a dark brown. A single bed stood beneath the window. There was a cooker, a sink and draining board with a length of white worktop, on which stood a large plastic container filled with fermenting beer. A wooden table housed a portable television and cassette player, and the room's only chair was also wooden with a hard back, and looked as old as the house itself.

'What brings you here?' he asked, ducking into a room Holly assumed was the bathroom, and emerging seconds later, rubbing himself down with a large towel.

'Message from Ashworth,' she said.

'What's the word from Boss Man then?'

'He says you're to stop following Cain and Bennett.'

'Oh, Jesus — Josh wasn't supposed to pass the message on word for word.' He threw the towel on to the bed, his dark looks smouldering with anger. 'Well, you tell Boss Man I'll back off, but he sure as hell needs to watch those kids.'

'Will do.'

Holly found her gaze transfixed on the bulge in Whitworth's trousers; the tightness of them did little to conceal his outline. 'You're still as cocky, I see,' she said, quite unintentionally, adding quickly, 'I mean, being suspended hasn't changed that.'

'No, it hasn't.' He stared at her. 'Come on, Hol, sit down.'

He pulled the chair into the centre of the room, and as she sat, he asked, 'Do you want a beer?'

'Yes, I'd love one.'

Behind the portable television there was a beer barrel. Whitworth pulled two half-pints from it.

'What's happening at the Sheriff's office?' he asked, passing Holly the drink, which was cloudy and smelt strongly of hops.

'The news is, Alistair's got one of the WPCs pregnant and he's done a runner.'

Whitworth chuckled wickedly. 'Good,' he remarked with relish.

Holly took a tentative sip of the beer; it bit the back of her throat and made her eyes water. 'God, Mike, what is this stuff?' she rasped.

'Devil's water. I brew it myself. Drink it — it'll put hairs on your chest.'

'Yes, I bet.'

Suddenly she felt an urgent need to talk to someone and she just hoped that Whitworth would be receptive. 'Do you want a really good laugh?' she asked.

'Try me.'

After taking a long drink — the beer seemed to be more palatable now — she said, 'You know I was friendly with Josh.'

He nodded.

'Well, he asked me to go to a concert with him . . .'

Whitworth sat across the bed, his back to the wall.

'. . . and I thought — this is it, Holly.'

'Then you found out he was gay.'

She closed her eyes and nodded. 'God, Mike, I feel so stupid. Everything I do in that department balls up.'

'That's a cow, Hol,' Whitworth sympathised.

Holly looked up, worried that he might be laughing at her, but she saw that his expression was deadly serious. 'I'll get over it, I suppose.'

The corners of his eyes crinkled. 'If you're that desperate, I could always give you a work-out.' Back to his old self now, he patted the bed.

'I'll never be that desperate,' she joked, lowering her eyes.

'That's what they all say.'

She drained her glass. 'Mike, I'm sorry, with all your troubles, you don't want to listen to mine.'

She was about to stand up when Whitworth said, 'No, Hol, don't go. You're the first person I've seen since I was suspended. Have another beer — yes?'

'Okay.' Holly was finding his company easy and relaxing.

As he pulled the drinks, he asked, 'How's the kidnap thing going?'

'That's something else that's bothering me,' she muttered. 'Oh, I don't know, Mike, Ashworth doesn't seem to share anything with us. I don't think he's up to the job at the moment — I've a strong suspicion he's having it off with the pathologist.'

'I hope that's a female.'

'Yes,' Holly laughed.

'Thank God for that — having Josh there is bad enough.'

Whitworth saw her face fall. 'Sorry, lousy joke.' He handed her the drink. 'Sit on the bed, Hol. You'll be safe.'

'That's what they all say,' she sighed, good-naturedly, as she sat down on the bed.

Whitworth sat beside her. 'Ashworth's a one-man-band, kid — a loner. Everybody who's worked under him has reached where you are now. That's why none of them have lasted.'

'What would you do if you were me?'

'Give him some space. The lads say that sometimes people think he hasn't got enough about him to find his way out of the station, but his brain's in overdrive, that's all. Which is probably why he's so detached.'

'But it's boring, Mike.'

'Hang in there, kid. The way I've heard it, Boss Man's going to be moved soon — something to do with the Home

Office. The plan was that Alistair would be moved up to inspector, but he's cocked that up with his . . .' He waited for Holly to finish the sentence. 'Come on, Hol,' he urged. Then waving his hands as if conducting an orchestra, he repeated, 'He's cocked that up with his . . .'

'Cock,' they chorused.

As they laughed, he said, 'So it's an open field. Could be a good job in there, Hol.'

'What will you do?'

'After they've thrown me out of the force?' He shrugged. 'I don't know. Security, I suppose.'

It came to Holly's notice then that every object she focused upon seemed to be fuzzy around the edges. Nevertheless, she gulped down what was left of her drink.

'More?' Whitworth asked.

She handed him the glass and watched his panther-like grace as he went to refill it. As soon as he handed her the fresh beer, she took the head off it.

Whitworth settled on the bed beside her, and for the first time, she became aware of his strong animal scent.

The alcohol had finally severed the link between her brain and her mouth, and she asked, 'Do you think I'm pretty, Mike?'

'You ain't a classic beauty, girl,' he admitted frankly, 'but you're attractive.'

She gripped his forearm. 'Do you find me attractive?'

'Steady, girl,' he cautioned, taking the half-empty glass from her hand and placing it on the floor.

Holly held his arm again, running her fingers up to his bulging biceps. 'Did you mean it, about giving me a work-out?'

Whitworth glanced at her hand, then looked into her eyes.

'I really need it, Mike . . . really.'

'Come on, Hol,' he coaxed, 'you're three parts pissed. Tomorrow you'd hate yourself — and me.'

She put her arms around his neck. 'You don't know how screwed up my head is, Mike. I need to be three parts pissed.'

Tears spilled from her eyes and ran down her cheeks. 'If I don't do it now, I'm never going to.'

Whitworth kissed her then, and his lips caused sensations within her that she had forgotten existed.

'I'm not a permanent guy,' he said as their lips parted.

'I don't want anything permanent. I just want a cock.'

Then the world swam around her. She knew her pants were being removed and that she was lying on the bed with her skirt pushed up.

Whitworth's skilful foreplay soon pushed her over the brink of control, and she pleaded urgently, 'Do it to me, Mike. Please do it.'

Holly felt him enter, and she gasped with the pleasure of it. His long sliding movements seemed to unlock every thwarted orgasm she had kept hidden over the last three years. They built, mingled, then exploded into one glorious feeling which filled her, and she cried out, tears streaming down her face.

Whitworth's movements became more furious, and there were tiny animal cries in his throat.

'Yes, Mike, yes . . . oh, yes.'

Then, with one deep growl of pleasure, Whitworth finally became still.

He rolled off her and, as the bed could not accommodate both of them, stood up. He was completely naked, and Holly thankfully saw, through a haze of fulfilment and inebriety, that he had managed at some point to put on a condom.

'Jesus, Hol, that was something.'

'It's right what they say about ugly women then?' she grinned.

'Don't say that. Stop putting yourself down all the time,' Whitworth chided, making his way to the bathroom.

Holly could hear the sounds of his bare feet on the floorboards. She looked down at herself and giggled. Her legs were still wide open and raised at the knees. 'You did it, Holly,' she whispered triumphantly.

The lavatory flushed and Whitworth, now wearing a white bathrobe, came back into the room, a lighted cigarette clamped between his teeth. 'Right, girl, I'd better get you a taxi,' he said awkwardly. 'You ain't in any fit state to drive that heap of junk you call a car.'

'I'm not going,' Holly said defiantly. 'I want another drink and I'm staying the night.'

'I think it's time you went, Hol.'

Whitworth was a man who shunned even the hint of involvement.

'Maybe you're not up to it again,' Holly teased.

'I'd wear you out, girl,' Whitworth retorted.

'Prove it then.' She sat up abruptly. 'Look, Mike, this is a one-off for both of us — right? A never-to-be-repeated offer. Let's make the most of it.'

He thought for a moment, then said reflectively, 'Ships that—'

'Mingle in the night,' Holly finished, deliberately misquoting.

CHAPTER 26

Ashworth stared at the flats and wondered how people could live in such contraptions.

In the late '70s, architects and designers, anxious not to compound their high-rise mistakes of the '50s and '60s, had gone to the opposite extreme and constructed double-tier flats in long uniform rows. To further distance these from the 'concrete jungle' image, they had added wooden cladding to their facades, which merely served to give the buildings a 'shanty town' appearance.

This row of thirty-two dwellings was within five minutes' walk of Paine's factory.

Ashworth located number 13, on the ground floor. Each double flat had its own porch housing the front door to the lower flat and narrow stairs leading to the one above. Ashworth squeezed into the confined space and rang the bell.

The door was opened by a man of about fifty-five, medium height and build, wearing grey trousers and cream shirt beneath a dark green cardigan.

'Mr Leonard Warren?' Ashworth asked.

'Yes.'

Almost everything about Warren was so average that he would have passed unnoticed in any crowd, but for the port-wine-coloured stain, about the size of an orange, running from the cheekbone to the corner of his mouth on the left side of his face.

'I'm Chief Inspector Ashworth—'

'Yes, I've seen you at the factory. What do you want?' Warren asked curtly.

'A few words, if I may, sir. Perhaps I could come inside?'

Warren seemed reluctant, but said, 'Yes, I suppose so.'

The hall was no larger than the porch. Ashworth was across it in two strides.

One look at the lounge confirmed that Warren was a bachelor. If the compact room had been furnished in a normal manner it would have no doubt appeared cluttered. However, one easy chair, a television on a stand, and a coffee table made it seem positively spacious.

A large bookcase covered half of one wall and Ashworth wandered over to it. 'A fine collection of books you have here, Mr Warren,' he remarked. 'You're interested in the works of the Bard, I see.' He pointed to a leather-bound edition of the complete works of Shakespeare.

'That surprise you, does it?'

'How do you mean?'

'That somebody working in a factory can enjoy the arts?'

'Not at all, Mr Warren, I was merely being pleasant.'

Warren appeared not to have heard. He said bitterly, 'When I was at school the powers-that-be categorised children as factory fodder or better at the age of eleven.'

'Yes, it was the same when I was there,' Ashworth said, then went back to scrutinising the books as Warren talked.

'Well, that system didn't allow for late developers, did it? God knows how many people successive governments have condemned to live as second-class citizens, just because they don't have pieces of paper to say they're clever.'

Ashworth saw a large collection of modern crime fiction, and some political works which were predictably far left of centre. Then, just as he was about to look away, something caught his attention. Resting between *The Workers' Struggle* and *Basic Rights in the Workplace* was a book on forensic science.

Warren was in full flow. 'Every staff job that's come up at the factory, every full-time official post in the union, I've applied for,' he complained sourly, 'but I've never even been considered.'

'You're interested in forensic science, are you, sir?'

'What? No, I'm not.' He looked puzzled. 'Oh, the book. No, I read a lot of detective thrillers and I like to check the writers have got their facts right. I don't know how much money those people get, but you'd be amazed at some of the technical mistakes they make. I used to write to the publishers, but they always came up with the same twaddle about artistic licence. Well, if I . . .' He jerked his thumb at his chest. '. . . or millions like me, made a mistake in my job, I'd get short shrift if I offered that as an excuse.'

'It's your job I want to talk to you about,' Ashworth told him, relieved to be changing the subject.

'What's my job got to do with you?' Warren asked belligerently.

'Nothing as such,' Ashworth answered mildly. 'I meant the factory really. You've heard about Simon Edwards's death, I take it?'

'Oh, that.' Warren sounded uninterested.

'You don't seem surprised or shocked.'

'I'm not. The only thing that surprises me is that somebody didn't bump him and Paine off years ago.'

Come the revolution . . . Ashworth thought. 'I find that strange. Simon Edwards seemed to be almost universally liked.'

'People will tell you that,' Warren sneered, 'because they haven't the backbone to say what they really think. Yes, Edwards had charm, and a certain amount of panache, I grant you, but underneath he was just the same. His policies were just the same as Paine's — lower pay, plus less rights, equals more profit.'

Ashworth feared he knew the answer to the next question before it was even asked. 'Would you know of anyone who might have wished Simon Edwards harm?'

'Just about anybody who's ever worked for him.'

'Thanks, it's been nice talking to you, Mr Warren. I'll let myself out.'

Tailor-made, Ashworth thought as he stepped out into the street. He began the hundred-yard walk back to where he had parked the Sierra.

If he had ordered a model to fit Gwen Anthony's profile of the kidnapper, Len Warren would have been delivered by return post. The man did not seem outwardly concerned by his birthmark, but the fact that he imagined that most of the world saw him as unintelligent matched Gwen's description exactly. And, by his own admission, he would go to great lengths to show how clever he was, even on such trivial matters as an author making a mistake in a work of fiction. Also, Warren definitely gave the impression that he disliked everything and anything that was breathing God's air.

'Tailor-made,' he said to himself, inserting the key into the car door.

* * *

Warren watched Ashworth until he was out of sight. Had he imagined it? Did that busybody of a policeman look back at his window to see if he was watching?

He was all right, he reassured himself, they were just trying to panic him. Yes, he knew what their game was — coming along here and chatting about books.

He went into the kitchen. There was something he had to get out of the flat. He stood on a chair, reached into the top shelf of a built-in cupboard and withdrew a large cardboard box. Balancing it, he stepped off the chair and placed the box on the table.

Opening it up he took out a black leather executive case. His hands were trembling.

He'd ring the factory and tell them he'd not be in today — make out he was ill.

Then he'd have time to think of a safer hiding place for this.

* * *

It was 10.30 a.m. when Holly pulled up outside her house. Her leg ached deliciously as she depressed the brake pedal.

'I'll give you one thing, Mike,' she murmured to herself, 'you really are macho man.'

She had telephoned the office; her official excuse was that she had overslept — the truth, however, was far more erotic.

Even her slight headache could not dampen her spirits. As is so often the case, when the route to a hangover has been a pleasurable one, its effects pass largely unnoticed.

She glanced up at the house and dread edged its way into her mind. She vaguely recollected telephoning Emily the previous night, but what she had said eluded her. She had made the call from the landing below Mike's flat; he had been there with her, and the fact that she was not even able to remember whether she was dressed or not did nothing to clear a path through the confusion.

Firmness, she told herself, that's what you need to deal with Emily Bedford — a firmness born of practicality and devoid of emotion.

She tried to shake off the gloom which met her whenever she entered the house, but it clung to her like an invisible cloak.

As her key turned in the lock it was obvious that Emily was advertising her presence in the kitchen by making as much noise as possible with the pots and pans. From the din, Holly half expected to find her juggling with them. But, in fact, when Holly entered, Emily was sitting at the table.

'Home at last,' she sniffed.

'Yes,' Holly said. 'I've just popped in to change, then I'm off.'

'The station phoned.'

Holly had visions of her overslept-alibi disintegrating. 'What did they want?' she asked, trying to sound casual.

'Don't know. Didn't answer it.'

'How the hell do you know it was the station then?' Holly could feel herself getting annoyed.

'Who else would it be?' Emily mumbled. 'It's no good you staying out all night, then coming home shouting at me and causing all this upset.'

Holly recognised the tactic but had no intention of playing the game. 'I'm going to change,' she announced.

As if on cue, Emily appeared in the bedroom doorway at the precise moment when Holly became totally naked. She could feel the old woman's eyes raking over her body.

'I called the station last night,' she said accusingly. 'They said you weren't on duty. I said, excuse me, but she must be, she's just rung me from there. But they said, no—'

'You had no right to do that, Emily.' Holly could no longer bring herself to call this woman 'mum'.

'You shouldn't tell stories. With this leg of mine, I could fall down, then I wouldn't know where to turn for help.'

Holly began to get dressed. 'You force me to tell stories,' she said evenly. 'The fuss you make whenever I do anything, or see anyone. You bring it on yourself.'

'You were with a man, I suppose,' Emily said slyly.

'Yes, Emily, I was with a man. I'm sure you'll want to know all the details.' With a great effort, Holly was managing to keep her tone completely matter of fact. 'Well, I got myself laid — for the first time in over three years. And I'll tell you something else — it was bloody beautiful.'

Emily staggered back in feigned shock as Holly fastened her dark blue skirt. 'May the Lord forgive you.'

'I'm sure he will.'

'You're just telling me this to upset me. My, you're a wicked daughter-in-law.'

'No, that's not why I'm telling you,' Holly corrected her. 'I'm serving you notice. I'm a young woman with the whole of my life in front of me, and I'm going to live it.'

'You want me out. I know what's behind this — you're just trying to get rid of me,' Emily wailed.

'You're quite welcome to stay . . .' Holly put on the matching jacket and studied her reflection in the dressing-table mirror, '. . . but the days of you making me feel guilty all the time are over. You must understand that.'

'I can't stay here,' Emily moaned, sniffing, her eyes screwed up but devoid of tears, 'not with you and men laying — or whatever you call it — all over the house. I'd rather be dead.'

Holly picked up her handbag from the bed. 'Your choice, Emily, your choice.'

Then without looking at her mother-in-law, Holly pushed past her, strode down the stairs and straight out of the front door.

* * *

She had a long drawn-out explanation ready for her late appearance, but Ashworth, sitting behind his desk, deep in thought, merely grunted as she bustled into the office, apologetically announcing that she had overslept.

Josh was at his desk looking lost and ill at ease, the VDU silent and lifeless.

Holly felt flustered and clumsy as she took her seat.

'I just thought you'd taken time off because you worked late last night,' Ashworth said with the air of a man emerging from a deep trance. 'I'll tell you both now, there's too much overtime being booked, so in future, if we work late we'll have to take time off in lieu when it's quiet.' He banged his palms on the desk and sat erect. 'Right, I'll update you on the Simon Edwards enquiry.'

For Josh's benefit he ran through the details of the French interview and then told them both about Len Warren. 'In my opinion,' he concluded, 'the man has a persecution complex, to say the least.'

'Just a thought,' Josh began hesitantly, 'but I think we should take a good look at Barbara Edwards.'

Ashworth's eyebrows arched. 'Whatever for?'

'Because I feel her drug dependency has got something to do with all this.'

Ashworth did not exactly sneer, but came pretty close to it. 'So Barbara Edwards killed her husband because he was about to send her to a rehabilitation clinic, and then proceeded to demand money from herself. Clever.'

'That's not what I meant, sir,' Josh faltered, feeling foolish, his cheeks glowing pink.

'No.' Ashworth shook his head. 'I've a fair idea who the murderer is, and why he did it, but I want some proof before I go into it with you.'

'Sir,' Josh said stiffly, 'can I take the tape and ransom notes home with me? I want to study them.'

'Yes, as long as it's in your own time.'

'It will be, sir,' Josh assured him.

'Good. Now I want some sort of watch kept on Len Warren.'

Holly, finally managing to push the memory of last night to the edge of her mind, was about to ask Ashworth to expand on his theory, but then when he ordered a watch to be kept on Warren she assumed that he was their suspect.

'I don't think it was Warren,' Josh said stubbornly.

Before Ashworth could deliver his acid reply, the telephone rang. He picked it up. 'Yes?' he barked.

'Jim, it's Gwen.'

'Gwen, I'm busy—'

'It's all right, Jim, don't panic.' She sounded serious. 'This is an official call. I thought I'd forewarn you — another body has turned up.'

'Where?' he asked curtly.

'Palmerstone Road, Ethelvale Estate.'

Mike Whitworth's warning flashed across Ashworth's mind.

'It's a nasty one, Jim,' Gwen went on. 'A seventy-two-year-old woman, raped and stabbed to death.'

Ashworth felt his heart and spirits sink as he listened to Gwen's now factual voice.

'The police surgeon's there,' she said, 'and I'm on my way.'

'I'll see you there.' He replaced the receiver.

* * *

Palmerstone Road was a long narrow street of terraced cottages, tenanted mostly by elderly people who had lived their whole married lives within the confines of these tiny two-up-two-down dwellings.

If any of them had felt a strong desire to leave behind the memories of a lifetime's joy, pain, triumph, and failure, the meagre state pension — which was, for most of them, their sole income — would have prevented it.

Ashworth had found out the house number from uniformed, alerted Forensic, ordered Holly and Josh to follow him, and driven straight there.

Turning into the road he saw Gwen's car, two panda cars, and a tight knot of neighbours and passers-by, speculating no doubt what could have happened to warrant such a large police presence.

He drew up behind a panda car and got out. Josh parked behind him.

Pushing his way unceremoniously through the crowd, he pointed to a constable standing by the front door, saying, 'Get rid of this lot.'

The house had no hall as such, just a narrow passage leading to a steep flight of stairs. Two doors led off the passage. The first opened into what most of the residents referred to as the 'front room'. But as sounds of activity were coming from the second, grandly titled 'breakfast room', Ashworth assumed that was where the murder had taken place.

Although Gwen and the two uniformed constables looked up as he appeared in the doorway, he did not acknowledge them. Instead he took in the room and could literally feel his flesh crawling.

Blood was splattered on the walls, the floor; three trails of it had oozed down the television screen and dripped on to the old carpet. It was splashed across the '70s-style three-piece suite, and the two faded framed photographs which stood on a pine dresser.

Ashworth looked at them closely. A young man and woman, smiling as they stood on a beach, the sea calm and tranquil in the background; the woman cradling a baby in her arms and proudly posing for the camera. In the second, the man — older now — holding a silver cup with equal pride. All that was left of two lives.

Above the woman's body, which lay on the floor in the centre of the room, was a small black and white mongrel dog, its pathetic body dangling from the light fitting by a piece of rope tied around its disjointed neck.

Ashworth looked down at the woman. Fifty or more years on, she bore no resemblance to the photograph. Her grey hair was thin and lifeless, a tiny bald spot stood out on the crown. The faded dead eyes stared unseeing towards her pet; the wrinkled mouth hung open as if in horror at what had been done to it.

Her torso was covered in stab wounds from which the blood had flowed so freely, it was impossible to tell the colour of her jumper. The body was naked from the waist down, and as he stared at the brown age spots on the thin white legs, Ashworth felt a surge of destructive anger well up inside him.

He could feel Holly and Josh behind him, could hear their breathing, sense their revulsion. 'My God,' he murmured. Try as he might, he could not disguise the edge of raw emotion in his tone.

Gwen's normally firm voice quavered as she told him, 'She's been raped, Jim, and then stabbed to death. But she was a game old girl — she really put up a fight. She must have scratched him, and . . .' she bit her lip, '. . . I think the dog attacked him, trying to protect his mistress. He's left so much behind, he might as well have left his name and address.'

'Good.' Suddenly Ashworth needed to be out of the room. 'A word outside, Gwen.'

She looked at him. 'Of course.'

'You two stay here,' he told his detectives. 'There's no need to wait in the room though,' he added, striding down the passage.

Outside he turned to Gwen. 'So you expect the assailant to be marked?'

'Heavily so — and of course he would be covered in blood.' She stared at his set, brooding expression. 'You get him, Jim.'

'It's "them", not "him" . . . and when we do, my people had better take great care not to leave me alone with the bastards.'

As she watched him getting into his car, Gwen knew the remark had not been made out of anger, or frustration — he had meant every syllable of it.

CHAPTER 27

Anyone not attuned to Spanish-style embellishments might well have considered the guitar and brightly coloured fans scattered around the walls of Dennis Paine's villa rather lacking in taste. The snow-white carpet was tasteful, however, and expensive, as were the ultra-modern pieces of furniture.

As he entered the lounge Paine paused to look at his sister, sprawled on a blue-and-white-check sofa. 'Babs, are you going to be all right, here on your own? I must put in an appearance at the factory.'

'Of course I'll be all right. I'm not an invalid, you know.'

'I know you're not, but those pills are getting out of hand,' Paine said tactfully.

'Don't start that, Dennis,' Barbara flared. 'That's what caused all the trouble between Simon and me.'

'I can't think how much they must cost you.'

'They're prescribed — you know that,' she replied evasively.

'No, they're not,' Paine said firmly. 'Not the amount you take. I'm only thinking of you, Babs—'

'Oh, why do you always pretend you're thinking of my best interests, when it's obvious you're just trying to prevent me from enjoying myself?'

'Oh, Babs,' Paine said sadly, 'if only you could get back to how you were. You were one of the best businesswomen I've known.'

'Don't keep nagging me,' she cried, burying her face in her hands. 'I wouldn't have come to stay with you if I'd known you were going to be like this.'

'All right, all right,' Paine said in a conciliatory manner, 'I don't want to make an issue out of it.' He disappeared into the hall and returned clutching a pile of papers. 'I need your signature on some of these.'

'What are they?'

'Papers that need the signatures of two company directors, and with Simon gone . . .' He paused. 'I'm sorry, that was a tactless thing to say.'

'It's all right, Dennis, just give them to me.'

'This is a letter to the bank confirming our overdraft will be settled by the end of the month.' He passed her the letter and a pen. 'If some of our customers pay up, that is.'

'You do worry, Dennis. Our credit's good at the bank.'

'It's the interest we're paying that bothers me. Now, this is a letter to one of our suppliers assuring them that in spite of what's happened we'll be continuing in business. There are two or three duplicates under that, for our other suppliers. If they get panicky and withdraw their credit, we'll go broke.'

He looked down at his sister as she scrawled her signature upon the letters. 'Do read them, Babs. For Christ's sake, don't just sign.'

'Don't keep on at me.'

Paine sighed. 'And this is one to Ashworth, thanking him for his help. I'm trying to rebuild a few bridges there. I can pop it into the station on my way to the factory.' As she signed, Paine's hand shot out to grab the letter. 'No, not there — it's a two-page letter.'

'Well, you should have said. I've signed it now.'

'I can Tippex it out. Just turn the page and sign it again.'

'There.' She handed back the blue notepaper and pen. 'Now just leave me alone.'

'I'm doing what I think is best, you know. I really do want things to work out.'

'I know you do, Dennis, and I know you have my best interests at heart . . . but please don't mention clinics.'

* * *

Holly and Josh were silent for some time as they drove away from the harrowing scene of rape and murder.

Josh was the first to break the silence. As they crossed the bridge which spanned the River Thane, he said, 'Have I offended you in any way, Holly?'

'No, of course you haven't,' she said breezily.

'Is it because I'm gay?' he persisted. 'I know some people have a thing about it.'

'It's got nothing to do with that.'

Josh steered the car into the high street. 'I know I've offended you in some way. I mean, until yesterday you were really friendly towards me.'

'Josh, it's not that you're gay, and you've done nothing to offend me in any way.' Then she relented. 'Oh, I just feel such a fool.'

'Tell me, Holly,' he urged, dividing his attention between her and the road ahead. 'I really do need a friend in this god-forsaken place.'

'I thought you were interested in me,' she said quietly.

He glanced at her. 'I am.'

'I didn't know you were gay,' she explained.

'Oh, I see,' he said slowly. 'I'm sorry, I didn't realise.'

'It's not up to you to apologise. It was my fault — and I would like to be your friend.'

'Thanks, Holly,' he said gratefully. 'Actually, I probably won't be here for much longer. I'm thinking of going home.'

'Why? I thought you were settling in.'

'No, I'm not. And it's Ashworth — I could almost picture him queer-bashing.'

'I think you're wrong, Josh. I don't think he's got anything against you.'

'No?' he asked bitterly. 'Have you noticed how he thinks he's got the Edwards case stitched up? There's no room in his world for an opposing opinion.'

'He's like that with everyone.'

'Maybe he is, but I did come here to work with computers, and he's ordered me out on to the streets.'

'What will you do?'

'There's a job going in telecommunications in Leeds. I've applied for it. If I get an interview I'll take a day's leave . . .' He paused, then continued in a passable impression of Ashworth's deep growling voice, 'or time off in lieu of overtime . . . and go for it.'

Checking the mirror, Josh turned right into the station car park, saying, 'But I'd love to prove Ashworth wrong before I do. I bet that hasn't been done before.'

No, Holly thought, I bet it hasn't.

He waited for an oncoming car to pass, then parked the Sunny. The station was a hub of activity. A harassed Sergeant Dutton was at reception, talking to Mike Whitworth. He signalled to them as they came through the swing doors.

'What's happening?' Josh asked as he surveyed the journalists crowded into the foyer.

'Damon Cain's given himself up — and this lot have got wind of it,' Dutton said, eyeing the journalistic gathering with some distaste.

The arrival of Holly and Josh had given rise to fresh speculation, and a young man — spotty-faced, with greasy blond hair, wearing jeans and padded anorak — approached the reception desk. '*Bridgetown Post*,' he announced grandly. 'Can you tell me what's happening?'

An exasperated Dutton was about to answer when Whitworth interjected. '*Bridge-town Post*, eh? Well, I can tell you this . . .' His voice was low, confidential. '. . . There's been a mass break-out at Rampton, and one of the escapees has turned himself in at this nick.'

The young man was scribbling wildly in his notepad. 'Do you know his name?' he asked excitedly.

'I do, but it's more than my job's worth to disclose it. I can tell you that he's a mass murderer.'

This led to renewed scribbling. 'And what's your name?'

'Detective Constable Elvis Presley,' Whitworth said in a southern drawl.

The journalist, realising he was being sent up, reacted angrily, 'Give me a break.'

'Okay, okay.' Whitworth held up both hands in a token of surrender. 'Which limb?'

The young man looked at the smiling faces of the police group as Whitworth added, 'Fade — like the man said, there'll be a press release as soon as possible.'

As the rather abashed reporter rejoined his colleagues, Josh remarked, 'Still the master of public relations, I see. It's good to see you, Mike.'

'Likewise,' Whitworth smiled, 'just don't follow me into the toilets — okay?'

Josh laughed good-naturedly.

'Hi, Hol.'

'Hello, Mike,' Holly said, blushing and staring intently at her shoes.

Whitworth's suit was crumpled, she had noticed, and beneath the knot of his tie a button was missing from his shirt. His black hair tumbled untidily over his forehead and hid his ears. If anything he looked more dishevelled than usual — and so bloody sexy.

Visions of the previous night's passion-filled hours flashed into her mind. 'What are you doing here?' she managed to ask casually.

Whitworth noted her discomfort and seemed to be enjoying it. 'Just proving I can stand up,' he replied nonchalantly. 'No, I came to see Boss Man.'

'Come with us then,' Josh said.

'I'm not sure I'll be welcome.'

'You will,' Dutton said cheerfully. 'He likes you, and the odds on him doing that with most people are as long as winning the jackpot on the pools.'

'I know,' Josh murmured quietly.

Ashworth's greeting was warm. 'Mike, what brings you here?' he asked, ignoring the other two.

'I heard about the rape and murder, guv . . .' he shrugged, '. . . and I've got a career tied up in there somewhere.'

'Yes, that hadn't escaped my notice. Let's go into the other office. I want to talk to you.'

Ashworth closed the door. 'This is a bad one,' he said before going into detail.

Whitworth stood, stony-faced, as he listened to the horrors that had been inflicted on the seventy-two-year-old woman before she met her death.

'It's what I expected, guv.'

'You know Cain's given himself up?'

Whitworth nodded.

'I'm just about to interview him. Mike, will you do something for me?'

'If I can.'

'I want you to watch a man named Len Warren.'

'Hold on, guv, you warn me off watching Cain and Bennett, and now you want me to keep an eye on this Len Warren.'

'That's right.'

'Got you.'

As Ashworth told him the address, Whitworth smiled; not at the irony of what he was being asked to do, but at the fact that Ashworth could not see it.

'And how do you want him watched?'

'High profile. I want him to know you're there because I don't know what it is I'm looking for.'

'Right, guv, I'll give it all the time I can.'

He went and sat on the desk which was his before his suspension. 'Your army's becoming a bit restless about the

Edwards case, you know,' he said, indicating the outer office. 'They feel you're pushing them to one side.'

'Yes, I know. I'm not quite as unobservant as people think. No doubt Holly told you that in her considered opinion I'm past it, and that she's based that assumption on my behaviour at the French interview.' His hostile brown eyes settled on Whitworth as if daring him to lie.

'She didn't mention 'past it', but she does seem to think your mind's not on the job,' Whitworth answered with customary frankness.

'No doubt she could hazard a guess as to where it was.' He waved his hand. 'No, I won't ask you to answer that.'

'Is there a point to this, guv?'

'Yes, Mike, a very valid one. What is it you call me when I'm not around? Now, let's see,' he mused, 'it used to be Dixon of Dock Green, but of late it's been Boss Man.'

'Guv—'

'Well, Mike, that's what I am. I'm the head of CID and I can't be forever running the gauntlet of what my junior officers think of me, or my methods. Do you know what I was doing at the Frenches'?'

'No, guv,' Whitworth said, realising that he was being offered a privileged glimpse at the workings of the great man's mind.

'I didn't need to look at their faces to know they were lying. No, what I was doing was looking around the room, at the half-empty decanters — one of whisky, the other gin. Now, do you know what that suggested to me? Those people are regular drinkers — they don't just play at it. And in their bookcase was a large collection of literature; nothing highbrow, but all recent and in hardback, and that's expensive. So, I calculated their possible earnings, and fitted their expenditure into their income — it didn't go. So from that I deduced that the money was from another source.'

'Shouldn't you be wearing a deerstalker, and saying things like 'elementary', guv?'

'Probably, Mike,' Ashworth replied in all seriousness, 'but where does the money come from?'

'Not from the kidnap, that's for sure.'

'No, but kidnapping is rarely a first major crime, if that's the path you want to go along. Detectives aren't made, Mike, they're born. Do you know, sometimes I can look at people and know what they're thinking,' he said passionately, 'actually what they're thinking.'

'Are you telling me you always know who did it?'

'I always know who didn't do it, Mike, and that eventually leads me to who did. And while that process is taking place, I'd much rather have an office full of people thinking I'm past my sell-by date, or that my mind's on other things, than have them clouding my judgement with their theories. It comes from here, Mike.' He hit his now slimline stomach with his fist. 'You can take a suspect in a murder enquiry and prove them guilty or innocent. Lawyers are doing it all the time.'

'That makes sense.' Whitworth's usual flamboyance had vanished. 'But where's this leading?'

Ashworth walked over to the glass outer wall and surveyed the town. 'That's my world out there, Mike. I've lived in this place all my life — spent over thirty years policing it. It matters to me, damn it, it matters.'

A puzzled Whitworth studied his superior's broad back.

'Just after you were suspended,' Ashworth continued, 'I got to thinking about you. Young man, you're arrogant; you show a total lack of respect for authority; you cut corners to get where you want to go. For ability to work as a member of a team, I would award you nil points. You're pig-headed . . .'

'These are just my plus points, I take it.'

Ashworth turned to face him. '. . . and you remind me of me,' he concluded with a slight smile.

Little did Whitworth realise that he had just been awarded the highest accolade Ashworth could ever bestow on anyone.

Ashworth said, 'You wouldn't know why Ken Savage wanted me back in this job. It was because my resignation would have looked bad on his record, so he brought me back, and now he has plans to sideline me with some little job of dealing with the Home Office. He thinks it's time I was put out to grass, and I'm beginning to agree with him.'

'Guv, half the people in this nick say you're the best copper they've ever met. If you're having difficulties with the Edwards case, I'll do all I can to help.'

'Bless you, Mike, on both counts, but no . . .' he shook his head vigorously, '. . . it's not that. I've been doing a lot of soul searching over the last few days, and I've come to realise I'm reaching back for something that's no longer there — it's gone.' He seemed distant all of a sudden, totally absorbed in himself. 'Yes, I can still do a hundred press-ups, run up the stairs without getting out of breath, and still — to use modern terminology — get it up, but that doesn't make me young again, because youth is up here.' He tapped his forehead. 'It's the ability to adapt quickly, easily. Do you know, I acknowledge that there are people out there with drug problems, and kids, barely in their teens, leading full and varied sex lives — I know these things to be, but I still can't believe them. The world's changed, but I haven't. Does that sound silly?'

'No, I don't think so, guv.'

'You asked me what this was leading up to,' Ashworth said, centring his gaze on Whitworth's perplexed face. 'Well, when it became apparent that I was going to be sidelined, I was determined to have a say in my successor.'

Whitworth's jaw dropped open. 'You want me to succeed you?'

Ashworth nodded.

'Why?'

'Maybe I want to wish you on Ken Savage as some sort of revenge,' he said with a wry smile. 'But think on it, Mike.'

'I'd need to be reinstated first.'

'I'm working on that.'

'Guv, there's something else — Josh. I know he's a wrong way round guy, but I think you're being unfair to him.'

'His homosexuality has nothing to do with it, Mike. I'm not a bigot,' Ashworth declared loudly, 'I just don't think he's a good policeman.'

'I think you're wrong.'

'I'm never wrong,' Ashworth said stiffly.

'Neither am I.'

Ashworth smiled as he recognised the trap into which he had fallen. 'While I'm wearing the big hat you are.'

Whitworth laughed, pushing himself off the desk. 'Right, guv, I'll watch this Len Warren for you.'

'Good, and I'll get on and interview Cain.'

He watched as Whitworth swaggered to the door. 'Mike?'

'Yes, guv?'

'I'd like this little discussion to have been off the record.'

'You can count on it.'

When Whitworth emerged, he found Holly alone in the outer office.

'Mike, whatever's the matter — you actually look thoughtful,' she said with mock surprise.

'Yeah, yeah.' He perched on the edge of her desk. 'Right, Hol, I regarded last night as a draw, so I'm demanding a rematch,' he said light-heartedly, all deep thoughts set aside.

'I don't know, Mike,' Holly replied doubtfully. 'You said you're not permanent.'

'Two nights suddenly turn me into a husband?' he grinned.

Those lovely white teeth in that attractive face sent shivers down Holly's spine.

There were others — besides Ashworth — in Bridgetown Station who were struggling to come to terms with themselves. Holly for one. The fact that, driven by pure lust, she could be attracted to sex which offered no security, no future, offended her middle-class morality. And the fact that she seemed powerless to resist alarmed her.

'Full treatment this time — I'll buy you a meal,' Whitworth promised. 'Anything you want — burgers and fries, fish and chips. For the sort of performance you turn in, I might even stretch to a Chinese. Shall I call you?'

She nodded. 'Yes.'

Whitworth jumped off the desk, patting her under the chin. 'Right, girl. Keep your knickers up unless you want to go to the toilet.'

Laughing, and shaking her head, she watched him leave the office.

CHAPTER 28

Damon Cain, in interview room number one, was contemplating the consequences of his recent actions.

He sat considering the brown Formica of the tabletop, in which he had burnt a hole with his lighted cigarette. The smell of smouldering plastic brought a reprimand from the uniformed officer by the door.

'Stop it, Damon,' the social worker, Rolands, snapped, lightly tapping the hand holding the offending cigarette.

Cain fingered the deep scratch marks on his left cheek. Jenny Rolands wasn't showing any sympathy, he thought moodily. Tell the police everything, had been her advice.

It wasn't his fault — why couldn't they see that? If the stupid old woman hadn't struggled, she'd have been all right. They just wanted a bit of fun, a laugh.

He would blame it all on to Delvin, he had already decided that. And in court, he would tell the magistrates how much he missed his dad, how he'd like to study and really make something of himself — but his mum was never at home, which made him feel lost and unwanted.

He knew what he had done was wrong, but he only did it to draw attention to himself. It was a cry for help, really.

Yes, that's what he would say — that always went down well with all the poxy welfare people.

He would spend a couple of years in care, behave himself, and then he would be out.

Stubbing out the cigarette, he began to feel quite cheerful. After all, he had given himself up — that should go in his favour. He would say that as soon as the drugs had worn off — the drugs Delvin had made him take — he had realised he'd done a bad thing and gone straight to the police.

Feeling so good now, he almost laughed out loud. When the filth came in to interview him, he'd just take the piss. What could they do?

Then the door opened.

Oh, Christ, it's the old geezer who always looks uptight, and that skinny bird. What's the matter with the old fart? Why's he looking at me like that?

Now the bird's mumbling some crap into the tape recorder, and the old bloke's sitting down. Right, let's go.

Ashworth came straight to the point. 'I'm not going to mess about — you can tell me what happened, or I can wait for the Forensic report, and then I'll tell you.'

Cain sniggered.

'Tell them,' Rolands commanded sharply.

Cain looked Ashworth in the eye and smiled. 'I can't remember nothing. I'd snorted some coke Delvin had given me. It's the first time I've had any, 'cause I don't do drugs, see.'

'So you don't remember stabbing the old lady?'

'I didn't stab nobody.'

'Oh, you remember you didn't stab anybody, but you don't remember anything else.'

'No, you're trying to trick me.'

Cain watched Ashworth's finger pointing towards him. 'You're in a lot of trouble son, and you're not helping yourself with this attitude.'

The boy considered his position. He would have to tell them, so why not put himself in the best possible light?

'Well, I snorted some coke, right? Then Delvin said, why don't we go and see this old woman he knew. He'd been doing errands for her and taking her dog out, things like that. I didn't know he meant to have her, honest. Then, while she was making us a cup of tea he said to me, do you want it with the old girl? I thought he was joking, but when she came back he tripped her over. The dog bit him on the leg and he lost his cool. He got the piece of rope the old girl used as a lead and tied the dog up on the light.'

Cain paused, and stared at Ashworth's tightly clenched fists on the tabletop, the cold anger in his eyes.

'Go on,' Ashworth said, his voice sounding strained and choked.

Cain shrugged. 'Well, we got the old girl's clothes off, and she lay still while I was having her, just looked up at the dog dangling on the rope, she did. But then when it was Delvin's turn, she went ape shit — scratched me . . .' He touched the marks on his face. '. . . and I couldn't keep her still. Delvin freaked out 'cause he couldn't get it in, and he grabbed the knife off me and just started stabbing her. I got frightened and ran off.'

He saw Ashworth and Holly exchange a look. 'And did you rape the woman on the Cherry Tree Estate?' Holly asked.

'Yeah,' Cain admitted quietly.

'Good, you're helping us now,' she said. 'Do you know where Delvin Bennett is?'

Cain noticed that Holly's tone was more sympathetic now that he was cooperating, and decided that this would be a good road to stay on. Surely if he told them all they wanted to know, they'd go easy with him.

Very quickly, Cain said, 'Yeah, he's gone to his sister's in Northampton.'

'One more question,' Ashworth snapped. 'Bennett's accused one of our officers of assaulting him while he was at Clifton House — is that true?'

'No, Delvin got one of the bigger kids to hit him, then blamed it on King Shit, 'cause he was bugging us, like, and Delvin wanted him off the street.'

'Right.' Ashworth stood up. 'Charge him, Holly, and get him out of here.'

* * *

For the umpteenth time, Len Warren peeped around the lounge curtains.

He was still there.

Warren could hear his own breathing, could feel the rhythmic beating of his heart as he stood in the darkened room.

He tried to reassure himself. The man could not be from the police, surely? He looked dirty, unkempt even, standing there in the drizzling rain, leaning against his car. And the car — that didn't look like a police vehicle. Dark blue, apart from the driver's door and one wing which seemed to be a dull grey colour.

He was parked on double yellow lines, though — only the police could get away with that . . . and he was watching the flat. It wasn't imagination; several times he had grinned as he stared straight at this window.

There, he's seen me again. He's touched his forehead in a gesture of salute, and he's smiling. God, he looks an evil bastard.

Warren hurriedly moved away from the window. The ticking of the clock sounded loud in the stillness of the room. Knowing that he was being watched unnerved him, lent a claustrophobic atmosphere to the flat.

Entering the kitchen, he stumbled into a chair. Cursing, he righted himself as it crashed on to the tiled floor. As the flats backed on to unlit playing fields, the kitchen was in almost total darkness.

The cardboard box was still on the table. A dark shape in the gloom. Touching the lid created a strange feeling inside him, a mixture of pleasure, fear, and fulfilment. Within it lay the payment that went some way towards compensating him for the injustice he had suffered over the years at the hands of Edwards and Paine.

But he had to get it out; conceal it where the police would not find it. If he could, they would never be able to prove anything, whatever they suspected.

Cautiously he made his way back to the lounge and peered, once more, around the curtain. The road was black, shiny. The wind was gathering light drizzle and smattering it against the glass.

The car and its driver had gone.

Warren felt relief tempered with suspicion. This could merely be a ploy to lull him into a feeling of false security.

Aided by the light from a street lamp he consulted his wristwatch. He would wait an hour; that would make it seven thirty. If the watching man had not reappeared by then, he would do something about disposing of the cardboard box, and its contents.

* * *

Holly leant closer to the Mini's windscreen; the rubber of its wipers had perished, and even on high speed they were failing to cope with the light rain.

The road ahead, the tail lights of vehicles in front, appeared through a thin hazy film.

Her earlier worry, that this relationship with Mike Whitworth — if that was what it could be called — was motivated by a part of her anatomy somewhat closer to the ground than her heart, had faded; pulled away by the fact that he had not said when he would call, only that he would. This had given way to a fear, prompted by her own feelings of insecurity, that he would not contact her.

She turned into the small drive at her house, almost colliding with the garden gate because of her impaired vision, and, making full use of her large vocabulary of expletives, she parked the car.

That feeling of depression, which attached itself to her whenever she came home, embraced her once more as she hurried to the front door. During the day her attitude towards Emily had changed. Although her basic requirements — her own space, her own life — had not altered, her approach had; rather than use confrontation, she would try conciliation. She would assure Emily that her future was secure, would explain her own needs, while at the same time making her realise that she need not see them as a threat.

She stepped into the hall, relieved that the house felt oven hot. At least Emily had not decided to play the martyr.

Television sounds were blaring from the lounge. Holly popped her head round the door; the light was off and she could just make out Emily sitting in the armchair, eyes fixed on the flickering screen.

'Hello, mum. I'll make us a cup of tea and bring it in,' she announced cheerfully.

Emily did not reply, did not even look in Holly's direction.

Oh dear, Holly thought as she wandered to the kitchen, it's going to be the silent, wounded act, is it?

Should she ring Mike, or would that seem too forward? She laughed at that thought as she poured the tea. Too forward indeed. If her rather hazy recollections were correct, Mike was far too aware of her requirements, and the fervour with which she pursued them, for her to play the shrinking violet now.

She paused by the telephone in the hall, an impish grin playing on her lips. No, better make peace first — that would be delicate enough without Emily overhearing her talking on the telephone to a man.

Taking great care not to spill the tea, she opened the lounge door. 'Tea, mum.'

Still Emily made no reply.

Holly stared at her mother-in-law's profile. Look at her, she thought, sitting in the dark, staring at the television and refusing to speak. Dealing with a troublesome child could not be more difficult.

She waited diplomatically until the couple in the quiz show had answered the final question to win the holiday of a lifetime, then she said, 'Right, mum, I'll pull the curtains and put the light on, because I want to talk to you.'

Holly turned on the light and carried on talking as the curtains swished across the window. 'I'm sorry I was rude this morning, mum, but I was late for work.' She closed the gap in the curtains and went to fetch the tea from a small table beside the door. 'Let's make it up, shall we? We've both got to live under the same roof, so we might as well try to get along.'

The hot tea burnt her fingers as she picked up the mugs. 'If you like, you can have a television in your own room. One way or another we'll pay the heating bill, and that way—'

She had turned around, stopping in mid-sentence. Emily's gaze was still fixed on the television screen, her eyes wide and staring.

'Mum?' Panic surfaced in Holly's voice. She put the mugs back on the table, her trembling hands causing some of the tea to spill over on to the highly polished surface.

Holly knew Emily was dead before she touched the rapidly cooling flesh of that pinched face which, even in death, had retained its vindictive expression.

'No, God,' Holly said in a dull voice, without expression, 'no, I can't take any more — please.'

Then she went to telephone Mike Whitworth.

* * *

Emily's death undoubtedly delayed the uncovering of Len Warren's guilty secret. If Whitworth had not been dashing across town to offer help and comfort to Holly, he would have been watching the man.

Warren welcomed the dark cloudy night as he rummaged around in his garden shed for a spade. The wooden construction smelt strongly of mildew and earth.

The cardboard box, now wrapped in a large polythene sheet, stood just outside the rickety door. He kept glancing back at it, not wanting to let it out of his sight.

At last his fumbling hands closed around the required tool: a very large, almost new, spade.

He went behind the shed and — as best he could in the darkness — marked out an area on the lawn, cut around its edge, and rolled back the turf.

He spread a polythene sheet upon the grass and began to shovel earth on to it as he dug.

CHAPTER 29

Ashworth climbed slowly from the Sierra; his weariness was born not of physical fatigue, but of a tiredness of mind.

He was missing Sarah.

Their brief separation had brought with it a fear that what had taken place in the back of his car had erected a solid barrier between them, dismantling a relationship which had been thirty years in the building.

Even if what Gwen had described as 'a bit of fun' was not discovered by Sarah, then the memory of it would haunt him, forever attempting to entice him back for more. Anyway, the law of averages suggested that, sooner or later, discovery would be inevitable.

He stared in astonishment at the kidney-shaped swimming pool, and wondered how anyone possessing such an abysmal lack of taste could have accumulated so much wealth. Walking around the edge of the pool, he headed for the front door of the villa.

Dennis Paine opened it in answer to his knock. He was dressed in a plum-coloured smoking jacket and light grey slacks.

'Ashworth.' He sounded surprised.

'Mr Paine. I just thought I'd call to give you an update, and to thank you and your sister for your letter.'

'Yes, yes, come in, old chap.' Paine, apparently in good spirits, stood aside for Ashworth to enter. As he passed, Ashworth was aware of whisky fumes on the man's breath; undoubtedly, these went a long way towards explaining his jovial mood.

'I see you like Continental architecture,' Ashworth observed.

'Love it. None finer,' Paine confirmed. 'Into the lounge, Ashworth. Yes, I spent a lot of time in Spain, before the blasted liberals took it over.'

Ashworth assumed that anyone who was less than a cast-iron dictator would be accused by Paine of having liberal tendencies.

'Do you like the Continent?' Paine asked as they entered the lounge.

Ashworth almost winced as he took in the room. 'I've a very open mind about it.'

'Sit down, please,' Paine said cordially, seating himself in an armchair.

Ashworth noted Paine's glass of scotch and soda, the fat Havana cigar burning in the ashtray by his side. 'Thank you,' he said, perching on the edge of the sofa. 'I really did appreciate the letter. We get such a lot of flak—'

'Forget it,' Paine said, trimming ash from the cigar on the edge of the ashtray. 'I just hope it in some way makes up for my rudeness in the past.'

'How is Mrs Edwards?'

Paine's face clouded. 'Not well. She's staying with me, of course. I've given her a couple of large drinks and packed her off to bed. Ironic really, isn't it? Pouring poisoned water down her throat in the hope of getting her off the pills.' He drained his glass. 'Can I offer you a drink?'

'Better not, I'm driving.'

Paine rose from his chair. 'A small one, surely.'

'All right, a very small scotch and soda then.'

Ashworth watched as Paine went behind the bar, which was festooned with gaudy fans and bullfight posters.

'In any case, I thought if you chaps got stopped, you simply flashed your warrant cards,' Paine said with a wink.

Ashworth, who disliked frivolous attitudes towards drinking and driving, ignored him.

'I blame that blithering idiot, Anthony, for this,' Paine continued, accompanied by the sound of clinking glass. 'I've been after him for days now to get Babs into a home for her own safety, then to get her on a course of treatment. But do you think he will? Just keeps dodging the issue — and do you know why? Because it reflects badly on the medical profession. They prescribe the drugs — people get addicted.'

He handed Ashworth the drink and sat down. 'How's the investigation going?'

'That, apart from enquiring after the health of you and your sister, is the reason I'm here. I've interviewed the Frenches and Warren. The results are very interesting.'

'Yes?'

Ashworth told him what he had gleaned so far from the Frenches.

Paine whistled softly. 'So, Simon was indeed going to bed with Julie. Well, I'll be damned.'

'Does that surprise you?'

'Nothing surprises me anymore, Ashworth, but why does that make you suspect them?'

'They're living way beyond their means, for one thing. And they won't tell me the name of the woman who made up the foursome.'

'There could be a good reason for that,' Paine said reasonably. 'She could be married, for instance.'

'She could well be, but until we find out who she is, we won't know. Now, Len Warren — he's concealing something, and he's also a very frightened man.'

'Ashworth, Warren's a small man in every sense of the word. Just because he's frightened, doesn't mean he's committed murder.'

'Are you trying to get rid of all my suspects?' Ashworth laughed.

'Oh no,' Paine quickly declared, 'you people are trained. You know what you're doing. It's just that I can't think of French or Warren being capable of murder.'

'Believe me, in these cases it's nearly always the person people least expect.' He sipped the drink, grateful that Paine's taste in scotch was far superior to that of his furniture and fittings.

'Well, you've accused me of trying to get rid of your suspects, and I'm wondering if you're trying to put me out of business.'

'How do you mean?'

'Neither the Frenches nor Warren have been to work since you spoke to them.'

'Doesn't that say something?'

'Yes, I suppose it does — except for the fact that they couldn't all have done it.' Paine emptied his glass in two huge swallows. 'Unless they were all in it together, of course,' he said, studying Ashworth's expression, trying to read his thoughts.

'You're beginning to think like a policeman.' There was a note of praise in Ashworth's voice. 'But the main thing I want to impress upon you and your sister is that it may well seem as though nothing is happening, but that's only because I'm deliberately keeping this low key. I don't want anyone to think they're directly under suspicion.'

Paine indicated Ashworth's empty glass.

'No, better not,' Ashworth said.

Paine refilled his own at the bar. 'So you won't be doing anything over the next few days.'

'On the contrary, I shall be doing quite a lot — interviewing the Frenches again, trying to establish the identity of the mystery woman. And I'm having Warren watched. I've a notion that if I make that man sweat, he'll make a mistake. So, far from doing nothing, you could say I'm making it happen.'

Paine's look was confused as he said, 'But what is it you need to happen?'

'I want some of the ransom money to turn up.'

'What good would that do? It's unmarked, isn't it?'

'So everyone believes, but we took the serial numbers,' Ashworth replied smugly.

'Ashworth, you cunning old fox,' Paine said incredulously. 'So all you need is for some of the cash to turn up and you've got the murderer.' The prospect seemed to excite him.

'That's about it,' Ashworth confirmed.

Paine stayed behind the bar, sipping his drink. 'I don't believe it. So simple. I'll be totally frank with you — I didn't think you'd find Simon's killer.'

'God, and the police, move in mysterious ways, Mr Paine, their wonders to perform.'

'You can say that again.' Paine shook his head. 'So simple, yet so clever.'

'I won't take up any more of your time,' Ashworth said, getting to his feet. 'I trust I can rely on your discretion. I'd rather you didn't disclose any of this.'

'Of course.'

'Be reassured, Mr Paine — everything is now in place for us to make an arrest within the next few days.'

'You seem very certain that some of the money is going to turn up.'

'I am. One develops a gut feeling for these things over the years. Well, I'll leave you in peace.'

Paine came from behind the bar. 'Look, I think it's about time we got on first-name terms. It's James, I believe.'

'It is, but most people shorten it to Jim, and I feel more comfortable with that.'

'Good, Jim, and please call me Dennis.'

'Right then, Dennis, I'll be on my way. Thanks for the drink.'

Paine followed him to the front door. 'Jim, you've taken a load off my mind. Thanks for coming.'

As Ashworth opened the door to step outside, he said, 'Tell me, Dennis, there's one thing that baffles me . . .' He studied the empty swimming pool.

'What's that, old chap?'

'Why have you got a swimming pool in your front garden?'

'Jim, it's only the British who hide their pools in their back gardens.'

They bade each other goodnight. Ashworth got into his car and drove home.

* * *

He pulled into the drive to the sounds of a ringing telephone and a barking dog. Thinking the call could be from Sarah, Ashworth left the car unlocked in his haste to get indoors, but as is so often the case, the journey from car to telephone took twice as long as it would have done if he had kept calm. He finally picked up the receiver and over the sounds of the dog, still barking merrily away in the kitchen, shouted, 'Hello.'

'Hello, guv.'

'Oh . . . Mike.' Disappointment showed in his voice. 'What do you want?'

'I'm at Holly's guv. Her mother-in-law's died.'

As he digested the news, Ashworth selfishly calculated the effect Holly's absence would have on CID numbers. Then he asked, 'Is Holly all right?'

'Shook up, but I've got a couple of brandies down her and put her to bed.'

Ashworth, trying to imagine Mike Whitworth in the role of ministering angel, said desperately, 'I need you back at the station, Mike.'

'I'm suspended, guv,' Whitworth replied, ever practical.

'I know, but you've heard about Cain?'

'Yes, more or less.'

'Well, the Northamptonshire police have picked up Bennett. When we get him back and charged, you can be reinstated. Do you know what's happened to Stimpson?'

'He's done a runner. The last time he was spotted, his wife was chasing him with a carving knife — and she didn't intend stabbing him with it, if you get my drift.'

Ashworth sighed heavily. 'What's the situation there, Mike? How long is Holly likely to be away?'

'Have a heart, guv, her mother-in-law's just died,' Whitworth said, surprised by Ashworth's display of insensitivity. 'I'm staying here tonight, and I'll make all the arrangements tomorrow.'

'Yes, all right, I'm sorry, it's just that the balloon's about to go up in the Edwards case and I need people.' He paused. 'Give my sympathies to Holly, and tell her to take as much time as she needs. I'll manage.'

This was the first time Whitworth had witnessed the single-minded determination that could drive everything — even good manners — from Ashworth's mind. And there was a discernible coolness in his voice as he said, 'I'll be in touch.' Ashworth, however, appeared not to have noticed.

After replacing the receiver, he paced about the hall, opening the kitchen door to let the dog out. She bounded around his feet, jumped at his legs, and whined when he ignored her.

The telephone rang again.

'Hello, Jim.'

'Sarah, I'm glad you've phoned. Look, I'm sorry, I know I've been selfish. Of course you need to do things on your own. I can't simply expect you to be here, waiting on me hand and foot—'

'Jim, Jim,' Sarah laughed, 'you're gabbling. Listen to me. I've realised what a terrible mistake I've made. It's all that stuff I've been reading about being a modern woman. Well, I've realised I'm not a modern woman. I'm fifty-three years old and married to a Chief Inspector . . . and I want to come home, Jim.'

'Oh, thank God, Sarah, thank God,' he said, much relieved.

'I'll get a train first thing in the morning.'

'In the morning?' Ashworth said doubtfully.

'Yes, you do want me home, don't you? You haven't got another woman there, I hope,' she laughed.

Ashworth felt an acute pang of guilt. 'Don't talk nonsense. It's just that I'm coming to the end of the Edwards case and—'

'You're going to be preoccupied. Goodness, Jim, I do know you, remember. I accept that for the next few days I'll just be part of the furniture. All right?'

'Yes.'

'And, Jim, I know it sounds silly, but I love you.'

'I love you too, Sarah. I've come to realise over the last few days just how much I do,' he said, with so much tenderness in his voice.

* * *

It was nine a.m. the following morning before Ashworth spoke again to another human being, and this time there was not a trace of tenderness. 'Abraham can't be ill.'

'Don't be illogical, Jim,' Ken Savage said, 'there's no 'can't' about it — the man's ill.'

They were standing in the reception area; desk staff and officers who were passing through eyed the obvious confrontation with languid curiosity.

'Ken, I can't function without personnel. Three of my officers are on sick leave, and Whitworth's suspended—'

'It's not my fault, Jim,' Savage interrupted sharply.

Ashworth ignored this. 'I've got the Frenches to interview, Bennett to question. I can't do it. You'll have to get the Northampton police to interview him.'

'I can't do that.'

'You'll have to,' Ashworth insisted. 'That type of interview requires two detectives, and there aren't two here.'

Without waiting for a reply, Ashworth turned and stomped towards the stairs. Savage watched his retreating figure, then made off for his office, wondering how he could butter up the Chief Constable of Northamptonshire.

Ashworth sat at his desk for a while, collecting his thoughts, allowing his anger time to subside, then he picked up the telephone and dialled.

'Hello?' Julie French's voice was in his ear.

'Mrs French, this is Chief Inspector Ashworth, Bridgetown CID.'

'Yes?'

He could hear the taut nerves betrayed in her voice. 'I wonder if you and your husband could come into the station. There are a few questions I'd like to ask you both.'

'What about?'

'I think that would be better discussed here, don't you? Shall we say two fifteen this afternoon?'

'We could come in now,' she replied, a little too quickly.

'No, it will have to be this afternoon.'

'Yes, all right.'

Ashworth replaced the receiver with a smile. The pair of you can stew for a few hours, he thought, because sooner or later, you're going to have to tell me.

He drummed his fingers on the desktop.

CHAPTER 30

Ashworth had fondly believed that he had the immediate future neatly choreographed, with himself directing every movement, every step, but as he stood with Gwen Anthony, staring down at the bed, Fate reminded him that she could still disrupt even the most carefully laid plans.

'How long has she been dead?' he asked.

'About eight p.m. last night, I'd say.'

'God, I was here then, talking to Paine.'

'Overdose, and a massive one at that,' Gwen said. 'The officers attending found a typed suicide note. Forensic have taken it away.'

Barbara Edwards's peaceful face suggested that she had slipped into whatever lay beyond this life without pain or torment.

'What did it say?' Ashworth asked.

'Couldn't carry on without her husband — that sort of thing. I didn't inform you until I was about to clear things up, but it's suicide, Jim, there's no doubt about it.'

Ashworth turned away from the body to study the room which, with its cream-coloured built-in units, its pastel pink curtains, was far more tasteful than the rest of the house.

As if reading his thoughts, Gwen told him, 'Paine had the room refurbished for her. She was going to sell her house and live here.'

Ashworth grunted. 'Paine found the body, I take it?'

'Yes, that's right, and he's pretty distraught.'

'Is he now?'

'There's something worrying you about this, isn't there?'

Ashworth shook his head. 'Not about Barbara's death, there isn't. I half expected it.'

'So did Dennis Paine. He was forever after my husband to send Barbara to a clinic for her own safety.'

'But your husband didn't share his concern?'

'No, he didn't, and for once I agreed with him. Barbara was not particularly close to her husband. All right, the kidnap and murder must have taken their toll, but I wouldn't have thought they'd have provoked this reaction.'

'So what did?'

'I don't know, Jim. The balance of the mind, once disturbed, is very difficult to understand.'

'I think you know more about Barbara Edwards than you're telling me, Gwen.'

She gave him an uneasy look. 'You do push friendship to the limit, don't you?'

'Yes,' Ashworth said dully.

'Can we get out of this bedroom then? It feels almost obscene, talking about the woman while she's lying there.'

As they walked out, Ashworth caught Gwen's fresh smell, and memories of the sensations which her body could invoke were, once more, vivid in his mind. For a few seconds he thought of man's eternal, impractical desire for the best of both worlds.

They crossed the landing and descended the wide uncarpeted stone stairs.

'Now much of this is just suspicion, Jim.'

'And the bits that aren't are the things you shouldn't be telling me,' he smiled.

'You have ways of getting things out of a girl — you know that,' she said with a long-suffering look.

They reached the hall and sat down on the bottom stair. Before them were the marks of many wet dirty boots scarring the snowy whiteness of the hall carpet.

Gwen said, 'This idea you have of Barbara spending the whole of her life in some twilight world is not so.'

'But most people who knew her described her as subdued, withdrawn.'

'Yes, Jim, but . . . oh, how can I explain this? Drugs have an effect of curtailing certain desires and impulses, while greatly stimulating others. I firmly believe that Barbara was a sexually active woman.'

'But she told one of my detectives that she and Simon no longer—'

'Jim, I would think even — or especially — you would realise it's possible to have sex with someone other than the person you vowed to forsake all others for.'

'Are you saying you knew she was having an affair?'

'No, I'm not. I'm saying she was on the pill, which suggests she wasn't exactly celibate.'

'A married woman on the pill — what's so strange about that?' he asked, eyebrows arched questioningly.

'God, Jim, sometimes I swear you know when someone isn't telling you the whole truth.'

He smiled and waited. Reluctantly, Gwen said, 'Eighteen months ago she had an Aids test. Now before you get carried away, there could have been many reasons for that. She could have suspected that her husband was playing around, for one thing.'

'But you don't think so?'

'No, something tells me Barbara lived life to the full.' She turned to Ashworth. 'You don't seem very surprised by any of this.'

'I'm not unduly, but why is it bothering you? You must admit it looks like suicide.'

'Oh, it is suicide, and when it goes to the coroner it will be an open-and-shut case. I just don't think she died because she lost her husband.'

'I know she didn't,' Ashworth said with an air of finality as he looked around the hall. 'Do you know, this place reminds me of a Continental brothel.'

'I didn't realise you'd frequented such establishments,' Gwen said with a wicked grin.

Ashworth chuckled at fond memories. 'I did two years' National Service,' he explained. Then, suddenly serious, he said, 'Gwen . . .'

'Oh dear, here we go — I enjoyed it, but I'm afraid it was just a one-off. That's what you're going to say, isn't it?'

'I'd have put it a little better, but that's the gist of it.'

'I knew we'd have trouble with that conscience of yours.'

'It's not my conscience.'

'Well, every other part of you seemed more than willing.'

'I can't lead a double life, Gwen,' he said earnestly, 'it's just not me. Having to lie about where I've been, why I'm late. It just doesn't settle with me — and there's always the chance I'll slip up and we'll be discovered.'

'We'll be careful,' she implored, touching his arm. 'Come on, Jim, we're not talking forever here. Six months and we'll probably be tired of each other.'

'You're such a romantic,' Ashworth joked, trying to lighten the mood.

'No, I'm not a romantic, but I am practical. This isn't love, it's simply lust, and it will wear off. Me? I just like to enjoy it while it's there.'

Ashworth, finding Gwen's offer extremely difficult to refuse, was disturbed by her next statement.

She said, 'Anyway, I don't think it's up to you.'

'Why?'

'Because the grass is greener, and forbidden fruits do taste sweeter, that's why. When we get to London for the conference, will we go back to the hotel, say goodnight, and go to our separate rooms?' She looked at him knowingly. 'I don't think so.'

Of course, Ashworth knew she was right, and each time he succumbed, his resistance would be further eroded, until the course was run and the act they had performed in the back of his car no longer provoked a sense of longing or urgency; it would go the way of all such liaisons, built on nothing more solid than a primitive urge.

'We'll see,' he said.

'We shall,' Gwen replied firmly, feeling herself superior in this game of power brinkmanship. 'I'll arrange for the body to be taken away for post-mortem . . . and I'll be in touch.'

As he drove back to the station, Ashworth was aware that this position, of not being in total control of himself, his destiny, was completely alien to him.

'You don't look much like a spider, Gwen,' he said to himself as open fields slid past the car windows, 'and I don't resemble a fly, but that's how this situation is beginning to shape up.'

* * *

The Frenches arrived punctually for their appointment. Bobby Adams showed them to the interview room where Ashworth was waiting.

Both were smartly dressed: Alan in a grey suit reflecting the latest fashion, as did the brightly coloured tie adorning the neck of his crisp white shirt; Julie in a short light grey topcoat worn over a pink blouse and black miniskirt which reached half-way up her thighs and showed off her shapely legs to good advantage.

They would have made a handsome couple but for the worry which showed on their faces.

'Mr and Mrs French, thank you for coming, and please sit down.'

As they settled themselves stiffly into the plastic chairs to face Ashworth, he said, 'You understand that you are here to help us with our enquiries?'

They nodded, but seemed unwilling to look at him directly.

'Good. I suppose I should first inform you that Barbara Edwards was found dead today. Everything surrounding her death suggests that it was suicide.'

Ashworth watched them both very carefully. Shock registered immediately on their faces, but more so on Julie's, so he directed his next question to her. 'Would you like to tell me the name of the fourth person involved in your games?'

'Tell him, Alan, for God's sake,' Julie pleaded, 'I can't take much more of this.'

Alan French closed his eyes, as if trying to blot out what was happening. Then he spoke softly, 'It was Barbara.'

'The fourth person was Barbara Edwards — is that what you're telling me, sir?'

'Yes, yes,' Julie quickly answered for her husband. 'You can see why we couldn't tell you before. If all this had come out, it would have killed Barbara . . . Oh, what am I saying,' she sobbed.

French, slipping a comforting arm around his wife's shoulder, said, 'You do see that, don't you, Chief Inspector?'

'No, I don't,' Ashworth said firmly. 'What I see is this — you both had some sort of sexual arrangement with Simon Edwards and another party, whom you refused to name. Now Barbara Edwards is dead and no longer able to defend herself, you say she was the fourth person.' He was fishing for information, hoping to wheedle the whole story out of them. 'That seems very unlikely to me — a respectable middle-aged woman taking part in that sort of thing.' He shook his head in disbelief.

'Respectable?' French snorted. 'She was oversexed—'

'Don't go into details, Alan,' his wife implored. 'I feel so ashamed.'

'We've got to. He won't believe us otherwise.' He turned his attention back to Ashworth. 'It all started out as a joke. I was friendly with Simon and we all four went out together occasionally. We went to their house one night. Barbara took something and then had a lot to drink. She was sitting next to me on the settee and she started coming on to me, touching me, that sort of thing. Both Julie and I were embarrassed, for Christ's sake.

'I kept looking at Simon but he just laughed. He seemed to be enjoying it. Well, I had to try to be diplomatic — it was the boss and his wife, after all.' He looked at Ashworth's fixed expression before going on. 'I said something like, we'd better be going, and Barbara said, not until you've taken me to bed. I tried to joke my way out of it by saying, what would Simon think of that? And she said, well, he and Julie can come too. I remember Simon laughing and saying what a perfect end to the evening.'

'Not good enough,' Ashworth said severely. 'You make it sound too easy, too convenient.'

'That's how it happened,' French insisted.

'No, it's not.' Ashworth was equally insistent. 'It doesn't explain why two very attractive young people should go to bed with a middle-aged couple regularly, over a period of two years. Once as a drunken mistake, yes, but there it would probably end.'

'I can't do more than tell you the truth,' French said hotly.

'That you can't.' Ashworth leant across the table. 'And when you've done that, I'll be satisfied.' He held French's gaze until the man averted his eyes. 'Shall I help you a little way along the road?' he asked, standing up, using his considerable size and bulk to intimidate them. 'How does this fit? You were friendly with Edwards and you hatched a plot for sex in return for money.'

'No, no,' was French's venomous denial.

'Yes,' Ashworth insisted.

'Tell him, Alan,' Julie French said quite calmly. 'He knows.'

'All right, but you make it sound so sordid and mercenary.'

And it wasn't? Ashworth thought, although his expression remained bland as he listened.

French said, 'The first time was exactly as I told you. After that Simon and Barbara began helping us with things, so we just let it carry on.'

'Now I have to be clear on this — when you say they helped you, did they give you money?'

'Yes, for the house and other things,' French admitted, 'but it didn't seem as if they were paying us for anything. They just wanted to help.'

'Yes, I'm sure,' Ashworth said drily.

'And you do believe us?' Julie urged.

'Yes, I believe you,' Ashworth assured her. But he did not add that he was certain Simon Edwards's membership of that little quartet had led directly to his death.

Ashworth surprised them then by asking, 'Do either of you know Len Warren?'

'Of course we do. He works at the factory.' French's shifty gaze told Ashworth that the man was not revealing the whole truth.

'Neither of you know him socially?'

'Before we moved we used to live quite close to him,' Julie said.

Ashworth looked at her; there was no doubt in his mind that she was the more intelligent of the two, and knew exactly where this line of questioning was leading.

'That's what I thought. Did he ever visit your house?'

'Sometimes,' Julie answered with a defiant toss of her head.

'What was your relationship with him, Mrs French?'

'What the hell are you getting at?' her husband shouted.

'It's all right, Alan,' Julie said quietly before addressing herself to Ashworth. 'I didn't have any sort of relationship with him. Len's just a friend. We both feel sorry for him.'

Ashworth sat down again. 'But surely, you being a very pretty woman and Mr Warren being a bachelor, he could very likely be attracted to you.'

'I've no idea if he is or not. I've never discussed anything of that nature with him.'

'This is ridiculous,' French stormed. 'Len's just an odd-ball with a chip on his shoulder and as Julie said, we just feel sorry for him.'

'My assessment of him is that he's a very clever man,' Ashworth said coolly.

Alan French said, 'I don't know whether he's clever or not, but I do know he'd walk a hundred miles if he thought he could get back at Simon or Paine.'

'Shut up, Alan,' Julie snapped.

'It's true,' French insisted, 'everyone knows it.'

'All right, thank you for coming in,' Ashworth said abruptly. 'I may need to see you again.'

'Is that it?' French said, the relief plain in his tone.

'For the moment, yes.'

Through the window of the interview room Ashworth watched them cross the car park. He was not a particularly religious man and when, on occasions, he felt obliged to address the creator of this universe he did so in a manner somewhat lacking in reverence. He thought now: I don't know, old son, when you invented sex you certainly stored up a lot of trouble for this world . . . maybe you should have given more consideration to the 'under the gooseberry bush' alternative.

Ken Savage was waiting outside. 'Jim,' he said, his smile indicating that he was in a rare sunny mood, 'I've faxed everything to Northampton. They've interviewed Bennett and charged him, so Whitworth's in the clear.'

'Good, that's good, Ken. Oh, I shall be needing some search warrants in the near future,' Ashworth said absently, 'but I want to check something first with Vehicle Licensing. I'll catch you when I've done that.' Then he strode off.

Savage, realising that he had been dismissed, muttered, 'I've bloody had enough of this. I'm the Chief Constable,' and his sunny mood evaporated as he headed back to his office.

CHAPTER 31

Josh Abraham was not ill, he had been attending an interview for the job in Leeds. That feeling of satisfaction he had felt on boarding the train home was still with him when he got to Bridgetown station. While passengers alighted, the train on the opposite line started to leave. As Josh watched, it created the illusion that his train was moving, and when the large carriage had rattled past he felt as if he had been jolted to a halt.

On the platform he watched idly as mail was loaded on to the train, then he made his way to the ticket barrier.

The day had been a great success. His interview with the giant electronics company 'Sonic — tomorrow's technology today' had gone well. He was on the short-list but had been more or less told that this was just a formality.

After a conducted tour of what, to Josh, was an Aladdin's cave of new technology, some of which was not yet readily available in Britain, he had been given a free hand to wander around by himself.

He had used that opportunity to good effect and by the time he left the factory he knew exactly who had killed Simon Edwards.

There was a call he had to make at the bank which — if he had the audacity to pull it off — would prove beyond doubt that Ashworth was wrong not to have paid more attention to Barbara Edwards.

Smiling to himself, he anticipated the spectacle of the so-called 'great man' making a fool of himself.

* * *

Ashworth wished that either the rain would set in or the skies would clear and herald a frosty night; this incessant drizzle was beginning to irritate him. A fine spray had settled on his hair and coat by the time Dennis Paine opened the front door of what had been the Edwardses' home.

'Jim,' he said, his voice slightly slurred.

'I've just dropped by to say how sorry I am about your sister.'

'Thanks. Come on in out of the rain.'

Ashworth closed the door and followed Paine into the lounge. He noticed that the man was unsteady on his feet and speculated as to how much alcohol he must have consumed to reach that state. The evening before he had watched Paine down three large scotches without any noticeable effect.

'Sit down.' Paine waved towards an armchair as he settled on the sofa, picking up his glass of scotch from the floor. 'I can't face my own house after what happened. I think I'll sell up and leave the district. There's nothing for me here now.'

Ashworth sat down. 'It must have been quite a shock finding your sister like that.'

'Shock? I think I'm incapable of feeling shock any more,' Paine said slowly.

There was no doubt that this affair was beginning to take its toll on the man; his face was drawn, tired; his grey hair had lost its sheen.

'Dennis,' Ashworth began diplomatically, 'there is something I need to ask you.'

'Ask away,' Paine said blankly.

First of all Ashworth passed on the information extracted from the Frenches. As Paine listened his eyes slowly closed.

'Do you think it's true?' Ashworth asked.

'I don't know what to think any more,' he answered morosely. 'You know someone all those years, your only living relative, and suddenly you realise you didn't know them at all. Jim, Babs was my little sister and I've always treated her as such. For so long I've tried to help the pair of them: get Babs off the drugs; get Simon to take some sort of interest in the business . . . and now they're both gone.'

'I'm sorry, Dennis. I know this is upsetting but time is of the essence if we're to catch whoever did this.'

'I'm just so empty. I can't even hate at the moment,' he murmured, staring into space.

'That will pass,' Ashworth assured him. 'I'll be going, then.' He stood up and stared across at Paine. 'Dennis, if I may suggest, it might be wise not to have any more to drink.'

Paine gave a hollow laugh. 'Perhaps you're right . . . I haven't anything to celebrate, have I?'

'No, you haven't really.'

* * *

Sarah had not expected her homecoming to be quite so warmly welcomed. Her husband was being so kind and considerate; he even engaged in conversation over dinner.

'The Edwards case is over then,' she assumed.

'Whatever makes you say that?' Ashworth asked, a forkful of Brussels sprout hovering half-way between his mouth and plate.

'Just that you seem so relaxed and happy. I thought you must be in your 'bathing in the glory' period, which comes just before your 'I'm bored waiting for the next case to happen' mood,' she joked.

'No, the case isn't tied up.' He chewed the sprout. 'Is that really how it is, living with me?' he asked seriously.

'It was a joke, Jim.'

'Perhaps,' he said, 'but in future I'm going to leave work behind when I come home.' He sternly waved his fork at her. 'We've drifted apart, Sarah, and I blame myself for that.'

The domestic pet is so often a conductor for the emotions and atmospheres of its world, and the Ashworths' Jack Russell was no exception. While peace and harmony prevailed between the two humans at the centre of her universe she was relaxed, contented. However, by ten p.m. she had become slightly agitated.

Instinctively Sarah looked towards her husband slumped in the armchair, eyes fixed on the television screen; but she knew, by his furrowed brow, his blank eyes, that he was not watching the flickering picture, he was gathering loose ends, weaving them into one strong cord with which to tie someone to the Simon Edwards murder.

Don't change, Jim, she thought fondly, stay just as you are.

* * *

Next morning Ashworth surveyed the empty CID office. He looked out over the town from his glass-sided perch. As it was Saturday, the high street was busy, shoppers jostling one another on the crowded pavements.

Suddenly he wanted people around him, a confidant to bolster his flagging confidence. What had seemed so unequivocally clear the night before was now painted with a sheen of self-doubt.

He picked up the telephone and dialled Holly's number.

'Yes?' Mike Whitworth answered. Ashworth could hear Holly laughing in the background.

'It's Jim Ashworth, Mike.'

There was a short silence. 'Guv?'

'Can you come into the station? There's something I want to discuss with you. They've informed you that you've been reinstated, I take it?'

'Yes, they have, but—'

'Mike,' Ashworth said firmly, 'everything's starting to happen in the Edwards case and I'm here by myself.'

'Yes, I'm on my way, guv.' There was another short pause. 'How did you know I'd still be here?'

Ashworth gave a humourless laugh. 'Elementary, my dear Whitworth, elementary,' he intoned before replacing the receiver.

The thirty minutes it took for Whitworth to get to the station seemed like an eternity to Ashworth. Just as he was checking his watch for the umpteenth time, Whitworth walked through the door.

To say that his appearance told of a woman's hand would have been an exaggeration, but he did look slightly less as if he had been dragged through a hedge backwards. His brown suit was not so crumpled, and his thick dark hair looked as if it had received some attention from a comb.

'Sit, Mike,' Ashworth said. 'I need someone to bounce this off.'

Even Whitworth, hard-bitten as he was, realised the honour that was being bestowed upon him. He draped himself ungraciously across the chair. 'Holly's coming in as soon as she can, and I rang Josh. I thought if the soft stuff's about to hit the fan we'll need as many people as possible here.'

'That's good.' Ashworth seemed preoccupied. He said, 'Just listen to me, Mike, and see if you think this is a plausible case.'

As Whitworth listened he occasionally shook his head, not in disbelief, but in admiration of the details Ashworth had accumulated to incriminate his suspect.

'There, Mike, what do you think of that?' he concluded.

'As far as it goes, yes.' He sounded doubtful.

'But?' Ashworth queried.

'There's a certain thing missing — like, proof.'

'That'll come when some of the ransom money turns up,' Ashworth said enthusiastically.

'But how can you be so sure some will turn up? You could be way off beam,' Whitworth counselled.

Ashworth was insistent. 'I'm not, Mike. Call it intuition, whatever you like, but I know some of that money is going to turn up today.'

'Even if it does, it could prove difficult to trace the source. The man could pass it in any number of places.'

'Then we trace where it didn't come from . . . use a process of elimination,' Ashworth replied doggedly.

'There are too many ifs and buts in it, guv, and working through all the people who haven't done it could take some time.'

'Yes, it could,' Ashworth agreed, 'that's why I want a course of action in place, because if the bulk of that money doesn't turn up, I can't prove a thing.'

'Guv . . .' There was a pleading note in Whitworth's voice. 'Like you say, the man's highly intelligent, the money may not be at his house, he could have buried it in the countryside for all we know.'

'No, his intelligence is his strength *and* his weakness because it makes him think he's superior to everyone else.'

'What do you want me to do if some of the money does turn up?'

'*When* it does . . .' Ashworth had no doubt that it would. '. . . I want you, and possibly Holly, to interview the Frenches at their home. I don't think you'll need to search the place, but I'm sure you'll find that car they're driving about in belonged to Simon Edwards.'

'I don't follow, guv.'

'No, of course you don't, I keep forgetting you've been out of action for some time. I'll condense it: basically the Edwardses were giving the Frenches a lot of money, as I told you. Part of that package was a car — the same model and year as Edwards was driving himself. For the tax advantage, it went through the books as a company car. My guess is that Edwards and French used to inter-use the cars.'

'Got you, so the one found on Parker's Farm could easily have been driven by Alan French the day before.'

'That's it, and now he's probably frightened that we'll ask why a car he frequently drove but didn't own was found abandoned at the time Edwards went missing.' His chuckle had an unpleasant ring to it. 'Although my guess is, he's just worried that Paine will take it back.'

'So if you're right, that'll eliminate the Frenches.'

'It should.' Ashworth seemed lost in his own thoughts. 'Right, after that I want you to get on to Len Warren. Let's find out what our working-class Marxist genius is hiding.'

As Whitworth studied the immobile, thoughtful face in front of him, he took a decision to leave Bridgetown. This subtle cat-and-mouse detection was not for him; he needed an environment where the war came to him of its own accord.

Josh sheepishly entered the room.

'Ah, returned from the sick-bed,' Ashworth commented drily.

'Hi, Funny Guy,' Whitworth winked.

Josh smiled his acknowledgement of Whitworth's greeting but ignored Ashworth as he took his seat in front of the VDU.

'Phone Holly, Mike, and tell her she need not come in until she's wanted,' Ashworth ordered. 'After what she's been through she'll need a rest.'

The day passed slowly. Ashworth sat facing his young detectives like an ageing, stern schoolmaster.

Dusk was creeping in and the whole of Bridgetown had become dots of yellow light on a dark canvas, when Sergeant Dutton poked his head round the door. 'You've got a tickle, Jim. Some of the ransom money has turned up in the takings at Booth's off-licence.'

Ashworth was already on his feet. 'How much and when?'

'Just one ten-pound note, and when's a bit cloudy. It was either after four thirty yesterday afternoon, or sometime today.'

'Right, Mike, you come with me. Josh, ring Holly and tell her I need her.'

Ashworth grabbed his coat and was out of the office.

* * *

Booth's off-licence was situated in the high street. It stood between the bank and the offices of the United Reform Church. From outside it appeared quaint, but that illusion was dispelled even before the bell above the 'In' door had stopped ringing.

Inside, potential customers were faced with piles of wire baskets and a long narrow aisle flanked by racked wine on one side and a mountain of mixers and fruit drinks on the other. At the top of the aisle a right turn led to the spirits section and the check-out, which today was manned by a young girl whose bored expression was highlighted by the fierce glow of an overhead strip.

The shop was quite crowded and Ashworth had to shoulder his way around the obstacle course to the till.

'The manager?' he asked.

Turning her attention away from the customer at the counter, she looked up. 'You'll have to wait, love, I'm busy,' she told him in a sing-song voice.

Ashworth produced his warrant card. 'I haven't got time to wait.'

The girl glanced at it, completely unimpressed. 'Mr Newitt,' she yelled, at a pitch which threatened to shatter every glass receptacle in the store. 'Police.'

A flustered Mr Newitt appeared at the rear of the shop. 'Come this way, gentlemen, please,' he called.

Ashworth, followed by Whitworth, made his way to the room indicated by the small man: it was a curtained-off stockroom with a desk to one side.

'Mr Newitt,' Ashworth began, 'I believe you reported that some of the money we're trying to trace has passed through your till.'

'That's correct,' Newitt said. He was smartly dressed, and his grey curling hair lent him the air of an ageing folk singer.

It soon became apparent to Ashworth that Newitt — in common with many other retailers — was a talker.

He went on, 'As I told your officer on the phone, I can't actually say when we took the money, but it must have

270

been after four thirty yesterday afternoon, because I cashed up then and took the takings to the bank.'

'So what time did you close yesterday?' Ashworth asked.

'Eight p.m. as usual. I always take the rest of the takings home with me to use as a float the next morning. Well, when I emptied the till this afternoon, I was sitting here checking the numbers off against the list and there it was — a ten-pound note.' He smiled, obviously contemplating the notoriety which would surround his discovery, and the sales potential accompanying it.

'Who visited the shop today?'

'Half of Bridgetown,' Newitt smiled broadly. 'An excellent day for me.'

'But not for us.' Ashworth's voice was beginning to show irritation. 'Can you remember who came in after four thirty yesterday?'

'Yes, I was on the till after I came back from the bank. Julie French came in . . .' He pursed his lips in a man-to-man fashion. 'Of course, I mustn't gossip in my business, but the things I've heard about her. I always spend a little time with her . . . just in case I get lucky.'

'How did she pay?'

'By cheque.'

'Anyone else?'

'The vicar.' He smiled ruefully. 'If people knew the interpretation he puts on the 'holy spirit', they'd—'

'I think we can eliminate the vicar from our enquiries,' Ashworth said shortly. 'Anyone else?'

Newitt paused for a moment. 'Some people from the new estates — I don't know their names, but—'

'Did Len Warren come in?' Ashworth cut in.

'Yes, he did as a matter of fact . . . that's right, it was about five. Two bottles of Russian vodka, wouldn't you know.'

'How did he pay?'

'Cash.'

Ashworth shot a glance in Whitworth's direction.

'Notes? Coinage?' He was finding it difficult to conceal his excitement.

'The bill came to fourteen pounds something, and he paid with a ten-pound note and coins.'

'Len Warren passed a ten-pound note in your shop yesterday — that's what you're telling us?'

'Yes, Chief Inspector. Is it important?'

'Very,' Ashworth said. 'Mr Newitt, you've been a great help. Thank you.'

'Always glad to help the police,' he called after them.

As they made their way down the now less crowded aisle, Ashworth grabbed Whitworth's arm. 'It's coming together, Mike, it's coming together,' he said passionately.

CHAPTER 32

Len Warren had not been arrested, he had merely been brought in to assist the police with their enquiries. He had not come willingly; indeed he had protested all the way to the interview room where he now sat slumped at the table.

Ashworth studied him, trying to work out how to get to the man. Holly coughed as if prompting Ashworth to start the interview. However, he was in no mood to be hurried. Having despatched Abraham and Whitworth to interview the Frenches, he felt the longer he kept Warren stewing, the better.

Eventually he said, 'Do you know why we want to talk to you, Len?' His tone was friendly as he sat down to face the man. Holly remained standing at the door.

'I've got no idea, but I want a solicitor,' Warren complained, all the time fingering the birthmark on his cheek.

Ashworth took no notice of the request. He said, 'You were in Booth's off-licence last night, Len, and you bought two bottles of vodka. You paid with a ten-pound note and some change.'

'So?' He appeared unconcerned, relieved even.

'Where did you get the ten-pound note from?'

'From my wage packet. I'm off sick so I went to the factory in the morning to collect my wages.'

'Have you still got your wage packet?' Ashworth asked.

'No,' Warren said, puzzled. 'Well, yes, but it's empty. I put the money in the bank this morning.'

'Have you got your wage slip?'

Warren fished around the inside pocket of his jacket and brought out a bank book and a brown envelope from which he took the slip, passing it to Ashworth who studied it for a while. 'So, Len, your net wage is one hundred and thirty-two pounds.'

'Yes.'

'If you spent ten, you must have paid somewhere around one hundred and twenty pounds into your bank this morning.'

'Yes.' Panic showed in Warren's eyes. 'No. Look, what's all this about?'

'How much did you pay in, Len?'

'I put a hundred and thirty in. I had some money over from last week.'

'And you still say you paid your off-licence bill from your wage packet.'

'Yes, that's what I'm telling you. I remember opening the packet and taking the first note.'

Ashworth sat back and stared at him. The room was so quiet, he could hear his watch ticking. 'Is there anything you want to tell me, Len? Anything that will make my job easier?'

'I've got nothing to tell you,' Warren insisted, his temper rising. 'What's the big deal about the tenner?'

'My officers are going to search your flat.'

'You can't do that,' he protested.

'I can, Len,' Ashworth said calmly. 'With a warrant, I can.'

Warren cradled his forehead in his hand as he looked down at the tabletop.

'You have a right to be there,' Ashworth said gruffly. 'My officers will accompany you.'

Warren looked around the room and the haunted, frightened look in his eyes reminded Holly of a cornered, helpless animal knowing it had little chance of staving off its pursuers.

They left him in the interview room. Whitworth was waiting with Josh in the corridor. Holly was intrigued; she had understood the Warren interview, but was having difficulty in fitting it into the larger picture.

Whitworth approached the Chief Inspector. 'You were right about the car, guv. The Frenches were relieved we knew about it, and miffed that they were losing it.'

'More the latter than the former, I'll wager,' Ashworth chuckled, for he now seemed to be in quite jovial mood. 'Mike, I want you and Holly to organise a search of Warren's flat. Take half a dozen uniformed officers with you.'

'I take it you've got a warrant, guv.'

Ashworth gave him a pained look. 'Of course. It should be with Martin Dutton by now.'

Whitworth signalled to Holly and they began to walk away. 'Keep in touch with me by radio,' Ashworth called after them.

'Where will you be, guv?'

'Offering comfort to a grieving man,' Ashworth said, almost to himself, 'who's trying to rebuild his world.'

As they passed through the swing doors to the stairs, Holly said, 'What's happening, Mike?'

'I'll tell you on the way. What's the matter with Josh? He's hardly said a word.'

'He's probably as pissed off as I am about being kept in the dark.'

'No, it's not that. I tried to tell him but he laughed and said he didn't want to know.'

Holly stopped in the middle of the stairs, pleading, 'Tell me, Mike . . . please.'

'Okay. Once upon a time there was a big bad Chief Inspector . . .' Whitworth began as they carried on down towards reception, '. . . who sent this handsome young detective and his nymphomaniac side-kick — that's our parts in it, by the way — to . . .'

'Mike,' Holly warned.

'. . . search Warren's flat because he knew that what they'd find there would tell him who killed Simon Edwards . . .'

* * *

The nine people inside the small flat almost filled it to capacity. Warren, looking very dejected, was sitting at the kitchen table.

Every book had been rifled through, every cupboard searched; even the space between the ceiling and the flat above had been inspected.

'We'd better look under the floorboards,' Whitworth said, 'but I'm beginning to think Ashworth could be wrong.'

'Mike,' Holly whispered, 'watch Warren every time one of the lads goes near the back door.'

'The shed . . . of course.' He joined Warren in the kitchen. 'Right, Lenny boy, let's have a look in the shed, shall we?'

'I'll sue,' Warren grumbled. 'I'll sue if this isn't all put back straight.'

The still night air was heavy with fumes from the nearby expressway. The uniformed officers worked quickly and methodically, taking every item from the shed and placing them on the lawn.

Holly stood beside Whitworth and viewed the lawn mower, assorted spades and forks, cardboard boxes filled with nothing more incriminating than packets of weed killer, lawn feed and empty flowerpots.

Holly could see that Warren was agitated; she watched his face, followed his darting glance which kept coming to rest at the rear of the shed.

Without speaking she took the torch from Whitworth's hand and walked in that direction. She felt her heartbeat quicken when she heard Warren's muttered, 'Oh God.'

In the powerful beam of the torch, the disturbed grass, not yet knitted together, was clearly visible. 'Mike,' she called excitedly, 'I think there's something buried back here.'

Whitworth laughed with relief. 'So you've buried it, have you, Lenny boy?'

Everything seemed to drain out of Warren; even the bitter hatred which characterised him. 'Yes,' he said softly.

'How far down?'

'About three foot,' Warren said, staring at the ground.

'Right.' Whitworth passed the spade to a constable with an ample waistline. 'You dig. You look as if you could use the exercise.'

CHAPTER 33

To Ashworth, there was something almost obscene about Dennis Paine's presence in the tasteful elegance of the Edwardses' house; not unlike a wart on the end of a beautiful model's nose.

The man in question was sitting on the sofa, the large check of his sports jacket clashing with the patterned covers. He crossed his well-tailored legs and took a sip of whisky from the glass which was fast becoming an extension of his arm.

'Len Warren?' He stared in amazement at Ashworth, who was sitting in an armchair. 'I still can't believe it. Who'd have thought he would be capable of planning and executing a caper like that? It was a master stroke of yours, Jim, taking the serial numbers and then telling the press you hadn't.'

'I like to think so,' Ashworth said, none too humbly.

If he could have felt Josh's eyes piercing into his back, he might well have rephrased that last remark, but Josh's resentment, as he stood by the door, was not strong enough to penetrate the armour of his superior.

'So, my nightmare is nearly over, is it?' Paine said gratefully.

'Almost. It will be arrest and charge tonight, and in court on Monday.'

'But then there's the trial,' Paine said suddenly. 'With our courts it's quite—'

'An acquittal is out of the question,' Ashworth assured him. 'This case carries a guaranteed life sentence.'

'Good.' Paine drained the last of his scotch.

There was a series of bleeps from the radio in Ashworth's pocket. He took it out and depressed the button. 'Ashworth,' he said.

Whitworth's voice crackled from the set. 'We've found it, guv.'

Ashworth turned the radio off. 'Sorry, Dennis, can I take this in the hall? I shouldn't really let you hear . . . procedure and all that.'

'Of course, of course,' Paine said grandly. When Ashworth was out of the room he stood up and looked across at Josh. 'A drink, young man?'

'No thank you, sir, I don't drink,' Josh replied politely.

'You don't drink?' He emphasised each word with incredulity. 'Well, I'll pour one for Jim. By God, he's earned it.'

He was doing this when Ashworth came back. 'A drink, Jim,' he said. 'I take it they found the money just as you thought they would.'

Ashworth took the drink from him. 'No, they didn't.' He took a sip. 'Thanks for this. No, what they found buried in Warren's garden were six briefcases made of Moroccan leather — worth about four hundred pounds apiece, I believe. Seems he's been siphoning them off from the factory for a couple of years. He doesn't see it as stealing, more as redistribution of wealth. The poor devil thought the ten-pound note was tied up in an investigation into their theft.'

Paine looked confused. 'I don't understand any of this.'

'Don't you?' Ashworth asked cordially. 'It's simple really. Poor old Len Warren has been a thorn in my side. I knew he was hiding something, but until I could establish what it was I couldn't eliminate him, so I decided to use him.'

'You're saying he didn't kill Simon?'

'Of course he didn't . . . you did,' Ashworth said quietly. 'And your sister too, I believe, by administering a large overdose.'

Paine laughed. 'You're mad, Ashworth,' he exclaimed. 'Why on earth should I do that?'

'Simply because they were taking a lot of money from the business. With them out of the way the factory is all yours, and you inherit this house.'

At the door Josh shook his head in disagreement.

Paine seemed to regain a little of his composure. He returned to the sofa and sat down. 'And how have you reached this absurd conclusion?'

Ashworth felt the first twinge of doubt, but he confidently said, 'I've suspected you from the first. It seemed odd to me that you were the only one who knew of the business trip Edwards was going on the day he disappeared. You collected his overnight bag. You made all the arrangements.'

'Yes, that's correct. So you're suggesting I kidnapped Simon.'

'No, I'm not. What I'm saying is, I believe you struck him a blow on the head and then pushed him into the river.'

'Fascinating,' Paine observed. 'And then arranged for someone to write letters and make phone calls demanding money.'

'No, you did that. It didn't escape my notice that on the night of the last ransom drop you were the only person to speak to the kidnapper.'

'What a flight of fancy,' Paine mocked. 'Pray tell me, why should I go to all that trouble when — if what you're saying is correct — I could have just let Simon's body turn up in the river? No one would have suspected me. Why the charade of a kidnap?'

Warning bells were ringing inside Ashworth's head; so much of his case depended on bluff and Paine seemed too confident. Nevertheless, he pushed on. 'Now, this is guesswork . . .'

He saw Paine's eyebrows rise.

'. . . but I believe you panicked because you knew if the body turned up too soon it would be apparent that Edwards had received a blow on the head. When I told you, just before the freeze was supposed to be setting in, that we would be searching the waterways, you dreamed up the kidnap to delay the body being found. You wanted it to be buffeted about in the river for a few weeks.'

'Bravo.' Paine clapped his hands. 'And then planted the ten-pound note on Warren to incriminate him.'

'Yes.' Ashworth was finding it difficult to keep his voice firm. 'When I told you we'd taken the serial numbers I guessed you'd plant money in either Warren's or the Frenches' pay packets.'

'You should really be writing detective stories, Ashworth. Now, before I ask you to leave, tell me how you're going to prove all this.'

'Simple . . .' Ashworth paused before playing his trump card. '. . . I intend to search this house and your own, and I'm certain I'll find the balance of the ransom money.'

Paine threw back his head and laughed loudly. 'Ashworth, I thought you were just lacking in intelligence — now I believe you're mad.'

The man's words and attitude lashed at Ashworth and, if he needed confirmation that he had made an horrendous mistake, Paine's next statement provided it.

'I'll co-operate with you in every way possible, of course. You won't need a search warrant — but I do insist that the press are present.'

Ashworth realised that his mouth was hanging open as he watched Paine walk to the telephone and begin dialling.

The front doorbell rang. As if in a trance, Ashworth went into the hall. Josh had preceded him and the door was already open, revealing Holly and Whitworth.

'Guv, there's been a cock-up,' Whitworth told him.

Ashworth did not need any more bad news just at that moment and as he listened to what Whitworth had to say he felt despair flooding over him.

'We've found the rest of the ransom money at Warren's. It was in a case hidden underneath the shed. We'd have missed it, but the thing's rotten and one of the lads put his foot through the floor.'

Ashworth's first inclination was to shoot the messenger; instead he rounded on Josh, irritated as he was by the slight smile playing on the Detective Constable's lips. 'You find something funny about this, Abraham — something that makes you want to laugh?' His tone was acidulous.

Most people would have visibly flinched at the onset of one of Ashworth's onslaughts but it brought no such reaction from Josh; not even the gaze of his steady grey eyes wavered, but before his lips could deliver the answer which was formulating in his mind, Paine's voice interrupted them from the lounge.

'Ashworth,' he called, 'the press want to have a word with you, just to make sure this isn't some kind of hoax.'

'I'll take it,' Josh said coolly.

All three watched in amazement as Josh strode back into the lounge and took the proffered telephone receiver from Paine. 'Yes? This is DC Abraham speaking. That's quite right, if you'd like to do as Mr Paine advised, the police will have a statement to issue shortly.'

Ashworth was finding it difficult not to forcibly remove Josh from the room, or even from the face of the earth.

'Now, Mr Paine,' Josh began confidently, 'you certainly out-thought us with the money. We didn't think you'd plant all of it on Warren, but that doesn't really matter, we have all the evidence we need.'

'Ashworth, control this imbecile,' Paine ordered.

But the Chief Inspector, standing at the doorway in front of Holly and Whitworth, found that he was incapable of speech.

'We have all the evidence we need, Mr Paine,' Josh repeated, 'so shall we stop playing games?'

'Yes, let's do that, young man.' Paine sat down, nursing his glass of scotch. 'Tell me what this proof is that you've got.'

'This first part is conjecture, but bear with me.' Josh sat in an armchair to face Paine. 'As you know, members of a police team work very closely together, collectively sifting through all the information that comes in . . .' He turned and smiled sweetly at Ashworth. 'Now, I don't know if Jim misunderstood me when I was telling him about you and your sister, or perhaps I didn't make it plain, but either way he's got the facts jumbled. You don't own any part of the factory, or you didn't until you murdered the two people who did own it.'

Paine's eyes narrowed as he looked at Josh.

'Simon and Barbara Edwards were joint owners,' Josh continued. 'Five years ago your sister's drug addiction began to affect her judgement and that's when you were called in. At that time I believe you were a travel courier in Spain.

'You became a director of the company, but on a salaried basis. You did not own any part of the company. True, because of your forceful personality you took over as managing director, and Edwards was more than willing to let you do most of the work, but that's where it started to go wrong: because of your sister's and Edwards's blasé attitude towards the company, and the excesses in their private lives, the factory began to go downhill. So there you were, working fourteen hours a day and not even being able to afford your own house.' Josh smiled. 'See, we've even found that out. And that's why you decided to murder them.'

'It's a different version,' Paine said, doing his best to appear nonchalant, 'but it sounds like the same fairy tale to me.'

Josh laughed. 'Yes, but you see when we collect information we use every method at our disposal . . .' Again he glanced over his shoulder at Ashworth. '. . . to unearth some proof, which is what we've done in this case.'

From his pocket he took his small tape recorder, placed it on the coffee table and pressed the 'on' switch. Immediately Paine's booming voice filled the room. Paine stared at the machine, mesmerised.

'I recorded that the night the ransom was picked up.' Josh switched the machine off. 'Now, this is the kidnapper's call to the house.' The muffled sound of the kidnapper jumped from the machine.

'So?' Paine asked.

Josh silenced the tape recorder and leant forward. 'Have you heard of voice prints? No? Well, basically, the chance that two individuals could have the same patterns of speech — use of the tongue, teeth, lips, etc., to form sounds — is so remote that it isn't even worth considering. Can you follow that, Mr Paine? However the voice is disguised, the voice pattern remains unique.' He reached into the inside pocket of his jacket. 'Here's a report on your voice and the kidnapper's. You'll see they're one and the same.' He passed the paper to Paine. 'And that proves that you killed Simon Edwards.'

Paine studied the report. 'I didn't kill Babs,' he blurted out, bowing to the inevitability of one murder charge and trying to find a loophole to escape the second.

No?' Josh said quietly. 'The suicide note will tell us more about that. Technology is a wonderful thing, Mr Paine.' He stood up. 'Holly, if you'd like to caution Mr Paine while I have a word with Jim . . .'

'Yes.' So powerful had his performance been that she almost called him 'sir'.

Josh closed the door to face Ashworth in the hall.

'What the hell are you doing, Abraham?' Ashworth demanded.

'Solving a murder case.'

'I'll have your job for this,' Ashworth growled. 'You've made a fool of me.'

'No, you won't — I'm leaving anyway.'

'Where did you get all that information about Paine's private affairs?' The guttural sound of Ashworth's voice was harsh on the ear.

'From the bank manager who handles the factory's affairs. His son was parked in Poacher's Wood, having it off with his girlfriend, if you remember. Well, I told him that if he didn't come across with the information I wanted, we'd do his son. I was quite forceful — poofs can be when they have to.'

'You deliberately withheld the information of the voice prints.'

'I did not,' Josh replied coolly. 'You'd have brushed it aside if I'd told you.'

'I'd have been forced to act on it.'

'No, you wouldn't.' Josh was becoming heated. 'God, why don't you just stop bollocking me up hill and down dale and think. It was you who told me that one of the attributes a good detective needs is the ability to bluff. Well, that's what I've been doing.'

Ashworth managed to look both confused and angry. 'None of this voice print thing is true?'

'Every word, but it's not admissible in a British court of law. So, instead of tearing into me, it would be wise to get Paine to the station before he comes out of shock and starts demanding a solicitor, because if he does that before we take a statement, our case collapses.'

Whitworth stepped in. 'That makes sense, guv.'

'Yes,' Ashworth said heavily.

* * *

It was eleven thirty that same evening.

Ashworth sat alone in the darkened CID office. Paine had made a full confession to the murder of Simon Edwards, although still proclaiming his innocence to the second murder charge, but Ashworth knew it was only a matter of time before that second confession would be forthcoming.

Whitworth had told him of his decision to return to Manchester which had saddened him.

He had attempted to make his peace with Josh but the words had come out all wrong, so he had decided to leave it until another day. Apologies to Holly had been in order for not mentioning the death of her mother-in-law, so he had made them.

Now, physically and mentally exhausted, he could not at this point allow himself to think of the battle which would ensue when he informed Ken Savage that he had no intention of taking up the Home Office appointment. He had decided that for the sake of his marriage he would stay well away from Gwen Anthony's web.

He picked up the telephone and so familiar was his home number he was able to punch it out in the dark. When Sarah answered, all the sounds that were home came to his ear: a good woman's voice, the barking of a dog, the low drone of the television. He could almost smell malt whisky, could almost feel a comfortable chair wrapped around him.

'Jim, are you coming home?'

'Yes, Sarah, it's all over. I'm on my way.'

'Are you all right, Jim? You sound funny.'

'I'm a little older, and a good deal wiser, but all right.'

'Hurry home, Jim.'

After the call he donned his waxed cotton jacket, stood looking out of the glass wall at the bright lights of the town, and for some reason he remembered an American television series he had watched some years ago.

Through gritted teeth, and with a fairly good American accent, he said, 'Jim Ashworth — I'm a cop, and that's my town out there.'

He looked out for several seconds before he spoke again, this time using his normal voice. 'Yes, it is,' he said with a warm smile.

Then he went home.

THE END

ALSO BY BRIAN BATTISON

DETECTIVE JIM ASHWORTH SERIES
Book 1: TIED TO MURDER
Book 2: THE PRICE OF MURDER

More books in the series coming soon!

Thank you for reading this book. If you enjoyed it please leave a review on Amazon or Goodreads.

We love to hear from our readers. If there is anything we missed or you have a question about then please get in touch: feedback@joffebooks.com

Join our mailing list to get new releases and great deals every week from one of the UK's leading independent publishers.

www.joffebooks.com